# 13 Haunted Houses

# 13 Haunted Houses

### Edited by

### Curtis M. Lawson and Joe Morey

WEIRD
HOUSE

First Paperback Edition

Text © 2021 by Ramsey Campbell, James Chambers, Douglas Wynne, Sarah Read, Emma J. Gibbon, Evans Light, Sara Tantlinger, Tony Richards, Jason Parentt, Simon Clark, Tim Curran, Richard Gavin, and Philip Fracassi

ISBN: 978-1-957121-11-6

Introduction © 2022 by Curtis M. Lawson
Afterword © 2022 by Joe Morey

Interior and cover design by Cyrusfiction Productions
Cover art © 2022 by Cyrus Wraith Walker

Editor and Publisher, Joe Morey
Copy editing by Curtis M. Lawson

Weird House Press
Central Point, OR 97502
www.weirdhousepress.com

# Table of Contents

# Introduction
## By Curtis M. Lawson

When I was a boy, my family rented an apartment in a decommissioned church. The apartment itself was nice enough and, as best as I remember, the years living there were some of the better ones of my complicated childhood. There was a big driveway that I would play in while my dad fixed cars for extra cash, and we had enough room inside that I could wage war for the power of Grayskull between the heroes of Eternia and the forces of Skeletor.

My father had a *magic drawer* in those days. There was always something in there for me whenever I was bored or upset—a roll of Smarties, a new Hot Wheel, or a pack of Garbage Pail Kids. He would act as surprised as I was to find out what was in there and I remember believing that it really was magic.

That drawer full of cards and candy was not the only bit of magic I found in that house. Our landlord, a friend of my father, took me to see the view from the steeple one day. It was littered with gray feathers and the bones of pigeons. Seeing those skeletons—feeling those bones crack beneath my sneakers—was the first time I remember pondering death.

I was also allowed into the chapel a few times. It was intact if neglected. A lifesize porcelain crucifix hung on the wall, and canvas tarps covered the altar, the pews, and statues of saints. I hadn't been raised with religion, so this abandoned temple was my first experience with Christian imagery. I remember that massive crucifix so vividly—Christ's brow, torn by his crown of thorns—the spikes driven through his hands and feet—the blood dripping from the wound in his side.

From then on, I was convinced that our house was haunted. Every clicking or scratching noise was the specter of a pigeon, trying to fly to freedom on skeletal wings. Whenever the wind whistled or the house creaked, I imagined the ceramic Christ moaning, trapped forever in his moment of deepest tragedy. At night I would hide beneath my covers, afraid that the porcelain messiah would crawl down from his cross, followed by dead birds, and take my life so that I would be trapped there with them for all time.

My house, where my father produced a limitless supply of tiny treasures from his *magic drawer*, no longer felt safe. Worse still, the danger was not something that could be dealt with. The police wouldn't arrest a malevolent statue. Exterminators couldn't kill that which was already dead. Grownups couldn't protect you from the things they didn't believe in.

My experience is far from unique. There is something particularly horrifying in feeling that your home—your sanctuary from a hostile world—has been compromised. For that reason, haunted houses are not only a staple of horror fiction but of human imagination. What could be scarier?

We human beings love to borrow trouble, almost as much as we love a good yarn. For as long as floors have creaked in the night, we have populated the shadows with creeping bogeymen and revenants. When tragedy strikes in our homes, or when we learn that it had in the past, we imagine that misery seeping into the lumber and the masonry—spreading beneath the walls like mold.

From the priests of the ancient world to the authors like Charles Dickens and Shirley Jackson to filmmakers like James Wan, many a storyteller has exploited this base and universal fear. We, the audience, keep going back for more, eager to see those ugly things that hide in the crawlspace and hungry for the static suffering of the restless dead.

This brings me to a hypothesis. Maybe it isn't the houses that are haunted. Maybe the dead don't cling to landmarks. The tragedies of the past—the suicides and murders, the bouts of agonizing sickness and toxicity of abusive relationships—perhaps they haven't permeated the plaster and lathe of our homes, but rather our minds and our souls. Maybe our specters don't reside in the shadows of dingy cellars or decommissioned chapels but in the labyrinthine grooves of our brains.

It seems to me that it doesn't matter if you sanctify a home, move away, or burn the whole thing down. Your ghosts will follow you. They will always look out from the windows of your eyes and creep around in the attic of your mind. The only way to rid ourselves of them, in my experience, is to bind them with chains of ink and imprison them on the page. But this method of exorcism, does it truly banish the spirits, or merely pass them on to the reader?

13 of today's finest horror authors have trapped revenants of their own within the pages of the book you hold. So, dear reader, I ask, have you the bravery to enter these 13 haunted houses? Do you have the nerve to release these evil spirits into your mind? Do not expect to be rid of them easily. I suspect these ghosts will haunt you for quite some time.

Curtis M. Lawson
Providence, RI
February, 2022

# UP ABOVE

## by Ramsey Campbell

"Time someone shinned up Slumber Mountain."

Carole keeps most of a frown to herself. "Grandad just means it's bedtime, Timmy."

"Of course that's all I meant," Paul says and wonders what his latest gaffe could have been. "I was only thinking of the film your mummy and daddy are going to see."

"It's called *Dream Higher*," the five-year-old appears to think Paul needs to be informed. "I want to see it too."

"It isn't what it sounds like, son. It's about people who want to be first on the highest place in the world." To the boy's parents Paul murmurs "I believe there's quite a lot of language in it."

"You can see it when it's streamed," Lawrence tells his son.

Paul suspects the boy will be very little older, but he has interfered enough – at any rate, he knows his daughter and her partner think so. "Say good night to grandad," Carole prompts.

In exchange for a fierce hug that smells of bathtime soap Paul says "Remember I'll be down here if you need me."

A series of creaks muted by new carpet recedes up the stairs to end in Timmy's bedroom overhead. Paul hears parental murmurs and a longer one from Lawrence, apparently a bedtime story. By the time Carole leaves Lawrence to it, Paul is more than ready to ask "Forgive me, what did I do wrong this time?"

"No need to make Timmy feel you're far away from him."

"Would it help if I went up to my room? Then I'll be next to him."

"We don't want him disturbed any further. Just leave it and let's hope he sleeps."

"Sorry if I've caused more problems than I've solved. I thought I'd give you both a night off after you've been so busy moving house."

"We do appreciate it, dad. Only perhaps you mightn't have come to stay quite so soon."

Paul feels as if her last remark has put paid to its predecessor. Rather than respond, he listens to the murmur overhead, and thinks Lawrence has begun to repeat words like a monotonous lullaby if not a prayer. Carole has fallen to glancing at her eighteenth-birthday gold watch by the time Lawrence reappears. "What were you reading?" Paul asks as he sees them to the front door.

"The wild things on repeat."

"That settles him, I take it."

"He wanted a story about a mountain, but I couldn't find one."

"We'll have our phones on silent," Carole says, "if you need to get in touch."

"I'm sure I won't. I looked after you often enough when you were Timmy's age."

Her late mother did more of that, which may be why Carole doesn't answer. Paul watches her ease the Audi out of the drive, reddening the bulky sandstone gateposts with her brake lights, and then he shuts himself in the massive Victorian house. It would have been too vast for him and Laura, but Carole and Lawrence plan to have more children, not to mention working as researchers at home. He listens at the bottom of the wide steep stairs, and when he hears no sound from Timmy he returns to the front room.

The fat white leather suite – not a wedding present but a hint that Laura would have liked it to be one – has gathered in front of the thin expansive television. Perhaps he'll find the sort of film he and Laura used to watch, some glossy monochrome relic of a past that never really existed, but first he wants to track down a fairy tale about a mountain, which he can read to Timmy tomorrow. Carole used to like him to read to her at bedtime, after all.

His phone lists three stories. Semsi Mountain sounds like sesame, and indeed the Grimm tale tells of a treasure hoard revealed by speaking the name. A poor man takes what he needs, but his rich brother is trapped in the cave when he gets the name wrong, and the robbers who stored the swag decapitate him. Paul doubts this would help Timmy sleep, and he brings up the story of the glass mountain, where an eagle attacks climbers searching for a magic apple. Eventually a boy succeeds by mutilating the bird, and Paul doesn't want to leave this image in his grandson's mind at bedtime, if indeed at all. Is the tale of the blue mountain more appropriate? It starts like the kind of joke that involves three men. While the Englishman and the Scotsman each pass a night in a castle without questioning their host, the Irishman discovers that he must stay three nights to rescue her from an enchantment and then wait for her without sleeping. Will this make Timmy reluctant to sleep? His parents won't thank Paul for that, and even the thanks he has received so far felt dutiful, but he's about to read on when he hears Timmy's voice.

It falls silent as he strains his ears. Though it was muffled by the ceiling, he's almost sure he grasped the single word. He could fancy it was prompted by the kind of story he has been reading, but if Timmy said something was granted, what was the wish? When Paul's efforts to listen bring him only his own thumping pulse, he returns to the tale. As the hero waits for the princess he rescued, a mysterious boy keeps putting him to sleep. Paul doesn't know how all this might affect Timmy at the edge of slumber, and he's nowhere near the end when he hears the boy again. This time he can't mistake the word. His grandson is calling to him.

Paul wants to think the tale confused him, but he's afraid his age let him down, by no means for the first time. He pockets the phone while he heads for the stairs, as he should have done earlier. The light from the downstairs hall illuminates the lowest landing, across which he can see Timmy's door, open a few inches. Silence lets him hope the boy has drifted off to sleep, and then Timmy speaks. "Grandad," he says yet again. "Come up."

His voice doesn't sound quite as it should. For a moment Paul imagines he's hearing it through the baby listener, the intercom system he and Laura set up long ago by infant Carole's cot. He'd kept it as a memory and eventually passed it to Carole, but Timmy had resented its presence in his room by the time he was two years old. What may be affecting the boy's voice instead? Paul plants a hand on the stout banister and has taken one step up when he realises why his grandson's pronunciation is so loose. He's talking in his sleep.

If Paul goes to him the boy may waken. The stairs he's standing on are signifying his indecision with a surreptitious creak when Timmy speaks again. "Can't you come up?" he just about articulates.

Of course Paul can. He undertook to sit, which means the opposite as well, and more. Carole and her partner aren't expecting much of him, perhaps because they feel it's inadvisable. He grips the banister and hauls himself up the stairs, which emit a series of creaks as though parodying his progress. He isn't quite so ancient, even if the house is. When he reaches the landing he keeps hold of the banister while he takes a necessary breath. As he lets go of the support, Timmy mumbles "Grandad's coming up."

He sounds as somnolent as ever. Paul is almost sure the boy is still asleep, but this isn't why he falters. The observation or the greeting didn't come from Timmy's room. His voice is further up the house.

Paul makes to call out, only to press his lips together. He shouldn't waken Timmy until he finds him. May the boy have walked in his sleep? That would explain why he isn't in his room, and it's meant to be dangerous to rouse a sleepwalker. Paul hurries across the landing and seizes the banister.

Are these stairs steeper than the lowest flight? Perhaps having to climb more than he anticipated makes them feel precipitous. He halts around the halfway mark to catch his breath and dab his forehead with the hand that isn't clinging to the banister. When Carole was young, he and Laura took her walking if not climbing every weekend in the countryside, but now he doubts he would be capable of conquering even a small hill. He rather regrets having joked about the mountain to his grandson. As if the thought is a cue Timmy was awaiting, the boy calls out "He's coming."

"I am indeed," Paul says, though only for himself to hear. He has deduced the boy is dreaming. Although Timmy doesn't sound nervous, Paul wants to reach him before the dream has any chance to turn unpleasant. Renewing his grasp on the banister, he plants a foot on the next stair to lever himself up, an action that helps him gather speed. "You can do it," he mutters despite begrudging the breath it takes. "It's your job."

Teaching used to be, but that's more than a decade behind him, and he feels he has lost the knack. Certainly his bids to educate Timmy haven't found much favour with the boy's parents, who plainly think the methods are outdated, no doubt like their perpetrator. So long as he can look after Timmy now, and he makes himself clamber up the rest of the flight almost as fast as he might have not too many years ago. He stumbles onto the second landing, and at once he's blind.

It's not the only disability he has hoped age won't spring on him. He clenches his fists as if this can squeeze some sight back into his eyes, and as he blinks so fiercely that they ache he begins to distinguish an unlit corridor ahead. The landing has cut off most of the light from downstairs, that's all, and he manages to locate a light switch beside the corridor. When he presses it down it yields with a crunch suggesting he has pulverised a fragment of plaster, but the floor stays dark.

He fumbles out his phone to send the flashlight beam along the corridor, where every door is shut tight. How could Timmy have been so audible if he's in any of the rooms? Perhaps he was talking in the passage and then dodged into a room. Paul plants his free hand on the cold wall beside the corridor while he takes several breaths, which taste increasingly musty. He's about to search the rooms when he hears Timmy once more. "Still coming," the loose dreamy voice says, and even now it's somewhere above him.

Is the boy playing a trick on him? Paul isn't sure enough to risk shouting. Instead he tramps across the landing in search of more stairs. The flashlight beam isn't as steady as he's determined to be, but it shows him a set of stairs with a banister on the left side and brownish wallpaper unappealingly reminiscent of mould on the other. The stairs must lead to an attic, even if he can't recall hearing there was one. The upper floor is unlit, and how dangerous may that be for Timmy, sleepwalking or otherwise? Paul makes for the stairs almost faster than his breath can keep up with him.

The banister is thinner than those below, and shifts in its sockets when he takes hold. The stairs are so steep he can't see where they end. When he aims the flashlight past them the enfeebled beam shows him only emptiness. They're uncarpeted, and each one has a creak in store for him. They feel less stable than he likes, which is one reason why he tries to clamber fast, but he has to halt before he's even halfway up. The breaths he sucks in taste much as the wallpaper looks. The tread he's standing on emits a loud harsh creak to speed him on his way, and he manages to labour to the top without stopping, though his pulse has begun to deafen him. He uses the banister to lever himself onto the landing, where he loses a breath in a gasp that falls short of expressing what he feels. He hasn't reached the top of the house. On the far side of the small landing boxed in by walls without doors or any access to a corridor, another set of stairs leads upwards.

He tries to recall how the house looks from outside, only to find he has no idea. He might as well never have seen the exterior. Has the light in the hall gone out? A backwards glance shows him unrelieved darkness, which the flashlight beam seems disinclined to penetrate. Why is he looking back? Timmy can't be down there. As if Paul's indecision has prompted his grandson to call out, the boy mumbles "Finally" somewhere above him.

What can he mean? Does that matter so long as it helps Paul locate him? Paul is at the stairs when he realises what he misheard. Of course, the boy said "Find me." It sounds like a challenge in a game, and Paul can't help wondering if he's being tricked into playing one. Suppose Timmy hid the baby listener up here and is really in his bedroom, where Paul didn't take the time to look? The suspicion provokes him to shout "Timmy, just you tell me where you are."

Silence is the answer. Straining his ears merely amplifies his vicious heartbeat. Suppose his shout woke the five-year-old, who wandered up here in his sleep and is terrified to speak, having wakened in a lightless unknown place? "Timmy, I'll find you," Paul cries. "Keep talking so I can."

This earns no response either, and he grows afraid for his grandson, so intensely that it feels as if the child's terror is infecting him. He clutches the scrawny banister, which rattles its uprights the entire length of the staircase, and lurches onto the first step. He mustn't falter until he finds his grandson. He has a dismal sense that if he halts even momentarily he may leave himself incapable of moving on.

He drags himself from stair to stair as rapidly as he can. Too many of them feel as shaky as the wavering beam makes them look. How deep is the darkness alongside the unsteady banister? He could fancy he's climbing beside an abyss, an impression that makes him reluctant to shine the light down. He flinches away from the unseen drop, and the back of his hand brushes the wall. Surely it's only the wallpaper that feels soft and moist and liable to wobble, not the bricks. He recoils from the sensation and grabs the banister again, which rewards him with a bony clatter of its uprights. He flings himself forward as an aid to clambering, though it feels like losing his balance if not unbalancing the staircase. His pulse is as loud as his dogged thumping footsteps, and seems close to blinding him. Just the same, when he staggers off the top stair he can see all too well where he is. He has reached another enclosed landing – doorless walls mossed with darkly glistening wallpaper, and no trace of a corridor – beyond which more steps ascend into the dark.

Are they steeper still? It can't matter. He's already tottering towards them, not so much at a run as in a bid to keep his balance. He hardly needs to hear his grandson say "Climb up," unless the indistinct words are "I'm up." He would call "Coming" if he had the breath. The banister wobbles in his grasp with a sound like bones grown restless, and beyond it darkness yawns as though it's tempting him to experience the fall. The stairs sway in a bid to fling him backwards, but surely that's just an effect of the light, and he struggles up them, panting in time with his pulse. When at last he gains the next landing he can only flounder across it to continue his helpless climb.

How many flights has he laboured up? He can't remember that, let alone anything earlier. All his memories are of climbing the stairs – of never having done anything else. Perhaps his age has sloughed off the rest of his life. He wants to believe he's dreaming or even that somebody else is dreaming his plight, but that can't make it go away. He's trapped within his laborious clambering, which has spread an ache through his entire body, exacerbated by his dull insistent pulse that makes his vision flicker like a repeated omen of a storm. By the time he wavers off the stairs he's forgotten how long he has been climbing them – an eternity, it might as well have been. The dusty landing leads to more stairs, beyond which Timmy is just audible. "I'm here."

Or are his words "Climb here"? They may as well be, since Paul can only comply. Each time he slides his hand up the skeletal banister, the support feels in danger of collapsing, pitching him over the edge. He can't bring himself to touch the wall, which appears to be pulsing in sympathy with him. That has to be his vision, and the instability of the light is why the stairs yaw from side to side like a rope bridge, however close he feels to being thrown against the wall or the insecure banister. He toils to the top, where he hasn't enough breath to protest at the sight of yet another landing with no exit except further stairs. "I can't find you," he pleads. "Find me."

Not just his breath feels worse than exhausted, in which case how did he manage to speak? Perhaps the voice was only in his head. His legs waver as if the muscles are being jerked with strings, and before he can react he's toppling helplessly backwards. He's several stairs down by the time he manages to seize the banister, almost dislodging it from the sockets. It feels lethally unsafe, so that for a moment he's glad when a hand reaches down from the landing to him.

It's pale and plump, and considerably too small for the length of the smooth bare arm, which is all he can see of its owner. Is it Paul's vision or the light that makes its shape look so undecided? He thinks the hand is hardly of a size to offer him support, even once the arm but not the hand begins swelling to compensate. Then the fingers fasten on his, and he loses his hold on the phone, which clatters down the stairs, taking all the light with it. The hand feels as soft and damp as the wallpaper did, but it's far stronger than it looked. He may as well have left all his weight behind, if not his substance, as it lifts him into the dark to meet its owner.

# EDDY BOY

## by James Chambers

I rolled up almost an hour late, and, of course, Duplass, that asshole, made a show of tapping his watch while I parked my pickup behind his snotty, white Beemer. One of four plots at the end of a cul-de-sac, the dilapidated cottage, with McMansions on either side, resembled a rotten tooth in an otherwise perfect mouth. In the grimy front window, a shadow moved. A kid watching me leave my truck? Nah, only a trick of the light. According to Duplass, no one lived in the dump anymore. Empty, neglected, decaying for years. The kind of disrepair obvious even through a four-inch crust of snow, overgrown brambles, and spider-webbed evergreens, the kind of distress and decay that provided me with job security.

"Hey, Reese," Duplass called. "No rush. I haven't frozen both my nuts solid yet."

I took my time zipping my coat, tugging on my gloves. "Should've waited in your car. Bet you even got heated seats."

"With the price of gas, I'm going to idle my car for an hour waiting on your lazy ass?"

"Ah, shove it, Duplass," I said. "I came straight from the hospital. Got held up waiting for the doctor."

Duplass's expression softened, but I looked twice to convince myself. For a moment, I thought he might apologize for busting my balls. Wishful thinking.

He straightened his cornflower blue silk tie. "Oh, yeah? How's Theo doing?"

I shrugged, held my voice steady, and wrestled back the tears that always gathered when I thought about how Theo was doing.

I wanted to spend every minute by his side, but I needed this job, needed all the jobs I could handle for when the doctors' bills rolled in. "Same as yesterday, and the day before, and the day before that."

"He's going to get better, though, right?"

"His body, yeah, but his brain? No promises, but they're optimistic."

"I hope he recovers soon, you know?"

"Thanks. I appreciate you throwing some work my way. Been a few years. You usually go for the big boys, VerminX and PestPro."

"Yeah, sure, but, y'know, I heard about Theo, and, hey, everyone else was booked up, right? You positive you can handle this?"

"A few rats? I'll get the job done."

"Good because the fucking recession is killing me. No one wants to buy a total teardown when people are out of work right and left. I've had this dumpster fire on inventory for years, like Marley's fucking chain. I want to let the place go, and I've got nibbles from a buyer, but the damn neighbors are threatening to petition to have the place condemned if I don't skedaddle the rats. *All* of the rats."

"Show me around," I said.

Duplass and I stomped through the snow along the front of the house. I scanned the asbestos shingle siding and cement foundation for entry points, saw nothing there or along the driveway side. Around back the circular, steel screen for the house vent hung half rusted away from the masonry, leaving a hole big enough for half a dozen rats to squeeze through together. On the far side of the house, I eyed a broken pane in a basement window.

"Got to keep things sealed tight," I said. "Rats will squeeze through the thinnest cracks. This place must look like the Ritz-Carlton with those big holes. They come for the warmth, make a nest. Got a landfill maybe a mile and half from here, a sump just down the hill. Probably where they started out. You ought to take better care of this place."

"Spare me the lectures," Duplass said. "Can you get rid of them or not?"

Get rid of them or not. Yes or no. Black or white. Thoughtless

Duplass. Like so many people who believed they lived in an off-or-on world, like computers, all ones or zeros, us or them, no time for uncertainty. Theo lived there too, lived in his head too much, in video games and TV shows about made-up stuff that didn't matter. It formed a canyon between us, a gap we couldn't ever seem to close and might never get to bridge now. Impatience narrowed Duplass' eyes.

I nodded. "Yeah, sure, I'll send them packing, but rats take time."

"How long?"

"Couple weeks. Maybe months."

"You're joking."

"No, sir, it's a process. First, I seal up the entry points. Then I put down exterior bait stations. I'll set up snap traps in the house so any we kill in there die fast, and we can clean them out easy. Check back in a few days, remove the carcasses, refill the bait, rinse, and repeat. Ought to knock off enough rats to keep your neighbors happy and clear the house soon enough."

"Soon enough would be today. But go ahead, do what you have to."

Duplass pulled his smartphone from a pocket in his coat, initiated a call, but as we started back to our vehicles, I froze in my tracks. A dead cat lay in the snow, sunken into a cavity melted by the heat of its steaming blood and viscera. Splayed on its back, belly open to the sky, its head twisted around too far, neck broken. I'd seen dead animals of all kinds in my line of work, but this wasn't the result of animal violence or roadkill. A person had done this. Cut a line from neck to crotch then peeled the cat wide, pinned down its hide with sticks, removed its organs, then arranged them beside it in a pattern. It nauseated me like no dead mouse or raccoon ever had.

"Holy Mother," I said, barely keeping down my lunch. "Duplass!"

He hadn't seen it, had walked right by it, and turned back to me, annoyed.

"What the hell is going on here?" I said.

"What? We're killing rats."

"How could you walk right past..." I said, then fell speechless again when I pointed to clean, white snow. The carcass vanished. No blood, no tiny heart and lungs, or any other sign of gore. Only a thin branch bundled with dead leaves, dropped there by the wind. I looked up at Duplass. He'd already resumed his call, stalking off to his Beemer. Wind whispered around the house, quiet and unyielding against it. Beyond the back yard, rows of dead trees shook, a buffer between the home and the sump downhill from the cul-de-sac, its surrounding chain-link fence visible in the distance.

I walked to my truck, thinking how little sleep and no real rest I'd had since before Thanksgiving, how sadness for Theo hollowed me out and sapped my vitality. Tired minds played tricks on the senses. That's all. I gathered my kit, four outdoor bait stations, treated steel wool, a replacement screen for the house vent, and then piled it all in a five-gallon bucket.

Duplass prattled into his phone. I pitied the poor soul on the other end of that call. Vermin made better company than hucksters like him. His voice faded as I trudged out of earshot. Along the driveway, on a patch of snowless ground, I staked the first bait station to the hard earth, pounding it in with a rubber mallet, then loaded the little poison brick. Next, I moved around back and pried away the old house vent cover, dropped it in my bucket.

The wind whipped up, howled across the opening in the wall. A tiny voice whispered from the hole. *Theo's.* I hadn't heard his voice for weeks, except in my dreams and those off-kilter moments when funny things he'd said floated to the surface of my memories. The sound chilled me deeper than the cold. Everything made me think of Theo now. Nothing that didn't relate to him mattered. I shivered and lined the opening with high-grade, chemically treated steel wool, which worked wonders deterring mice and made rats think twice. They might eat through it, but the sharp fragments would kill them from the inside out if they swallowed them. The new cover fit, almost perfectly. I fastened it with the old bolts, still solid enough.

Around the side of the house, I measured the frame of the broken window.

The filthy glass made the basement inside a dank mystery.

A puff of warmth escaped through the shattered pane. I wiped one of the other panes with my glove, rearranging grime into thick smears. Another warm breath came. Barely enough light reached the interior to give a sense of the space inside. All shadows. I wiped the third pane. More filthy streaks. In the basement, a shape moved and something thumped.

Surprise set me back on my heels, stole my balance, and dropped me on my ass.

Duplass, coming around the corner just then, shook his head. "Smooth move, Reese."

"Hey, man, you got people living here?"

Duplass stared at me the way a teacher stares at a student who asks the exact question they just answered for the class.

"No. I told you, the place has been abandoned for years."

I pointed a thumb at the house. "Those folks inside know that?"

"You saying you saw someone inside?"

A child in the front window. A dead cat. A shadow in the basement. *My weary brain.* I pulled off a glove and rubbed my eyes, pressing against the ache behind them, then scooped a handful of snow and held it to my brow. The cold refreshed me.

"Maybe a kid in the window when I pulled up. Someone in the basement just now."

"Un-uh, no way."

"Well, you got the heat on in there? Warm air's coming out."

Duplass frowned. "Why would I heat an empty house?"

"Keep the pipes from freezing."

"Water and electric have been off for years. Pipes flushed dry. Shit, you think someone's squatting?" Duplass rushed to the window. Want a tightwad's attention? hit him in the wallet. "Where?"

He knelt beside me as I pointed to the broken pane. After slipping off his glove, he held his hand to the opening. "Cold as hell. Hasn't been any oil delivered here for years anyway. No fuel for the furnace." He stood, replacing his glove. "How long is this going to take, Reese?"

"Another hour, maybe."

"It'll be dark before then."

"I got a late start, sorry."

"Well, hurry it up. I don't want to be here after dark."

Duplass stormed off. I scribbled my measurements on a notepad from my toolkit then returned to my truck, set up my sawhorses, and, from scraps I kept, cut a piece of quarter-inch plywood to cover the window. I drilled holes then brought it to the house and screwed it tight to the frame with my electric drill. The hardware bit eagerly into the wood.

The wind rose, speaking with Theo's voice again. I took my finger off the drill trigger and listened. The mechanical whir died. Icy air bit at my nose and cheeks. On the other side of the window, something banged, then—hell no, was that a *scream*? Wind. Rustling branches. Duplass on his phone. Car engines on nearby roads. From the house, though, silence. Not a scream, only the wind and the whine of the drill in my ears. Nights of shitty sleep in a hospital recliner. My exhausted mind making things out of nothing. Made-up things that didn't matter in the real world. Black-and-white things.

I revved the drill and tightened the last screws. Yanked the board, and it held solid. I shoved tufts of steel wool into the cracks around its edge.

After staking the remaining bait stations, I returned to my truck.

The edge of twilight descended. Christmas lights blinked on at the neighboring houses. Bright lights painted me as an SUV pulled into the next-door driveway. The engine died and then the driver hopped out, a middle-aged man in a camel-hair overcoat. A teenage girl in a pink ski jacket and a white pom-pom hat exited from the passenger side. She came around to help the man—her father, I assumed—ease an elderly woman from the back seat. The girl noticed me and waved.

"Hey there! Happy New Year," she said.

Her father looked at me, read the lettering on my truck. "You here about the rats?"

"Yes, sir. I'm going to get this place all cleaned up," I said.

He approached me through the street. Over his shoulder, I

watched the old woman lean on the girl and tremble. Her watery eyes locked with mine, frightened of me maybe, or anxious from the cold. Or did she glance at the house first then me—and not frightened but sad? As if she saw the fatigue in my face, the dark, rundown cottage, and thought my work an awful burden, or—she eyed the house again. Then as if the sight of it offended her, she pulled down her hat and turned away, speaking to the girl, her granddaughter, I guessed.

"Thanks for coming out," the man said, snapping me out of my thoughts. "That moron, Duplass, kicked and screamed before he hired you, but I appreciate you taking care of this. He says he can't sell the place, but I swear he doesn't even try. I heard he's refused at least three good offers from property developers. Just lets it sit here and rot." He dug into his pocket and then handed me a business card. "I'm a lawyer. That guy hassles you, tries to short you, cut corners, anything like that, give me a call."

"Oh, uh, sure, thanks."

I couldn't take my gaze off the old woman. What the hell had she seen?

The lawyer rushed back to her. He and his daughter helped her up the walk and into their bright, high house. A boy Theo's age opened the front door, all smiles and wide eyes, happiness, and energy, and hugged the old lady as he guided her into the warmth and light.

Twilight turned the cul-de-sac into a shadowland. I hated this time of day. Difficult to see, visibility for driving worse than full dark. I'd always warned Theo about walking or riding his bike at twilight. You're almost invisible to drivers. Just another shadow at the edge of the road. He rolled his eyes, yeah, but I knew he listened. Even though kids his age felt invincible, they listened, sure, even if the next minute they ran out of the house and forgot everything they heard. In one ear, out the other. Onto the road. Into the hospital.

I waved Duplass over to my truck.

He ended his call. "Yeah?"

"Ready for inside now."

He sighed and led the way to the front entrance. I carried a bucket full of snap traps and supplies. Duplass shoved his weight against the door as he clicked the key in the lock. It creaked open into blackness and the tangible mustiness of a place closed off for too long.

"No electric. You got a flashlight?" Duplass said.

I dug a headlamp out of my bucket, tugged it over my hat, and switched it on. Sterile LED light pierced the gloom.

"Got one for you too," I said.

"No fucking way I'm going in there." Duplass glanced into the house then at the last of the sun going down on the other side of the trees. "That's your job."

"It'll take longer if I have to find my way around."

"I don't care." Duplass backed away down the front steps. "Gonna be dark soon. You should've been on time."

Duplass talked a tough game, but that's all. I wondered why the house frightened him so much. Rats, I figured. No one likes being in the dark with rats. I could refuse to go inside without him, but that would gain me nothing but an hour of listening to him bitch. And how hard could it be to find my way around a two-bedroom cottage?

"Fine, guess I'll take my time then."

I lifted my bucket and walked into the house.

Like the door, the floor creaked. Hell, everything did. The walls and windows, the ceilings, it all groaned and sagged with my presence, as if the house had atrophied from disuse and no longer had the strength to bear the weight of someone inside it. Where the hell had that thought come from? Like something out of one of Theo's video games or TV shows. Houses were houses. Wood, cement, Sheetrock, shingles. Glass. Tiles. Insulation. Wires and pipes. Only people made them anything more than fancy boxes to keep out the elements. Only families gave them warmth. I'd learned that lesson hard and sure.

In the living room, I dropped two rat traps: spring-loaded devices with enough tension to break your wrist or damn near take off a finger. Two more in the kitchen. One in each bedroom, one in the cramped bathroom that reeked of mildew. The floor there bowed underfoot, dislodging tiles from long crumbled paste and grout. Everywhere, droppings that testified to the presence of rats.

As I searched for the basement door, enough daylight remained outside so I could see through the front picture window. Duplass paced at the edge the driveway, waving one hand, the other pressing his phone to his ear. Beyond him, Christmas lights on the neighboring houses shimmered like jewels in the dirty glass. The warmth of those houses seemed like Earth seen from the moon in those old astronaut pictures. I detoured to the love seat by the window and looked for signs of the child who'd been watching through the front window. Threadbare, dust-furred upholstery looked utterly undisturbed. The only footprints in the dust, mine. The only child, a shadow. Or a stray memory of Theo staring out our front window the same way.

With a sigh, I promised myself an eighteen-hour catch-up sleep binge in a real bed. Next week, when Marcy returned from her Dominican Republic vacation. Let Theo's mother sit with him a few nights. To hell with what her newest sugar daddy wanted. Couldn't guilt her into canceling her trip for her hospitalized son, but once she set foot back in town, she'd have to pay attention, if only for the sake of appearances.

The basement door stuck in its frame. A quick jolt with my shoulder freed it.

My headlamp revealed a rickety staircase. Ugly and splintery. I leaned my weight against the wall and bannister, tested each sagging step until I reached the bottom. Except for the cone of light cast about wherever I looked, darkness filled the space. I grabbed a Maglite from my bucket. Sitting on my heels, I selected three snap traps and considered where to place them. Under the furnace oil tank, near the house vent, and by the broken window seemed obvious to start.

Broken window first. I set a trap, eased the catch into place, then slid it against the wall. House vent next. I pulled the snap back toward the catch.

"It's not what you think," a woman said.

I jerked so hard with shock, her voice right in my ear, that I triggered the trap. It bit hard on my hand, crunching bone, muscle, and tendons through my thick glove. I howled. With a long, flathead screwdriver snatched from my bucket, I wedged the mechanism open and freed myself. Spinning around with the screwdriver in my good hand like a knife, I lit up a woman against the furnace with my beam of light.

"It's not what you think."

She wore a filthy, black turtleneck and a skirt with a high hemline. Dark, tear-ruined makeup streaked her cheeks. Leaves, bits of mud, and other debris hung from her matted hair. Dirt smudged her cheeks and bare legs. An earthy, rotten odor rolled off her. I guessed her age, around mid-thirties, and wondered how she could last in the cold with such thin clothes and bare feet. She pressed to the steel furnace like a trapped rodent.

"What the holy hell?" I said. "Shit, lady, you should *not* be here."

"I can't leave. He might hurt someone if I leave."

My legs felt too rubbery to move. "Who else is here?"

I swept the basement with my lights. Empty and small, a storage place, utility for the furnace, oil tank, and water heater, few places to hide.

"You should go now," she said. "Right now. Go."

"I got to finish my job first. You and anyone else here got to get out right now. You don't belong here. This ain't your house."

"You should go be with Theo."

My heart skipped a beat. "How do you... know about Theo?"

The woman shrugged. A scuffling noise came from behind me.

"No, don't look! Please, don't," she said.

I ignored her. In a far corner lay a boy, age thirteen or so, belly down, face resting on its right side, left leg twitching, dirty sneaker scraping the floor. I tracked his body with my Maglite, then choked back a cry. Folds of brain poked through a crack in the side of his skull. Blood slicked his short hair, pooled around his head like a halo on the floor. Pink froth bubbled from his lips. A broken boy. Theo by the side of the road. Mangled bicycle beside him. Blood on the curb. Eyes as blank as an overcast night sky. Grief twisted through me.

I whirled back to the woman, gone, glanced back at the boy, gone.

A stony weight gripped my heart. I blinked away hot tears

welling in my eyes. Wind scraped and scratched at the house. Whispers floated from every crack, wordless voices warning me, pleading with me, for things I couldn't understand. How much was real, how much in my tired, overtaxed brain, I had no idea. I clamped my hands to my ears, focused on Theo, on finishing this job, getting paid, then pulling my head together to take care of him if—no, *when*—he left the hospital. *When.* My eyes locked to the patch of lit floor before my feet. I reset the sprung trap by the window then hurried to the furnace and set another. Head down. *Get done, get gone, get back to Theo.* The house vent, done. At least three more for good coverage. Basement empty. Voices quiet. My body running on adrenalin and desperation, fast-burning fuel. One into a bare corner, another under the stairs. Another corner, and call it done, but only the one where I'd seen the boy remained.

I raised my light, inch by inch, exposing only empty space.

Hunched down, I set and placed the last trap.

"We loved Gorf, that goofy old dog. At least, I did. Eddy Boy couldn't ever love."

I shouted and spun around to confront the woman—no sign of her. In the middle of the basement, lay a dog carcass, opened and disassembled like the cat. The name on its tag, attached to its collar, read *Captain Gorf.* The stench of its innards nauseated me. My breath came heavy. My head spun. I loosened my coat zipper, releasing body heat.

A deep throb swelled in my injured hand. Sweat beaded on my forehead. Spots flashed across my vision. The smell of fresh blood and meat choked me.

"You ever watch them shows about cold cases and serial killers?" the woman said.

As the dog vanished, she emerged from the shadows, naked, her torso cut open, skin peeled away in flaps to either side, her organs glistening behind and below her cracked ribcage, heart and lungs missing, blood dripping, plopping on the floor, evaporating. I shrieked. Afraid to look away, I backed up the stairs, rushing, careless. My foot crunched through a weak step, toppling me backward, my body snapping more steps, falling through, until I landed on my back with a bone-jarring slam. Pain erupted through me. The Maglite bounced from my hurt hand, rolled away, its light painting wheels of brightness on the far wall, casting the shadow of a tall boy.

I tightened my grip on the screwdriver.

"Who are you?" I said when I'd caught my breath.

The woman knelt beside me, her organs squishing, held in place by an invisible force. "I'm Nikki. Me and, Edmund, my son, Eddy Boy, we used to watch those shows. That's how I knew what my little Eddy Boy is."

"You should *not* be here, no one should *be* here, how can you be alive?" I said, talking to myself more than Nikki, keeping my head about me as I grappled onto my feet, every inch of my body aching from my fall. The back of my neck and skull pulsed. "I'm leaving now, calling it a day, did my job, heading home to rest, God, I need rest, real rest, fuck Duplass for sending me in here."

"Penny-pinching bastard never did anyone a damn bit of good," the woman said. "Thought he could hide us away, forget about us."

"Why'd I ever come into this house?"

"Same reason I'm here." Nikki grinned, creating hideous patterns in her dried makeup, arcing gray lips cracked from dehydration. "For your son. Your Theo. My Eddy Boy."

"Sure, sure, Eddy Boy. Who the hell is Eddy Boy? Dammit Marcy, you should help me, help Theo. I need sleep. I am absolutely losing my shit." Rest would put this right, get my head back on straight. Can't go so long without sleep. Brain playing tricks. Hearing voices. Seeing ghosts. I shuffled to the stairs, eyeing the broken steps.

My foot bumped something soft. I tried not to look, couldn't stop myself, as if a hand cupped the back of my head and forced my gaze downward. The corpse of a girl lay between me and the stairs. Dissected like the cat, like the dog, like Nikki. Nude. Her killer had folded her clothes and tucked them beneath her head for a pillow. A crutch lay beside her. A milky film covered her open eyes. Her heart and lungs lay above her head, forming the same pattern I'd seen by the cat, the remaining organs within her open body rearranged to match. Coarse rope bit into her ankles, binding her feet together. I dropped to my knees, gagged, and dry-heaved. By the time the convulsion passed, the girl had vanished.

"The first time Eddy Boy pulled the wings off a fly, I worried. Next, he cut a cicada in two with his pocketknife. Then a bird with a broken wing. All those crime shows say the signs start young." Nikki hovered at my shoulder, her voice much too close, breath frigid and damp on my neck, but I couldn't bring myself to look at her. "I told myself, just a cat, just a dog, just bugs and rodents. Poking dead birds with a stick. Stepping on ants. Hard enough raising a son alone with his asshole father keeping us a secret from his wife. Then here Eddy was, in the basement with that handicapped girl from the next block."

*Stop talking to me. Go away. Stop. Talking. To. Me. You're not real. Go away.*

I dragged myself to the bottom step, climbed, reached the gap where I'd fallen, threw my body across it, clutched the threshold of the upstairs door, spread out my weight, pulled, kicked as boards cracked, my feet dangled, and my muscles sparked with pain— then I rolled over onto my back upstairs. My chest heaved. So little light came through the picture window. Everything draped in murk except for my headlamp.

I crawled to the decrepit love seat, pulled myself up, legs throbbing. Outside, Christmas lights, snow, Duplass a silhouette pacing at the bottom of the driveway, his breath forming long horsetails of mist against the fresh night. I banged on the window, hollered his name.

"Poison seemed best. Perfect for vermin."

The plip-plop of blood dripping from Nikki's torso.

"Worked too slow. Maybe I used too little. Eddy Boy figured out what I'd done. Cut me open. Dragged my body to the sump in his little red wagon. Then the poison hit him hard. He fell and smashed his head on a rock. There we lay while rain came and covered us over, washed us to the bottom, into the mud and silt."

*Not real. Go away.*

Theo, I'm coming, I'm coming back, I promise, son, I won't leave you alone ever again, never leave your side.

"He did something with the animals, with their guts to trap us here. Something he read on the internet. God, you should've seen his browser history. Stuff I never even knew existed when I was thirteen. Torture. Magic. Cults."

I pounded the window. Duplass finally, looked, all the bright lights behind him.

*Yes, come, help me get out of this place.*

I shouted his name again. He walked faster, up the steps. The door opened. I pushed myself onto my feet, as he stepped across the threshold.

"What the hell, Nikki, aren't you done in here yet?" he said.

*Nikki.* How the hell did he know her name?

In a singsong voice, Nikki said, "Eddy Boy, Daddy's home!"

A shadow rushed across the room. Black ropy limbs gripped Duplass, covered his nose and mouth, yanked him inward. His cell phone dropped, cracked on the floor. He struggled for balance, for escape as the shadow dragged him deeper into the house. The substance of it rippled. Rats. Dozens of rats. Their fur, tails, and claws giving the darkness form. A flash of sharp-edged white. Then a red, wet line appeared along Duplass' torso, staining his tailored dress shirt and that damn cornflower blue silk tie, spraying his overcoat as his chest split open and the rat-dark shadow dragged it apart, cracking his ribs. His heart lifted on a thick coil of hairy shapes. Turned in the air. A soft hand fell on my shoulder as Nikki whispered in my ear. "Parents have to do what's best for our children even if it rips the heart out of us. Duplass liked to keep us neat and tidy right here. Sooner or later, though, we've got to send our kids out into the world. All they need is someplace to go, something sacrificed. He thought you'd do for that, but I think children turn out best when a parent makes the sacrifice."

Nikki spun me around to face her. I knew no name for what I saw in her eyes. Devotion. Despair. Love. Self-loathing. Pain. Resignation. Grief. All those emotions and others I couldn't identify, had never felt, hoped to never feel.

"I can't keep him any longer," she said. "At least his father found him a new home. I told you to go be with Theo. I gave you a chance. He won't be Theo much longer."

My headlamp died, dropping her face into darkness. The

sounds of teeth gnawing bone, rending flesh, the wet scrape of organs pushed around on the floor, the scrabbling rhythm of tiny claws filled the room. The truth about rats was you never could get rid of them altogether, only chase them off to another home, a new nest. They traveled like ghosts. You wouldn't know they were there until they'd already taken over.

"Eddy Boy knows the way now," Nikki said.

I shrugged off her clammy touch. The rat-dark reached for me. I swung the screwdriver, slashed at fur, meat, bone, teeth, tails, and flesh. By the grimy glow of the neighbor's Christmas lights, I found my way to the door, the cottage now ripe with the smell of death, and the squeal of rats maddened by something beyond instinct. Theo filled my mind, the imaginary worlds he loved, where impossible things happened. For a moment I almost understood: black, white, on, off, chase a rat from one home, it finds a new, better one. I slashed with the screwdriver. Duplass screamed.

A blank space exists in my memory after that.

One moment, those noises and the whisper of Nikki's words—next, sitting behind the wheel of my truck as if snapping out of dream, swerving on icy roads, missing a tree by the curb then skidding to a stop, disoriented while wind shrieked and my screwdriver, slicked in blood, jangled in a cup holder, a scrap of blue silk from Duplass's tie matted to it. Theo's name echoed in my head. My cell phone rang, rang, rang. The hospital number onscreen. Fresh dread replaced my horror as I lifted the phone from its holder, swiped the green icon, and, in a trembling voice, answered.

# THE BIRD HOUSE

## by Douglas Wynne

Compared to the photos, the place looked pretty ordinary to Emily in the noonday sun. Like most of the rentals on Scare BnB, the lake house had been showcased from odd angles with bad lighting that lent it a creepy vibe, and now, stepping from the car, she worried it would disappoint. If Steve—still peering at it over the steering wheel through the bug spattered windshield—found it disappointing, she couldn't tell. But his criteria would be different, and he didn't need to know where she'd found it. Not yet. She would come clean in the end, but for now, she intended to safeguard the blind experiment from undue influence. And for that to work, she had to get into the house ahead of him and stash the guestbook somewhere he wouldn't find it.

They'd parked beside a maple tree on the gravel drive, and while Steve pulled suitcases from the hatch of the SUV, Emily trotted up the footpath to the front door where she found a combination-locked key box hanging from a metal loop around the doorknob. She punched in the lock box code she'd memorized from the host's last email, opened the compartment, scooped out the key, and let herself in. Steve didn't complain that she wasn't helping with the bags. They might be down to the dregs of romance these days but apparently chivalry died a slower death.

She found a light switch just inside the entryway and inadvertently turned on a set of ceiling fans suspended from rough-hewn beams beneath the skylights before finding the right one to turn on the lights. The guestbook was hard to miss, set out on a lace doily on an end table by the staircase. The book was the only overtly Gothic item in sight, and the host had spared no expense—a leather-bound journal with raised bands on the spine and an elaborate Celtic knot stamped into the cover, lending it a dash of occult flair. A fountain pen lay beside it.

Emily hastily stashed the pen in her pocket and wedged the journal under a couch cushion. Steve's nosy curiosity about the vacation homes of strangers didn't extend quite as far as whether or not they dropped pocket change and guitar picks between the cushions. Nor did it extend to the cracks and seams in the universe through which people lost other things—pets, parents, and tragedy-stricken loved ones. Well, maybe this weekend, with its charade of an anniversary getaway, would change that.

The door clattered open behind her and Emily started. Steve wrangled a pair of suitcases by the handles and stepped sideways through the doorway, a canvas grocery bag stuffed with dry goods draped over his elbow swinging at his side almost spilling its contents. He dropped the bags on the living room floor with the absolute minimum of finesse. Was that a passive aggressive commentary on her lack of help after all?

Emily pecked him on the cheek on her way out to fetch the smaller bags, leaving the cooler for him. They hadn't packed much in the way of food. Mostly beer, wine, and light snacks. The plan was to shop on Saturday morning at a nearby supermarket and maybe pick up takeout somewhere on Saturday night, but they had enough to make a simple meal tonight: crackers and cheese, pasta and a jar of sauce.

When she returned from the car, Steve was standing in the middle of the living room, hands on hips, taking the place in. The house definitely had a history, a fact she was sure Steve was absorbing. Most Maine rental cottages favored the generic hunting lodge kitsch that would appeal to a general audience seeking a different vibe from what they had at home. This was not at all the MO on Scare BnB, where the photo galleries were chock-full of Victorians with creepy dolls and shacks with rusty saws and other menacing miscellany tucked in amid a décor that generally looked more preserved than staged. As if the places were living museums, which Emily supposed the authentic ones were.

The interior of the Taggart House looked ordinary at a glance. Red-and-white checkered curtains, moose-shaped bookends perched on a mantle made from a railroad tie above a fieldstone fireplace, a folk art stenciled sign framed with birch twigs: LIFE IS BETTER ON THE LAKE. But there were also darker flourishes mixed in, giving the appearance of two different geological strata of décor. And that made sense, based on what she knew about the history of the place. Glen Taggart, the infamous previous owner, had inherited the house from his mother, Connie Taggart. His father had built the place as a retirement home for the couple but had died of lung cancer just seven months after putting the final coat of paint on it. Connie continued to use it as a vacation home until her own retirement from teaching in the 1990s when she moved up to the lake full time and became something of a socialite. Emily didn't know if their only child, Glen, had spent much time at the lake before ownership fell to him, but when it did, the entertaining stopped abruptly. Soon, the long, rutted driveway, once crowded with cars belonging to members of Connie's book club or knitting circle or the RTVs of the young men who cut firewood and cleaned the gutters and ice damns for her, was overgrown with weedy grass.

Glen was a loner. Not rude, but never chatty. Often spotted prowling the woods at dusk and dawn with his camera and bird watching binoculars. The only relationship he cultivated was with a local hunter, trapper, and taxidermist who lived in a small cabin on the far side of Shale Hill.

Emily had learned the backstory from the well-thumbed paperback currently residing in her purse. *Haunted Vacationland* devoted a six-page entry to the Taggart House, a fact of which Steve was blissfully ignorant as he transferred the contents of their cooler to the fridge. According to the book, Taggart had abducted and murdered a small parade of hikers and leaf peepers who went missing around Marasco Lake during his tenure there. When the sheriff's department put the house on the market, an out-of-state buyer, savvy to the interest it held for the ghost hunting community, snatched it up and ensured it was kept well preserved.

The lighthearted folk art vibe Connie Taggart had bestowed upon the house was likewise left undisturbed by her serial killer son, who'd merely augmented it with his own strange aesthetic. Where once there might have been family photos, there now hung a series of framed black and white portraits of what Emily imagined were otherwise colorful birds. She couldn't be sure which was creepier—the taxidermy mounts of glass-eyed pheasant, red fox, and raccoon running rampant across the shelves and walls of the house or the grainy, colorless photos of birds that somehow managed to look even more lifeless through Glen Taggart's lens than their stuffed counterparts.

"Weird place." Steve's two-syllable assessment. He rummaged in the kitchen drawers for a bottle opener and popped the cap off a Sam Adams. Another stenciled sign above his head proclaimed: SING AS IF NO ONE CAN HEAR YOU. Emily only nodded, wondering, not for the last time that weekend, if she'd made a terrible mistake.

By the time they were finished unpacking, the sun had dipped below Shale Hill across the lake, leaving the house gloomy with shadows. Steve went around searching for more light switches while Emily put the water on to boil. She cooked, nursing a glass of wine, while he downed another beer. They ate in near silence except for Steve complaining about the lack of a TV and musing on whether or not it was worth using his data plan to watch Netflix on his tablet.

Contemplating another glass of Cabernet, Emily suggested that the absence of a TV was supposed to encourage conversation in a rustic lake house. Steve, whose tendency to talk obsessively about his job had dried up in recent months, shrugged and set about pillaging a closet full of puzzles and board games, stacking the boxes that caught his eye on the braided wool rug in front of the hearth where he'd given up on starting a fire. When Emily came in, she found him counting Scrabble tiles.

"Leave the dishes in the sink," Steve said without looking up. "I'll do them before bed."

"Don't worry about it. They can wait until morning. *Ooh,*

Parcheesi! I haven't played that since I was a kid. What else have they got?" She moved to the closet to take stock of the games he'd rejected, and felt his eyes tracking her as she stood on tip-toes, slid a box out of the stack, and carried it to the dining room table without asking his opinion.

"*Really?*" he said, the word almost a sigh. "The Ouija board? That's your go-to for a romantic evening away from home? You are still such a Goth girl."

She raised an eyebrow, gave the planchette a flick, and set it spinning between the thumb and middle finger of her left hand. "What other game encourages you to dim the lights and huddle close?"

"*Game?* So you've had a change of heart. Did you read up on its origins like I told you to?"

Emily nodded, her mischievous smile defiant in the chill wind of his condescending contempt.

"So you know it's not some ancient gypsy oracle. It's a parlor trick, barely more than a hundred years old, designed to cash in on a bumper crop of widows after the Civil War. You can—"

"Even look up the patent," she finished for him. "I know. I did, after our last debate about it. I also read some interesting theories about how it works. Want to test them?"

Steve was on his feet now, sensing that there was more flirt than fight in her demeanor. He drifted toward the table and looked at the board.

"I mean, since neither of us believe in it... what's the harm?" she said. "You're not afraid of talking to the walls in a remote cottage filled with dead animals. Are you?"

Steve laughed and took in the room again. "Yeah, what's up with that, anyway? Is it our hipster host's idea of irony or something?" To Emily's ears, he sounded relaxed, good humored. The beers had washed away the irritability she'd sensed earlier when he was still blaming her for blowing their vacation budget on something that wasn't up to his standards. He still clutched a Scrabble tile in his hand: a Q. She plucked it up and tossed it at the rug with the others. "You showing off your vocabulary isn't sexy, darling."

He shrugged. "So tell me what is."

"Séances. Séances are sexy. Get those candles from the living room."

The red fox and the raccoon watched him go.

The planchette roamed the board aimlessly.

"This is stupid."

Emily shushed him and repeated the question. "Who is here with us?"

A... N... Y

"Any?"

The planchette paused on the letter M, then repeated the rest: MANY.

"Many. Who are *you?*" Emily asked. Then, in a whisper, "Steve, light touch. Let it lead."

"I can't believe I'm doing this."

The planchette moved to G, then T, then to the empty space at the center of the board. "That's not even a name," Steve said.

"It's initials."

"How do you know?"

Emily shrugged.

"What? Tell me."

"They're the initials of the previous owner of the house."

"And you know this how?"

"I read about it in one of my local lore books."

Steve removed his fingers from the planchette, shook his head in disdain, and almost got up from the table but then changed his mind, set his fingers down on the plastic again, and asked, "Is Emily fucking crazy? Did she lure me here on false pretenses?" He shoved the planchette to YES.

Before he could let go of it again, Emily asked, "Has Steve ever cheated on me?"

The planchette traced a fast circle around the board, dragging their fingers along for the ride and landed right back where it had started: YES.

Steve stood up, nearly knocking his chair over behind him.

"You asshole," Emily said. "I knew it."

He didn't protest or try to pick a fight with her about how gullible she was. Didn't tell her that she'd pushed the thing to try and distract from her own deception. He just stared through the archway at the kitchen sink, eyes wide, mouth agape. Emily followed his gaze. The pots, pans, and dinner dishes floated in a red bath, as if the tomato sauce residue had spread to overtake and stain the soapy water she'd filled the sink with to soak them. The red wave sloshed over the side, and pattered on the floor in thick stars.

The stenciled sign over the sink had changed. It now read:
SCREAM AS IF SOMEONE CAN HEAR YOU
She did.

"Give me the keys, Em. I'm not kidding."

"Why? Are you scared? Admit it. You are."

"I'm not fucking scared. You set this up. This whole thing. It's some kind of trick house, right? That's why you booked it. To play a prank on me? Well, I'm not amused. There are better things I could be doing with the weekend if this isn't about our anniversary, which clearly it isn't."

Emily stood between Steve and the car door, the key ring clutched in her fist behind her back. "Yeah? You have something better you could be doing? Like what, exactly? Like Jenna from work?"

"Oh, come *on*. You pushed it where you wanted it to go, just like I did."

She scoffed. "It practically dragged us."

"You think a ghost told you some secret I'm keeping from you? That is insane."

"You said the Ouija works by... what did you call it? Micro motor movements. The subconscious impulses of the users. So, by your own reasoning, if you don't believe in spirits, it was your guilty conscience talking."

"I can't believe you're talking about honesty after you switched that sign."

Emily opened her mouth to fire off an angry retort, but stopped herself and exhaled. This was not going the way she'd planned. Everything was accelerating to a confrontation too fast, before she even had a chance to explore the house or ease him into the weirdness she'd hoped to encounter. She didn't know what she'd imagined would happen here, exactly. That he would see a ghost with his own eyes and have some great moment of conversion to her worldview? That he would turn to her, wide eyed, and whisper: *you were right. They're real.* Whatever it was she'd expected to find here, it wasn't folk art signs that changed their lettering. And she couldn't expect *him* to just change. To not look for other explanations. Occam's razor and all that. God, how he loved that phrase. So, of course, her tricking him was the simplest explanation.

"What did you see, exactly?" she asked, as calmly as she could manage. "You saw what the sign said. Did you see anything in the sink?"

He looked confused. "Just the dishes." And was that a new look in his eyes? Was he wondering if she was unwell? If the quirky beliefs he'd thought were mostly harmless actually signaled mental illness?

"Okay," she said, raising placating hands, the key ring looped over her ring finger. "Let's start over. Can we start over? Just forget about the Ouija board and the sign and... my paranoia? We just got here. It's paid for. Let's just start over and try to have a nice weekend. We can play Scrabble if you want or... I don't know. Just don't leave."

Steve looked up at the dark silhouette of the lake house, its tall windows reflecting the hazy moon, the towering pines looming over it frosted with tarnished silver. The candles burning in the kitchen looked small and dim against the night.

"So, this place is supposed to be haunted? That's the deal?"

Emily nodded and laced her fingers through his with the hand not holding the keys.

"I hope you didn't pay extra for that."

"No. It was cheap. Not cheap enough to let it go to waste, but..."

Steve sighed. "All right. Let's turn on some lights and play Parcheesi."

Steve woke early out of habit and wandered the house in his flannels watching the salmon-colored dawn seep into the condensation on the big windows. The wood floor was cold under his bare feet as he padded to the kitchen to put on a pot of coffee. The sign above the sink was back to its more innocuous message about singing, as it had been when they'd come inside after their fight last night. Emily hadn't explained how it worked, and he'd decided he would rather ignore it than stoop to a display of curiosity by taking it down from the wall to examine the back. Probably some kind of photosensitive ink and a battery. He found another sign in the same style above toilet:

## MY AIM IS TO KEEP THIS BATHROOM CLEAN
## YOUR AIM WILL HELP

In a better mood, he would have found it funny. Alone now, while Emily slept in, he did examine this one, easily within reach, hanging from a single screw on a standard saw-toothed bracket. There was no battery compartment on the back, and when he rapped his knuckles against it, the sound and feel confirmed what his eyes told him: it was just a wood plank. Maybe the one in the kitchen was different. Whatever. He stripped down and spent the usual five minutes figuring out the best setting on the unfamiliar shower control.

The water was hot, the pressure strong, and he stepped out feeling revived, his enthusiasm for the weekend getaway restored. He usually jacked off in the shower, thinking of his greatest hits with Jenna from HR, but today he'd decided to save it for Emily. If she felt sufficiently guilty about her accusation last night, she might even work for it.

He toweled off, dressed, unzipped his shaving kit, and lathered his face. A few strokes in, he shook the clogged blade under the running faucet and watched bright roses of blood bloom in the shaving cream swirling around the drain. In the mirror a deep, dark gash ran across his throat from ear to ear like a lewd smile. Behind him, the shower was beaded with ruby drops, as if he'd bathed in blood, not water. The sign over the toilet read:

MY AIM WITH A BLADE IS CLEAN
PLEASE AIM YOUR VEIN AT THE DRAIN

Steve shut his eyes and clamped a hand over his throat. He felt only stubble and the bulb of his Adam's apple, and when he opened his eyes and examined his palm, it was smeared with shaving cream, not blood. Deliberately averting his eyes from the sign, he grasped the doorknob and cranked on it, fearing it would be locked, but it flew open, and he spilled out into the living room.

Emily stood in front of the bay windows with a steaming mug of tea cupped in her hands, a shawl draped over her shoulders, her hair still a bird's nest from sleep. She looked up at him and her sleepy expression went taut. Steve caught his breath and swallowed. He could feel his face flushing with heat under her gaze.

"You saw something," she said. "What did you see?"

He touched his throat again, then stomped past her to the kitchen, opening and slamming cabinets looking for a coffee mug. Emily trailed behind him and set her own cup on the counter. "Top right," she said, and took the milk from the fridge for him. "What was it, Steve?"

"You know goddamned well what it was. Another trick sign. Trick mirror, too. This is getting tiresome, Em. I'm barely awake. It's not funny."

But she was already gone before he finished his rant, speed walking to the bathroom, tossing her shawl at the couch on the way. When she returned, he was sipping his coffee. It tasted cheap and bitter, but it would still do to clear the cobwebs from his head. They'd come up here to relax and unwind. But fucking Emily and her woo-woo Wiccan bullshit couldn't let that happen. She had to go and get hustled by some huckster. Two tickets to Bumfuck Maine's version of Disney's Haunted Mansion.

The red fox stared at him from a low partition between the kitchen and living room.

"What are *you* looking at?" This was all so stupid. He was angry at Emily, sure, but he was more angry at himself for getting caught off guard in the bathroom. He should have expected another cheap scare when he saw the sign over the mirror. But he fell for it like a punk.

*Only, you* did *expect it. You even took the sign down and examined it, and you still have no idea how it changed.*

Emily crept back to the kitchen table, picked up her tea, and quietly sat down across from him, the way she did when she was trying to discern how much of a hair trigger he was on. After a moment, she asked, "What did it say?"

"Huh?"

"The sign in the bathroom. It changed, right? Like last night?"

"Doesn't matter. It's another stupid trick. Take a shower. Maybe you'll see it and get your money's worth. How many more surprises are there?"

"I don't know. The place has a reputation but I wasn't expecting this."

"What's the reputation? Clearly, you're dying to tell me. You said those initials last night belonged to the previous owner. The ones you spelled on the board."

"*I* spelled?" She scoffed. "*Still?*"

"Jesus, I don't want to fight with you about it but I don't see how we can just settle in and enjoy the prank. How is that a relaxing weekend for me? And for you... You actually *believe* this place is haunted and you want to what? Hang out and get terrified? How romantic."

"You know what's not romantic, Steve? Pretending that we don't have differences. Pretending that you don't think I'm stupid and gullible. Or that you don't have this smug, condescending attitude about my interests and way of looking at the world. Pretending that it's not an issue. That it hasn't put distance between us. And I'm just supposed to ignore that, like it doesn't matter. I'm just supposed to be *intimate* on demand with someone who looks down on me. Grow old with someone who doesn't think there's anything beyond death's door." Her eyes fixed on the scratched tabletop, her tea going cold, she shook her head slowly. "I don't know how to do that."

"That's what this is all about? You brought me here to have it out."

Emily shrugged. "Maybe I did."

"To see if you could convince me that the bullshit in those books you're addicted to is real." He laughed. "Have at it. Convince me. But I'm warning you, if there's a security deposit on this place, it's on you because I will tear it apart plank by plank to show you what a sucker you are for cheap tricks."

But she wasn't hearing him. She was staring at something over his shoulder. When he turned to look, the sign they'd seen upon entering read:

LIFE IS BITTER AT THE LAKE

A keening wail rose through the house, emanating from all directions at once. It began as a moan, almost a sob, then rose in pitch and intensity, morphing into a ragged scream that set loose objects buzzing and rattling against every adjacent surface. The sound lasted for no more than ten seconds, but it seemed like it might never stop. The hair on Steve's arms rose with it. He shot up from his chair and looked around for the source, heart pounding like he'd just sprinted a quarter mile, the sudden adrenaline dump setting his fingers trembling in imitation of the ceramic robin's eggs that just a moment ago had rattled against each other in a nest of woven twigs on an end table. The sound system required to produce the effect would have to be phenomenal. He rubbed the gooseflesh down, embarrassed by his animal reaction to the effect.

Emily held a hand to her heaving chest. It had scared the hell out of her, too, but there was more than that in her eyes. She looked exultant.

Steve dropped to all fours and looked under the couches and chairs, scanning for hidden speakers. Nothing. He moved through the first floor on a mission, tilting the framed bird portraits to look behind them at bare wallpaper, sweeping curtains aside, and even gazing up the fireplace flue into the darkened chimney. But he found no speakers or wires.

He climbed the stairs to the loft, surveying the open floor plan from above the rough-hewn beams, inspecting the ceiling fans and light fixtures.

"Steve? You're not going to find anything, you know. I promise. Just save yourself the effort and I'll tell you what I know about he house. About Glen Taggart."

Another wavering peal of anguish slashed through the floor like a shark fin breaking still water. This one came from below, from the basement. He took the stairs two at a time back to the ground floor, rounded a corner at speed, and came to a narrow door beneath the stairs. It was padlocked. He took a poker from the fireplace, wedged the tip in the latch and cranked on it. The short screws that held it in place screeched out of the wood and the lock tumbled to the floor with the bent hardware still attached. He turned the knob, threw the door open on a rectangle of darkness, and felt the wall for a switch. He was moving fast, like he always did when he was angry or frustrated. Too fast for fear to catch up with him.

There was no light switch, and the sky through the high windows of the living room had darkened with storm clouds, lending scant light to spill through the slim door onto the top step. Steve tromped down the creaking planks into the gloom, the smells of wet cement and old gasoline crowding into his throat along with a coppery tang that might have been his own spent adrenaline.

"I wouldn't go down there, if I were you," Emily said behind him.

He shouted back over his shoulder, his tone bolder than he felt, his volume pushing any tremor out of his voice. "This is where the equipment is, Emily. That's why it was locked. Come on. I'll show you. God, this is stupid."

A beaded chain hung from a bare bulb fixture at the bottom of the stairs. When he clicked it on, the circle of light only extended about a dozen feet, but he could tell from the sounds of his own motions reflected back from distant walls that the basement had to run most of the length of the house. It sounded vast and empty.

Emily appeared behind him with a flashlight she must have found in a kitchen drawer. She swept the beam around the dank space, then tracked back to linger on black letters splashed across the cement wall.

## SCREAM AS IF NO ONE CAN HEAR YOU.

"This is where he tortured them," Emily said. "The hikers and tourists he hunted. He was a birdwatcher and amateur photographer, but he also collected bird songs with a handheld tape recorder. Eventually, when he started collecting people, he recorded their screams. Here in the cellar."

"Give me that." Steve wrenched the flashlight from Emily's grip. It was a heavy, black job with a long metal barrel, the kind a night watchman might have used fifty years ago. For its size, the amount of light it threw was meager compared to modern models, but it felt good in his hand. Like a weapon. Ignoring the hokey message on the wall, he walked the length of the room, scanning the pipes and wiring and exposed insulation in the ceiling joists, looking for evidence of a digital audio player, a timer, any kind of A/V system at all. But he found nothing.

"The police took his photography and recording equipment as evidence. But by the time he was caught, he'd already stopped using it."

Steve turned to look at her. She flinched at the light and he aimed it at her feet.

"According to a woman who became his prison pen pal, he came to believe that electronics weren't necessary for collecting the death songs of his victims. He believed he could save them in taxidermy birds that would sing them back to him on command. Hey, I'm just telling you the lore. In the end, he even stopped using birds. He thought the house itself was recording the screams and echoing them back later, for his enjoyment."

Steve found a broom in a corner and used the handle to poke at the fiberglass insulation strips in the ceiling. Nothing. No wires or audio components. The place was empty and clean, except for stains in the concrete floor that would probably never come out. Oil or paint. Had to be. He leaned the broom against the wall and brushed past Emily on his way up the stairs. "Whoever rents this place? They should hire you. You do half the work for them."

When Emily reached the top of the stairs, she could hear Steve rooting around on the second floor, opening closets and tossing the place like this was an FBI raid. She leaned in the doorway of the master bedroom where she found him on his knees, shining the flashlight beam into a heating vent in the floor. The room was cast in a pewter colored gloom, and rain pattered on the windows. Thunder rumbled somewhere over the lake.

"You check the attic yet?"

He looked up at her. "There's an attic?"

She nodded and led him to a nook at the end of the balcony landing where she pulled a dangling cord and released a folding ladder from a trap door in the ceiling. Springs groaned, thirsty for oil as she swung it down. "After you."

Steve hesitated, then to spite her climbed up and switched on a light. "Jesus Christ."

If the basement had been a vacant disappointment, the attic more than made up for it. Every corner was crowded with dusty boxes and bins. Racks of dresses and coats jostled for space. Furniture draped with dusty white sheets loomed beyond the circle of light. But all of the clutter had been relegated to the outer perimeter of a clear space in the middle, where a row of antique bird cages hung from hooks driven into the ridge beam.

The cages rocked gently—whether in response to the stirring of the air from the opened trap door or the storm outside drafting through vents in the eaves, Emily couldn't say. Each held one or more taxidermy birds, their claws wrapped around wooded perches or affixed to the bars of their cages, their plumage dark and glossy in the dim light, eyes dead, beaks frozen open in silent mimicry of song.

"Well, I gotta hand it to you, babe. This is some creepy-ass shit."

Emily touched the tarnished bars of the nearest cage, half expecting an electric shock. Thunder crashed and she jumped, setting the cage swinging and clattering against its fellows. The rain picked up, drumming on the roof shingles mere inches from their heads. A chorus of screams and moans rose with it, lingering in a wavering dissonance when the surge subsided. Sounds of anguish, insanity, and despair.

Shadows shifted in the corners, moving among the coats and dresses. Shadows of birds thrown by the bare bulb through the rocking cages, but also... something else. Shadows of people.

*Who are you?*

*Many.*

Scott saw them, too. His gaze tracked them nervously, flitting around the attic. He didn't look like himself anymore, but it took Emily a moment to put her finger on what was missing. Then it came to her: his smug condescension was gone, leaving the impression of a house without a tenant. She'd never realized just how much of his personality it constituted.

"What's the matter, Steve?" she whispered. "I'm sure it's just funhouse mirrors. Tape loops and motion sensors."

Something else was emerging from the gloom now beyond the birdcages. A blurry, man-sized shape radiating menace in its every movement. The birds shrieked at its approach. Their beaks remained static, their bodies frozen in time, but the sound that filled the attic was a chaos of fluttering wings, restless talons, cries of pain and alarm.

Steve took a backward step, and with it, lost a foot of height as his leg dropped through the hole in the floor and caught on a rung of the ladder. His ankle twisted and he barked his knee against the trapdoor frame before falling backward through the gap, flailing for purchase. The shape swept over him and he tumbled down the ladder, trailing a cry of alarm until his head hit the floor with a *crack*, cutting the sound short. The riot of noise crowding Emily's ears ceased with it, the birds and rain muted to a near pristine silence marred only by the echo of Steve's cry ringing in the rafters. Within the space of a heartbeat the house had absorbed that as well.

Emily sat on the couch with the shawl wrapped around her shoulders, the guestbook in her lap. She didn't have time to read all of the entries, hungry as she was for those other stories, but she leafed through the pages, scanning for confirmation of her own experiences in those of the previous guests. And she found it in spades. References to the changing signs, the echoing screams, the restless bird cages in the attic. The ambulance would arrive soon, and the temptation to steal the book was overwhelming. To take it home where she could linger over the things others had discovered that she hadn't had time to explore. But the host would hit her credit card for the loss and trash her rating with bad feedback. The fee she could live with, but she couldn't risk the damage to her rating. There were still so many places she wanted to visit.

She uncapped the burgundy fountain pen and paused to gather her thoughts, the gold nib poised over the empty page. She wanted to believe she would sleep here tonight. The place was paid for, and Steve might be in a nearby hospital bed. She could make a fire and stay up late with the book, a cup of tea by her side. But who was she kidding? He wasn't just unconscious. The police would have questions.

She had to be careful. To write anything at a time like this was crazy, but she had to leave her mark, contribute her verse to the song of the house, just as Steve had done. She hesitated, and omitted the date.

*Thank you for the opportunity to experience Taggart House! It has such a powerful atmosphere, and really brings another time back to life. Such sights and sounds! Drifting off to the lapping of the lake, waking up to birdsong. We can imagine never leaving. Sadly, we've had to check out early, but hope to one day return.*
*—M.*

# DEATH PLATE SEATING FOR 1,000

## by Sarah Read

The house would never fall. That's what the seller's listing promised. But the listing of ancient beams promised otherwise, as did the eroded cliffside that weathered closer to its doorstep with every storm.

"That's just the soft rock," said the seller, an old man with a face as eroded as the cliff. "The bedrock is stronger stuff. Hasn't gone anywhere for two hundred million years; isn't going anywhere anytime soon."

Dad believed him. Mom didn't. But she wasn't moving with us, anyway.

The house was ten times bigger than her city apartment and cost ten times less. Fixing it up would narrow the gap, but Dad didn't want to fix it *too* much.

"Just think of everyone who has ever lived here," he said, running his hand along the shaking banister where countless hands had worn away the stain and polished the wood to a natural shine. Polishing, I thought, is just another kind of erosion. Less violent than a cliff face. Or a crumbling marriage.

But the house's dark past was exactly why Dad had bought it. *Smuggler's Cove*, it was called, the seaside destination for Jacobean criminals.

"Maybe we'll find their cache of treasure," Dad said.

I nodded. They had mostly smuggled priests and potatoes. Discovering a cache of four-hundred-year-old potatoes did not seem unlikely.

I got the master bedroom—a trade for losing everything else. I had my own hearth and a bathroom with a clawfoot tub, an enormous closet, and a bay window with a seat that overlooked the sea. And the cliff, which had crept so close to the foundation that I had to press my face against the glass to see any land at all. But from there, nose and brow held against the cold windowpane, I could see sideways along the edge of land. That was how I saw the stairs. They had been cut into the rock itself, steps worn low and smooth at the center, some crumbled away altogether, tracing a sloping line down the seven-hundred-foot precipice. Iron spikes for handholds protruded along the steep path, weeping rust stains down the rock face.

Our first meal in the new/old house was cheese and crackers, the cheese not cold enough because all the ice in the cooler had melted and the fridge, of course, did not work.

"Go check the fuse box in the basement. I'll tell you if anything comes on." Dad brushed cracker crumbs from his lap and stood, handing me the small flashlight from his pocket. It was uncomfortably warm.

An earlier trip to the basement had revealed that the network of pipes that crisscrossed the low space created a kind of maze that was impossible for a grown man to cross. A scrawny sixteen-year-old girl like myself could squeeze through, if I waved a stick ahead of me to gather all the webs that filled the space like insulation. I made my way through the tangle of old pipes, some rattling, some warm, some coated in oily deposits.

The basement spanned the whole width of the house, irregularly shaped with an odd number of dark corners that swallowed the flashlight's glow. Only the cliffside wall ran straight.

An orange glow caught my eye. It came from the wall—a flash that disappeared when I moved my head and suddenly sparkled back into view.

As I got closer, the light grew in intensity—neon orange, then magenta. It poured through a crack in the damp stones of the basement wall—the setting sun beaming through the cracks in the old stone foundation, the only skin between our basement and the open air of the cliff face. Irregular rocks piled against the wind, moss and lichen for mortar. The stones were oddly patterned, writhing lines and sunburst sprays etched into the surface of each, and the shifting light cast the shapes into motion.

I pressed my eye to the hole and felt a breeze against my lashes. The view of the sea through the cracks seemed distant, but the percussion of the waves at the foot of the cliff below felt near enough that my toes curled as if to avoid the splash. It shook my heart free of frozen dread, and I backed away from the wall, pressing against the sticky, web-covered pipes.

"Dad!" I called across the dark basement. He didn't answer. I turned and scrambled across the floor, web stick left behind, fuse box forgotten. I wanted to get out from under the house, out from the crushing weight I could feel pressing down on me, as the foundation groaned under the lash of the sea. I crawled out of the basement and didn't stop, running hard for the front door.

"Callie!" Dad called after me.

"Get out!" I shouted back over my shoulder.

He followed, more concerned for me than alarmed by my words, I was sure, but relief washed over me as soon as we were both clear of the porch.

I stumbled to a stop in the weeds of the overgrown lawn.

"Callie, what's wrong?" Dad grabbed my shoulder, pulling me to face him. I gasped to catch my breath, wiped web and dust from my face, the grit of the basement floor rough on my fingers.

"That house is coming down," I said. "Any second. The basement wall isn't even there anymore. It's open to the air."

"Callie, the house isn't going anywhere. I'm sure it needs patches, yes, but it's not at risk of coming down. I did have that checked, you know."

"I promise you, the foundation is broken. It's not stable. None of this is safe."

Dad let go of my shoulder, his hand dropping limply to his

side. I thought for a moment that he was finally listening. "Did your mother put this idea in your head?"

My breath left again in a rush. "No! I saw it myself—the wall has crumbled away, and there are holes in the stone big enough to look through."

The sun had set further, dipping into the waves, and the house's shadow fell across us.

"I'll take a look at it myself," Dad said.

"I don't even think you should go in there. You can't fit through the basement, anyway."

"Then will you come and show me? Here." He held out his cell phone. "Take a picture of the wall. Show me what's got you so upset."

My knees felt weak at the idea of going back under the house, back to the broken wall.

"It's going to be fine, Callie. I promise."

I took the phone from him and gripped it tight.

The basement was darker without the orange glow of sunset. It would be hard to even see the cracks in the dark. Would they show up in the picture?

"Flip the fuse while you're down there, please." Dad's voice chased me through the dark maze of pipes.

I made it to the wall, hands shaking. I could still feel the crash of the waves below, and the soft fall of old stone turned to sand. I set the flash on the camera and snapped a few shots, inspecting the photos after. The holes were just black spots on the grainy wall. their nothingness appearing as solid black—solid, though they were anything but.

I switched the camera over to video and filmed my own hand receding into one of the spaces. I pressed a finger against a small stone and filmed it falling away into the dark, the hole it left behind now wide enough to reach through.

A shaky sob caught in my throat as I pulled my trembling hand back through.

"See?" I whispered to the camera, as if it alone might believe me. "There's nothing here."

I stood another moment, listening to the wind pass through the holey wall. What if Dad didn't believe me? Would anyone? I switched off the camera and emailed myself the video, just in case.

I made my way to the fuse box, my path lit by the phone's flash, and pried open the rusty door. The inside was all web and corrosion. There were no visible labels and no switches, just old glass plug fuses that looked like they might crumble if I touched them. Just like the wall. I snapped a picture of them, too.

I turned and made my way back, trying not to panic, trying not to rush. Dad was waiting at the basement door.

"None of those fuses do anything," I said, and handed him his phone. I moved toward the front door.

"Where are you going?"

I turned back to him. "We can't stay here. Look at the pictures, the video. No one should stay here."

He thumbed his screen to life and swiped through the photos. The static rush of the wind filled the house as he played the video. I heard my own frantic voice: *"See? There's nothing here."* I heard the wind howl through the open spaces like a rough voice: *"I'm here."*

Dad's head snapped up to look at me. My heart stuttered.

"Is this a joke?" Dad asked.

"I didn't say that! I didn't even hear it!"

He shook his head. I reached for the phone, but he slipped it into his pocket.

"I'll ask the contractor about the wall. But I'm done talking about it tonight. Now, get inside." He turned away and walked deeper into the house.

I stood in the doorway, half in and half out. *I'm here.* Just the wind.

The wind blew through the cracks in my bedroom window as it had in the basement, eroding the face of the house as the waves eroded the cliff below. I opened my laptop on the dusty desk.

There was a red sliver of battery left, despite the fact that I had left it plugged in. Whatever fuse supplied this room was as dead as the one in the kitchen. I opened my email and clicked the message from my father's phone. The computer screen dimmed to conserve power, but it seemed bright in the dark room as the video played. So many dust particles flashed across the screen, blowing every time I exhaled, that it was hard to see past them. The camera's focus slipped in and out as my hand disappeared into darkness, reappeared pale and shaking.

*See? There's nothing here.*

*I'm here.*

Wind buffeted my window so hard that the curtains swayed in the draft. The computer screen went black, the red glow of the power light fading, then winking out.

I switched on the camping lantern on the dresser and eyed the corners of the room, every shadow unfamiliar and stark. The draft's subtle movements made the LED seem like flickering candlelight. I carried the lantern into my closet, changed out of my clothes covered in basement filth, and put on my robe. The thick fabric had trapped the smells of home, releasing them as I pulled it close, my eyes stinging with tears that had stayed hidden until now. I crawled under the blanket, flinching as the bed groaned, and I pressed my head into the pillow, trying to block out the wind's rough voice.

*I'm here.*

The wind both pushed and pulled, knocking me back, then tugging at my jacket, unsure if it wanted to drive me away from the cliff or drag me over. I had to stand close to the edge to see the stairs. The top few had eroded away so that it was a drop of two feet, at least, to the next intact stair. The iron handholds were long railroad nails, jutting out, rusted to sharp points. But the stairs were broader than they had appeared from my window, carved deeper into the rock so that they didn't seem quite so treacherous as I had first thought. They cut back and forth across the cliff at a steady decline, disappearing from view below a scrub-covered outcrop.

I sat in the tall grass so I could scoot closer, hanging my feet out into the air, lowering them over the edge so that I sat with my feet on the first solid stair. I looked back to the house.

Dad had begun to demolish the kitchen, fuses be damned, tearing into the old cabinets and plaster walls—a force of erosion himself at high-speed, wearing it all away from the inside out. My gut fluttered. One heavy drop of his hammer and the whole house might come down.

Would it come flying past me on the stairs? Would we wave to each other in midair?

I pressed away from the reeds and stood. The stair felt solid beneath me, more so than the house did. Perhaps the wind would pluck me off the cliff face and I would disappear, tossed to the sea.

I wrapped a cold hand around the first iron spike and took a step. The open air to my right felt like a gnawing threat, and I pressed myself close to the rock face. Here, too, it was patterned like the stones of the foundation. I traced the shapes with my eyes as I walked down, clinging to the vining impressions of some long-lost life in stone. The turn when the stairs switched back was almost enough to send me scrambling back up the cliff face, but I spun, faced the wind and the sea. At the next switch I was low enough that the spray of a wave hit my face.

And then I came to the scrubbed outcrop, the protrusion of stone to which desperate, stunted trees clung and somehow lived. Their branches were stripped by wind, beaten by the constant force, and where they crooked, sea birds had built nests. They all stood empty, now. I hadn't seen or heard any birds since we'd arrived. That seaside sound had been absent. It would have felt more like a holiday with reeling gulls.

I edged below the outcrop, gripping the iron spikes as the stairs stopped in the shelter below the overhang, the tree's roots forming a curtain along its edge. I took a deep breath and looked down. Only waves and foam below, reaching up for me, and where the rock wall had been, gaping between the hanging tree roots, an opening. A cave.

I turned myself toward that darkness and stepped inside. The wind was instantly silenced. My ears rang in its absence, their numbness fading to a sting in the cold stillness.

The cave was not natural. It had been carved out of the cliff face; the scars of old tools marred its surface. Fragments of broken crates and glass lay scattered across the entrance. It tunneled far into the darkness, an unknown depth. As far back as the light hit the walls, I could see the now-familiar markings, depressed shapes crossing the stone surface, and here, away from the wind and waves, they were bolder. The crisp outlines of fish, and twisted plants, and curling, thick tentacles. Some even looked like bones—an eye socket, a joint. And wings. So many birds. They grew larger and clearer the deeper into the cave I walked. I wished I'd brought my lantern.

I pressed my hand against the stone, tracing the curve of a feather. Stone crunched under my toes. I bent down and ran my hands over the cave floor and picked up a slab of stone as broad as my palm. A fossil. I traced the surface along a stem or twisting spine. I tucked it into the pocket of my jacket, intending to come back with the lantern, maybe with Dad, to show him this strange wonder. The smugglers had only left garbage, but the real treasure had always been here.

I hesitated at the mouth of the cave. The stone felt so strong, secure. Safe compared to the flimsy house, safe out of the whispering wind.

Climbing up the stairs was harder than descending had been, and by the time I reached the dry grass of the cliffside meadow, my legs trembled both from exhaustion and strain. I wrapped my fingers around the fossil in my pocket and made my way back to the house.

The seller's blue truck stood parked in front. He crouched on the porch, peering through a window.

"Hello," I called out. He started and turned to me.

"Oh, there you are. How you settling in?"

I frowned. Politeness and honesty warred in my mouth. I shrugged, not trusting myself to speak.

He laughed. "I'm sure it's not much of a fun project for a young woman like you."

I didn't like his smile. His comment decided the outcome of the war on my tongue. "You really shouldn't sell people houses that aren't safe."

He shoved his hands into his pockets and I pulled my hands out of mine, the stone gripped tight under white knuckles.

"Now, don't worry hun. Like I said before, nothing ever leaves these cliffs. What's here has always been here."

*I'm here.*

His eyes lowered. "See there for yourself." He pointed to the rock in my hands. "Two hundred million years and it's still here, intact, undisturbed—until you picked it up." He raised his eyebrows.

I lifted the fossil and looked at it again. Outside of the shadow of the cave I could see it was speckled with hundreds of small fossils—a matrix of stone shapes.

"It's called a death plate. Stone that once was seabed. Everything that died settled on the seabed, layered over, fossils on fossils, all the way through."

I turned the rock over. All sides were covered in shapes, in death.

"Nothing ever leaves this cliff. Even in death." His lurid smile had fallen away, but his slack intensity was even worse. A strange light shone in his eyes, like the light piercing the cracks of the foundation. "The house is part of the cliff. It always will be."

I wanted to throw the rock, to hit him in the face and make those strange lights go out. I resisted. I wanted to show the rock to Dad more.

As if he heard my thoughts, the man smiled again. "When your dad gets back, have him give me a call. He said he had a question about fuses."

I nodded and backed farther into the weeds as the man passed me on his way to his truck. I watched the truck disappear across the field before I turned my back to it and headed inside.

"Dad," I called. There was no answer.

*When your dad gets back*, the man had said. Had he gone somewhere? Perhaps he'd gone in search of tools, hopefully for some food. I rubbed a spot clear on the dining room window and peered through. The tail of the car poked out of the shed. He hadn't gone anywhere, unless he'd walked. It was twenty miles to town.

"Dad!" I called again. Silence, not even wind. Anxiety gnawed at me. What if he was hurt? I raced into the kitchen, empty, up the stairs to his room, the bathroom, all empty. Might he have tried to get in the basement? Cold sweat sprung up on my face as I raced back down the main stairs to the basement door.

"Dad?" My feet felt heavy on the steps, this enclosed stairwell somehow more terrifying than those on the cliff face. The basement was dark save for the swords of sunlight cutting through the walls, crisscrossing the maze of pipes and web. My eyes followed the sunbeams, tracing their paths over the stones of the foundation to a place where one disappeared into shadow. In the dark of a corner, a shaft of sunlight was swallowed. I climbed over pipes and under wires to that corner, to the mouth of a tunnel in the rock. Another room? Another level of basement? The smuggler's storage?

I breathed into the space and the sound echoed back, hollow.

"Dad?" It echoed.

*I'm here*, the wind whistled through the stones. It froze the cold sweat on my lip, my brow. Was this a part of the cave? The end of the cliffside tunnel?

*I'm here.* Louder this time, less wind and more voice. Was he lost? Trapped? How stable was the rock of the tunnel?

My heart raced. "Stay there, I'm coming!" I shouted into the echoing darkness and the stone shouted back.

I stepped into the narrow space, remembered the darkness at the back of the cave, the way the stone shapes seemed to move, and I pulled my foot back. I turned instead and raced for the stairs, up through the house and up again to my room, my legs straining, my lungs aching for air, choked on the dust and damp of the house. I grabbed my lantern and swung back toward the stairs, thundering down over the wooden treads that screamed in protest, my footfalls enough to bring the whole house down. With Dad beneath it. I slowed my pace, tried to step softly, but still swiftly, willing myself to fly.

The basement felt darker, the sun, having arced high, no longer shot its beams through the wall; instead light fell in weak streams to the floor. I clicked on the lantern. It glowed dimly, exhausted from a long night of keeping the shadows of this house at bay.

I made my way into the tunnel. The stone walls were narrow here, more roughly cut, as if fresh, and the patterned facets of stone felt like eyes tracing my progress into the heart of the cliff.

"Dad! I'm here!" I followed the tunnel farther back, the weak light of the lantern reaching only as far as my own outstretched hand. Grit on the floor of the tunnel rolled roughly underfoot. Stones scattered against my toes as I pushed ahead. Still, I felt wind on my face, like the whisper of a stranger standing too close.

I do not know how far I had gone before the rock ceiling grazed the crown of my head, stone scraping and tumbling away from my shoulders as the passage shrunk around me. The walls seemed to constrict and relax with the rhythm of my breath, as if I were an obstruction in some stone creature's throat.

As the light grew dimmer, the patterns in the rock grew larger, teeth as big as my palm, eye sockets that could have swallowed my arm. Plant fronds like sails, tentacles like grasping ropes. I tried to shrink myself to fit the space, to peel away from ancient stone faces.

"Dad," I whispered.

*I'm here.*

The stone breathed against me. I knew, then, that he would not have come here. Would not have gone this far into the dark, into the close, heavy stone inside the ancient cliff.

The space was too tight for me to turn around, my shoulders wedged as I tried, abraded by ancient corals, stuck fast against calcite bones.

I wrenched myself loose and stepped backward, toe to heel, eyes stuck on the dark beyond the lantern's reach. I slipped on a loose stone under my heel, feet sliding out from under me, and instinctively I grabbed for the walls, hands raking across the stone surface, palms tearing on sharp rock. The lantern fell, blinking, and rolled away down the slope, farther into the tunnel.

I sat, panting through the sting in my hands, watching the light recede. My own breath became the wind in the tunnel, swirling off the walls and back at me. The orb of light grew smaller as it rolled away, disappearing to a pinprick then winking out.

The dark pressed in like a thick blanket against my skin. I gripped the walls and tried to pull myself to stand, and my fingers slipped in the wetness of my own blood. I struggled to my feet, pulled my arms in close, and held my hands protectively under my chin. A shaking sob escaped my chest, echoing off the stone.

"Callie?" a voice came from down the tunnel.

My voice caught in the pain that choked my throat. "I'm here," I struggled to whisper.

A spot of light appeared far down the tunnel. I squeezed my eyes shut, convinced it was an illusion, firing neurons or a specter born of pain. When I opened my eyes, the light had grown. A soft crunch of stone approached.

"Dad?"

"I'm here!"

I moved forward toward the light as it advanced. I pressed past the tightness of the stone, beyond the hollow eyes that once again grew visible as the light approached. I stooped, crouched, then crawled as the tunnel tightened, so low my head scraped the ceiling, my shoulders pressed between its walls. I folded myself into the tight throat and knelt in the crumble of loose rock that littered the ground, all death plates patterned with a thousand lost lives.

The lantern rolled to a stop in the dust against my knees. It flickered. Its glow did not reach even as far as my breath as another sob escaped me. Faces peered out of the stone. The curve of a brow, grinning rows of teeth, the shape of human hands gripping at my hips and shoulders. My father's face, wrought in stone, poised as if to kiss my bleeding forehead.

"Dad?"

The stone around me groaned.

I screamed, the sound tearing through me like a knife as the rock walls screamed back at me in violent echoes.

I writhed backward, setting the lantern rolling away again, its light disappearing almost instantly, the faces winking out in darkness. I pushed against the stone with my torn hands, leaving pieces of myself behind, another fine layer in the cliffside, another death on its plate.

The flesh of my arms became the mortar between the ribs

of trilobites, the skin of my knees cement to build a stronger foundation. As the tunnel constricted around me, the howling breath of wind narrowing to a whistle that piped through my ears like a million screams, I stopped pushing and lay in my stone bed.

And I knew then that I would be here forever, one among thousands, holding the cliff in place. Holding the house up.

The house will never fall. Because I'm here.

# HOME, SAFE AND SOUND

## by Emma J. Gibbon

We hadn't been in the condo long before the lockdown started. It was April. The daffodils had bloomed, then were crushed by snow. We were told to stay home. It made little difference to me. I didn't like to leave the house. I couldn't get comfortable, though. Everything in the condo was too new, the edges were too sharp. I couldn't get the plastic and paint fume smell from out of my nose. I blew it and blew it until it bled.

"You're being dramatic," said my wife. She insisted we eat breakfast together before she left for work. I would rather have slept in. All she did was look at her phone anyway.

I showed her the bloody tissue. "It's bleeding," I said.

"Because you keep poking it." She snatched the tissue out of my hand and folded it into a neat square before putting it in the trash can then washing her hands. She paused, then took a deep breath before she kissed me. "You'll get used to it." She picked up her laptop and walked out the door.

My wife is very good at her job. She's an accountant for a company in town. She works very hard. We moved to the condo so she could walk to work. I work from home. I'm a medical insurance coder, so it doesn't matter where I live. I don't go out. I liked our old house. I liked working from home there. I couldn't get used to the condo. Whenever I looked out of the window, there were never any people. Just our small front yard with a path and the smashed daffodils, the pavement, other condos. No people. No one washing their cars or walking their dogs or getting the kids into cars. I knew people lived in the condos; we had got the welcome email from the condo association. There used to be woods here, but now the trees had been massacred to build these condos. I was relieved they hadn't named the streets after what was gone. Living on Oak Street or Maple Drive would have been too much to bear.

I grabbed a coffee and flicked on the TV. It was all about the coronavirus. I flicked it off and scrolled my phone. The same thing, coronavirus trending everywhere. I sighed and looked up, thought about how much I disliked the color of the walls. My wife had called it apple. To me it looked institutional. There, on the white ceiling, was a shiny, amber-colored stain. I stood on the sofa and poked at it. It was sticky and smelled like pine. Pine resin on the ceiling? I went and got a magic eraser from under the kitchen sink, wetted it a little and scrubbed it off. I heard a noise behind me. I startled and fell backwards off the sofa, hitting my back on the other wall. It winded me. The condo was too small.

The noise was my wife. "What are you doing on the floor?" she said.

"I fell," I said. "I was cleaning the ceiling."

My wife shook her head in disbelief. "Why aren't you working?"

"I haven't started yet. Why are you here?"

"They sent me home," she said. "The virus. I've to work from home until further notice."

I smiled at her. "We can work at home together."

"I suppose," she said. "I have a lot to do."

I didn't mind when she asked if she could take over my home office to work in. Truth be told, I hadn't spent any time in there anyway. Again, I couldn't settle. It felt like my chair was wrong, in the wrong place. Again, the new smell, even overcoming the comfort of my regular everyday things. I much preferred to sit at the kitchen table with my laptop. There was a large window that let in a lot of light, and a view of the small yard. I could see squirrels busying themselves at the tree line, but they never came close like they used to at the old place. At the old place, at least I was able to walk in the yard. I would go and fill the bird feeders, there and back, once every day. Here, I got the sense that the squirrels knew I was trapped in here. They didn't want to get trapped, too. I'd stood at the back door a few times and thought about walking over to where they buried acorns. But I couldn't quite get myself to do it. I just had to step down onto the patio. I couldn't do it.

My wife settled into a schedule immediately, just like she always did. We would eat breakfast together, she still insisted on that, and then she would go to my office, now her office. She would work until lunch, come out and grab a sandwich, and then go back to work again, often late into the night. I would make dinner and take it over to her, and she would still be in there when I went to bed, her eyes scanning spreadsheets in the darkened room.

I remember the first thing that happened. I don't know for sure if it was the condo or not, but I have my suspicions. I hadn't been able to work. I don't know if it was the condo or the pandemic or just me, but I stared at my screen a lot, and then I scrolled on my phone a lot. Doomscrolling, I suppose they would call it. I've always felt pretty filled with doom, so I suppose all scrolling is doomscrolling if you are me. I got myself a sandwich and as I got up to clear my plate my wife came in for her lunch.

"Is that YouTube on your screen?" she said. "I thought you had work to do."

I pressed my foot on the pedal of the trash can and started to scrape the crumbs from my plate in the trash. "I couldn't concentrate," I said.

"Some of us don't have the option," said my wife.

And then the lid of the can slammed down on my wrist.

The trash can is made of metal. A light metal, aluminum. But it came down with such force, lifting my foot up off the pedal, that it hurt. I felt the bones in my wrist vibrate. I yelped.

"Are you ok?" My wife rushed over to me.

"My wrist," I said, and held it over to her. It was already bruising. "The lid closed on it."

"Your foot must have slipped. Get some ice on it."

I did what I was told. How could I tell her I knew my foot

hadn't slipped. How could I tell her that somehow I felt the condo was *pleased*.

The next morning, the sun was bright and shining. I managed to stand on the back step. I curled my toes over the concrete edge. It would take one step to get onto the patio. I couldn't do it. I couldn't step into the yard. I noticed my toenails needed cutting. They were like claws. I went back inside and tried to work again.

I'd always known that my wife had a difficult job, and that she worked very hard, but I had no idea how angry she got, at least not at work. I knew she got angry at me, but she was always so good at managing it. After all, she shouldered most of our responsibilities. I had made her a cup of tea, mid-afternoon. I stood outside the office, her office door, and I paused before I went in. The door was slightly ajar. Inside, I could hear her muttering. I could tell she was angry, the way she was speaking through her teeth. I didn't know if she was on the phone. I went to knock but thought the better of it. I leaned in closer.

"Then why is it not fucking done, Charles?" she said. I knew Charles was one of the clerks at her office. "Why do I always have to ask and ask and ask for something so fucking simple?" I heard her sigh, and I imagined her running her fingers through her hair, something she did when she was stressed. "Why do I have to do everything myself?" I walked away with the tea going cold. I knew it wouldn't help to interrupt.

Later, I sat on the edge of the toilet, attempting to clip my toenails. I couldn't stop running through my head what she had said, the hiss in her voice. She was always so calm and collected. I looked at the nail clippers and suddenly felt afraid. What if I were to slip, cut my skin? I put them back in the cupboard and left my nails long for now.

A couple of days after, the doorbell rang, making me jump. I'd been sat at my computer pretending to work. I was logged on, so my boss could see I was there, but I'd been avoiding zoom calls and pretending I had connection difficulties with the new move, so being online made me vulnerable to being contacted and asked to explain myself. I felt like I was walking on a tightrope. What if I got fired? Could I hide it from my wife? I hadn't even noticed we had a doorbell. Our old house did not have a doorbell. I imagined my wife sighing in her office. I got up and answered the door.

A woman stood there. She was smiley and wearing bright colors. "Hello," she said. "I'm Angela." I stood in silence, trying to work out if I should know Angela. "From the condo association?" She must have been the one who emailed.

"I'd invite you in," I said, "but corona."

"Of course, of course," she said, "That's why I'm here."

She held out a basket full of items. I did not take it. I took a step back. She held them in the air awkwardly before putting them on the step.

"Ok, so, I put some masks in the basket and some sanitizer, along with our usual welcome pack—coupons for local stores, important phone numbers on a fridge magnet, a key ring. We usually put in baked goods but, you know."

"Thank you," I stammered.

"But if you need anything, groceries if you have to quarantine, more masks, anything—" She kept ducking her head down, trying to make eye contact with me. Why do people insist on eye contact? "–then just give me a call. My number's on there, ok?"

I nodded. She made her way down our garden path and back down the road. My wife appeared behind me. "Who was that?"

"Angela," I said.

"From the condo association? I wish you'd called me. I have some things to ask her." She stepped in front of me, stooped down, and scooped up the basket. "Well, this was nice of them," she said, and carried the basket back to her office. I poked my head out of the door to see if I could see anyone else. No one. I closed the door and went back to the kitchen to work.

I stared at the screen again, but something was off. Something was bothering me. A drip. Dripping water. Was there a leak somewhere? I stood up and tried to locate where it was coming from. I checked the faucets in the kitchen. They were dry. I followed the noise out of the kitchen and into the hallway, through the bedroom and into the master bath between our bedroom and the office where my wife was working. I could hear the tap of her keyboard, making it harder to hear the noise. She stopped typing. I heard the drip again. I moved closer to check on those faucets. The floor must have been wet. I slipped, my feet flying from under me. I cracked my head on the tiled wall before landing flat on my back on the floor, my legs crumpled against the bath. I reached my hand to the back of my head. It was wet. Blood. My wife appeared at the door. At first, she was frowning, but her face softened. She pointed to the wall. "You cracked the tile," she said. I looked up and there on the wall, a tile had been cracked it half. It was smeared with blood. "Do you want to go to the hospital?" she said. I shook my head. "Ok," she said. "Let me help you clean up. I'm sure it's fine. Head wounds always bleed dramatically. What were you doing in here?"

"There was a drip," I said. But I couldn't hear it any longer, and the floor was dry.

My wife helped me into the living room so I could lie on the sofa. "You probably shouldn't sleep," she said. "You might be concussed." But after she left the room, I couldn't keep my eyes open. I stayed there until the next morning, drifting in and out of sleep. Sometimes, I thought I could hear my wife calling my name, but when I tried to respond I couldn't move. I kept dreaming of a dark figure, tall, just on the edge of my peripheral vision, in the corner of the room, but I couldn't turn my head to focus on it. I dreamed of roots coming up from under the floor, ghostly white and gleaming, covering the carpet and climbing the sofa, holding me down to I couldn't move. I mentioned it all to my wife the next morning. She said it was probably sleep paralysis. The bump on the head or sleeping on the sofa for too long, either could have caused it. "Why don't you try to get some fresh air," she said, "take the day off." I couldn't bear to tell her I hadn't done a day of work since we arrived at the condo.

I tried the front door first. Once again, there was no one on the street. No evidence of human life beyond our condo. I could feel myself starting to panic, so I quickly stepped inside. The back door felt better. There was no sign of the squirrels by the tree line, but it was getting warmer. Summer was on its way. I could hear the buzz of insects and the chirps of birds. The wound on the back of my head still throbbed, but I was feeling brave. I took a step forward onto the patio. As I did so, a small brown bird flew past my head and smashed into the window next to me, the window I looked out of when I tried to work. I confess, I screamed and rushed inside. Looking through the window, I could see it was dead, its neck broken. I went to get my wife to ask her to move the bird. I knew I wouldn't be able to reach it. Before I got to her room, I heard a crash—something breaking against the wall, a dish or a cup—then I heard her shout. "Fucking hell." I poked my head around the corner. Her office door was open. I could see my wife sat at her desk, my old desk. She turned her head to me. "What do you want now? Go away." I could feel waves of resentment coming from her, washing over me, nourishing the horrible atmosphere. The door slammed shut. It only occurred to me later that the door had slammed on its own. There were no drafts. I hate this condo.

It's hard to say what came next. It all came in a flurry. I don't remember anymore what happened when. My head continued to hurt. I continued sleeping on the sofa instead of in the bed. I did not see my wife. How was it possible in such a small space? I saw evidence of her existence. The bird was removed from under the window, the pieces of the smashed cup swept up and put in the trash can. I heard her though; I heard her throughout the day and night. Shouting and screaming. Poor Charles seemed to bear the brunt of it, but I had no idea if he was on the phone or whether she was ranting to the air. There was no way that I was going to approach her. I couldn't sit at the kitchen window anymore, not after the bird. I closed my laptop and ignored all the messages and phone calls from my boss. I spent some time in the laundry room, at the other end of the condo from my wife's office, so I could have some respite from the noises she made. I knew there were things being smashed. I wondered what had survived her rages. I would have worried about what the neighbors thought, but I still hadn't seen any. I had heard no more from Angela. There was less and less food in the cupboards. I wondered if I could call her and ask for groceries based on my condition. I couldn't bring myself to pick up the phone.

The wound on my head was a pulse I couldn't stop. Occasionally, it would reopen and bleed. I stuck a pad of tissue on it and took

Tylenol, painstakingly counting the pills and writing a note to make sure I didn't overdose. I could feel the condo's satisfaction at my confusion, especially when the notes would disappear, and I knew I had left them on the counter. The amber stains started to appear everywhere: on the institutionally green walls, on the ceilings, on the beige carpets I hated. The smell of pine, which I'd once enjoyed, was overpowering, taking over the plastic and paint smell, making me even more nauseous. Every time I tried to clean the pools of residue up, I would have an *accident*. I banged my elbow or scraped my knee, opened my head wound again or knocked my temple. I felt dizzy and disoriented. Eventually, I gave up, magic erasers littering the house, forlorn and abandoned. I let the stains proliferate, get bigger and join together, covering the surfaces. I don't know if my wife noticed, but I was sure she'd have something to say to the condo association when she did. I'd tell her, when I saw her, that I had told her it was a terrible idea to move to the condo, that it was bad, and that she never listened to me. It was eerily quiet in her office at that moment, but still, I didn't want to go in and disturb her. I'd wait.

There were more birds. After the first couple of times, I closed the blinds. It did not muffle the sound of them hitting the glass, their necks breaking, but it meant I didn't have to look. The darkened condo took on a different aspect, like I was lost in dark woods or sunk in overgrowth. It meant I walked into things more, barking my shin on a chair leg, catching my smallest toe on the metal bed frame, ripping off the nail.

The scald came next, or maybe the burn. They were in quick succession. I found myself pacing around the condo. I'd completely abandoned work; surely I was unemployed by that point. I'd crept out from the laundry room when there was a lull in my wife's screaming. The steady thump of the birds continued, and it weighed on me, all those poor little things. Someone must have noticed them all. I decided to make a cup of tea and look up what I could do to help the birds. I filled the electric hot water kettle and switched it on. I grabbed my mug and put a tea bag in. I waited, stock-still, until the kettle clicked off, just like I always did. I grabbed the kettle to pour, and something grabbed by elbow and jerked my arm, sloshing boiling water over my other arm and wrist. The shock stopped the pain at first, and I turned, trying to find who had grabbed me, but of course no one was there, but then the pain started, my skin turning bright red. I had the presence of mind to stick my hand and arm under the cold water faucet, and from the corner of the kitchen came a deep sigh, a sound of contentment. "Fuck you," I hissed. My wife started screaming again.

The burn was on my other arm, an almost perfect match to the scald. I had tripped in the kitchen and fallen on the stove, but I couldn't remember turning it on. Again, I jammed it under the cold faucet immediately, but I knew I should have sought medical attention for both. Each were red, livid, and began to peel in unison.

I stopped taking my medication. I couldn't keep straight what I had taken and when. I thought about ordering one of those organizers from Amazon, but I couldn't muster the energy. I found some crackers in the cupboard and ate a few of those throughout the day, spread with whatever I could find in the fridge that hadn't molded. I had no idea what my wife was eating. I found no evidence of it as I had before. I drank cold water only, my head aching and fuzzy from caffeine withdrawal. Every time I picked up a knife, it sliced me; I stubbed my toe and rolled my ankles endlessly. I hobbled around, covered in Band-Aids and using packaging tape on my ankles and broken toes, my clothes and skin and hair stained and sticky with resin.

I let my phone run out of battery power, and I hid when the doorbell rang, even though the blinds were closed. I could hear Angela calling our names. I heard snatches of her voice "Just checking you're both ok... If you need anything... Need to do something about these birds." Then the thump of another one meeting its end at our windows. "Oh, no."

When I was sure Angela was gone, I rifled through the cupboards until I found electrical tape. I moved the blinds and taped crisscrosses on the windows to try to save the birds. I cut my fingers on everything I touched, the scissors, the edges of the blinds, paper cuts from the tape, my ankles giving way as I moved from room to room, bruises blooming on hips and shoulders as I hit the angles of the doors and walls, trying to dodge furniture as it suddenly appeared before me, desperately trying to protect my injured arms. I daren't enter the office. I could hear my wife in there shouting gibberish, and I apologized out loud to the birds that would perish thanks to my cowardice.

Once all the windows I could reach were done, I slumped to the floor. I could still hear my wife, but the thumping of the birds had stopped. When I looked up, I saw those hideous green walls that surrounded me start to warp and move, in and out like breathing, the condo being sustained by our pain and misery. Something inside me snapped. I stood up. "That's it," I screeched. "That's enough." I began to pick up the discarded magic erasers and tape and Band-Aid wrappers and cracker boxes. "I'm going to tidy this place up then I'm going to call Angela to get some food and then check on my wife." I limped around, gathering more detritus. I could feel a warm trickle of blood behind my ear; my wound had opened again. I carried everything to the kitchen. The trash can was full, overflowing. Enraged, I moved over to the sink, switched on the garbage disposal and began stuffing everything into it, recognizing a moment before it happened, that this was exactly what the condo wanted. The garbage disposal grabbed the tape around my fingers and pulled my arm down into those sharp, sharp blades. As soon as they bit flesh, the condo was filled with bird call, loud and shrieking and discordant.

By the time I got my arm free, my hand had been shredded so badly it was no longer recognizable for what it was. Just a ragged lump of skin and blood. I lurched to the front door, my joints popping as some unseen force tried to dislocate them, household items thrown in front of me to impede my progress. I threw the door open, and there was Angela, on the path. She yelped at the sight of me and dropped the basket she was holding, paper masks floating down the street. "Ambulance, ambulance," I managed to say. I saw her shakily take her phone out of her purse. I took a step to walk towards her, but then stopped. I looked down at my broken toes gripping the edge of the doorframe, refusing to go forward. I had to leave. I had to go outside, but I couldn't. I stopped dead, unable to move. I could hear the condo laughing at my back, the bird call gone. Then, from behind me, something rushed like a whirlwind. I felt two strong hands on my back shove me forward, so hard my feet left the floor, and I landed on the path outside. I turned around to see my wife's anguished face, just before the door slammed closed on her. I knew she had saved me as the condo swallowed her. I heard the sirens make their way down the cul-de-sac as I lost consciousness.

# DEEP DOWN INSIDE

## by Evans Light

I've had the same nightmare every night for two weeks, ever since I moved into Forester House after Dad died.

In my dream, I'm trapped inside a giant silo filled with black sand as a silver moon shines overhead. Grit fills my mouth and eyes as I struggle to stay on the surface, but my efforts are futile. Each night I'm pulled down into the silo, crushed and smothered by the deep black sand.

I awoke from this dream last night to find myself naked in the kitchen. Black sand, very real, was inexplicably caked on my lips.

The experience left me so shaken I couldn't go back to sleep.

It's well past noon now and there's a half-empty cup of coffee on the table beside me. I've been staring at the phone in my hand for almost an hour.

Finally, I dial Bryan's number.

It's been a long time since we last spoke, so I know he's not expecting my call. Hell, I don't even know if he'll answer.

I haven't been much of a friend. Bryan and I were inseparable during elementary all the way through high school, even stayed friends during college. After earning my degree, I opened a restaurant in the state capital and lucked into it becoming the hottest thing in town.

To be honest... I'd pretty much forgotten Bryan even existed after that.

The tinny sound of a line ringing chirped from the earpiece of the flip phone, the best phone the trust allowed me to purchase. Smart phones are too good for me.

Even with my restaurant closed and bankrupt and Dad dead, I wouldn't be calling Bryan if it wasn't for this house. I have nowhere else to turn, no one left to talk to. None of my restaurant *friends*, always so available when money was flowing, will return my calls. The few who accidentally answered told me not to call anymore, blaming the lawsuit and my lawyers, even though I doubt they give a damn about me anyway.

The good times are over.

Now it's just me and this fucking house.

Bryan's line rings twice, three times. Still no answer.

Things have been happening here in Forester House, little things that are slowly driving me mad, death by a thousand cuts. I need to hear a friendly voice, someone who knows me, someone who might be able to tell if there's something wrong with this house or something wrong with me.

The deviations were minor at first, nearly imperceptible, impossible to prove they'd even occurred. The changes often happen as I sleep: a minor shift in the wallpaper's pattern, a switch of which step on the staircase was the creaky one, always something subtle.

But the changes are becoming more significant: a bookmark swapping pages from where I'd left it in a book, the rug in the living room flipped so the pattern faces the opposite direction.

This morning I'd found all my pants hanging in the closet even though I swear they were folded in drawers the night before.

All things I could be misremembering.

"You son of a bitch."

The voice startles me and I almost drop the phone.

"Bryan?"

I breathe his name so weirdly I creep myself out.

"That's the number you called, ya bastard, probably by accident. Butt-dialed, didn't you?"

"No, not at all. It's good to hear your voice. Been a long time."

"No kidding. You need a loan or something?"

"No, not why I called. We need to talk. In person, if possible. I miss you, man."

I meant what I said.

"Seriously?" Bryan sounds surprised.

"Seriously. Can you come? I'm staying at Forester House now."

"Yeah. I guess so. When?"

I glance at the clock hanging on the living room wall. Mother's silver urn sits beneath it on the mantel. Has the clock always been square? I swear it was round the last time I saw it.

"It's five-thirty now," I say. "How soon can you get here?"

I don't want to be alone after sundown.

"I'm on my way. Should I pick up an eighteen-inch pepperoni and sausage pie for old time's sake? My treat."

"That would be amazing. The executor barely gives me enough money for ramen."

"Executor?"

"I'll tell you when you get here. Don't forget the Parmesan."

Forty minutes later, Bryan is hunched down over the table, half-eaten slice of pizza in hand. He's brought along a much-welcomed case of cheap beer, the same brand we used to drink together.

"Your parents gave us the tour right after they bought this place, remember? When was that? Before your restaurant. Two years ago?"

"Sounds about right."

"And your mom passed away soon after they moved in, as I recall."

"Mom and Dad got to live four whole months together here. So much for spending their golden years preserving a piece of history," I say.

"This house could be incredible, with a little love." He slides a fingertip across the grimy kitchen tabletop, holding it up for me to see. It's black enough to fingerprint him into the county jail.

"The place is impossible to keep clean," I say. "If I dusted now, it'd dirty again by sunrise."

"Was there a fire? Looks like soot." Bryan sniffs his finger. "Doesn't smell burnt."

"Anything's possible. It's a very old house."

Bryan shrugs and rubs his fingertip clean on his pants.

"I really miss your dad, he was a kind man. Such bad luck, for him to find out he had cancer as he was burying his wife."

"Mom's not quite buried," I say, and gesture towards the mantel in the living room.

Bryan turns, jaw freezing mid-bite as he sees the silver urn.

"Man," he says, gulping down his mouthful. "I don't know what to say. I'm really sorry I didn't go to your dad's funeral, but I never received an invite. Wish I could have been there."

Bryan's words spiral me back in time to that awful morning: the blaring phone rousing me out of a bender-induced blackout, unfamiliar voice on the phone saying Dad's name, asking if I knew him, saying he was dead.

That he'd been that way for several days.

Being stuck living in this majestic shithole serves me right. I hadn't been there for Dad when he needed me most. Had I been his biggest disappointment of all?

"You okay?" Bryan asks.

His words bring me back to the present moment and I lie.

"Yeah, totally fine. What were you saying?"

"Sorry for missing your dad's funeral."

"He didn't have one. His body had decomposed too much for viewing, and I didn't feel like tracking his friends down back home, to be honest. His ashes are still sitting at the mortuary right now, waiting to be picked up."

"Oh," Bryan says, and we sit in awkward silence.

I can't help but look at the faint stain on the kitchen floor where Dad's blood had soaked into the hardwood. No matter how much I scrubbed, it was never coming out, an everlasting monument to my traitorous neglect. Nothing I could ever do would change the fact my father had perished naked and alone atop a crumpled towel, brained on the corner of the granite countertop after slipping on a wet floor. Carelessness got him before cancer could finish the job.

*How long had it taken for him to die? How much had he suffered?*

"Arm wrestle for the last slice?" Bryan offers, desperate to inject levity into what is quickly becoming a sullen reunion.

"Nah, you're welcome to it."

"I'll stick it in the fridge for later," he says, and lets out a low whistle as he opens the icebox. "I guess you weren't kidding about living on ramen. Looks like a North Korean supermarket in here."

"Yeah, bare essentials only. Unlimited funds to fix up this money pit, but austerity measures for the caretaker. Let's move to the couch and I'll tell you all about it."

We move into the living room—*parlor*, I suppose it should be referred to in a place such as Forester House—and settle into opposite ends of an antique burgundy sofa with fluted mahogany legs. The velvet cushioning has a light coating of the same black dust that's settled on everything throughout the house. I brush it off as best I can.

There's a box of old keepsakes from our childhood days I've pulled out in case conversation should flag, but I needn't have worried. Our friendship picks up right where we left it.

I tell him everything: about how my high-flying restaurateur days came to an abrupt end, about the elevator shaft accident and the lawsuit, about how the lawsuit led to audits, and how the audits uncovered my creative accounting for the restaurant.

It's hard to admit to Bryan that I'm now nothing more than the poorly paid caretaker of my dad's old house, that anything I earn for the rest of my life is going to be garnished by the government or settlements from the lawsuit, but each confession made lifts a bit of heaviness from my soul.

I want to tell him about the strange happenings in this house, but I don't yet have the courage. I'm afraid he will leave if the conversation gets too weird.

"Can't you sell this place? Even without renovations it'd bring a small fortune. This house is a landmark."

"I can't sell it because it doesn't belong to me. Every bit of Dad's money was bequeathed to a trust established for Forester House. It's good, in a way, since the trust protects it from my misfortune. Technically, the house owns itself. Otherwise, it would've been liquidated along with the rest of my assets."

"Wait," Bryan says, making the *time-out* gesture with his hands. "Back up. I'm confused. Your restaurant was in the big white building with the fancy pillars, corner of Seventh and Trade, right?"

"Yep. That's the one."

"You mentioned *Sharon*. That's who got hurt and sued? Is she the girl you were dating when I ran into you at Midwood's last summer?"

"We weren't dating, but yes—that was Sharon. She was a server at my restaurant."

Bryan lets out a low whistle.

"Dude, she was smokin'. She's paralyzed now? I'm so confused."

"I said *possibly paralyzed*. I think she's exaggerating her injuries to try to get more money."

I'm surprised by how defensive I sound. I'd seen the poor girl lying tangled at the bottom of that shaft with my own eyes, watched rescue workers lift her mangled body out of that hole, her screams louder than the sirens outside. She was lucky to be alive.

"Okay, *possibly paralyzed*," Bryan says. "Why are you responsible? Shouldn't the restaurant's liability insurance cover it?"

My lawyers have told me not to discuss it, but I trust Bryan. I need to talk to somebody, so I spill details.

"The restaurant had a working vintage elevator in it when I bought the building. Sold it for a nice sum when renovating the building—it's amazing the weird shit people collect. A crew came and pulled the whole damn contraption right out of the building, leaving an empty shaft.

"Downstairs, in the dining room, we sealed off the opening and painted it to match the rest of the wall, but the upstairs entrance to the shaft was never closed off. That area was only used for storage, so I tacked up a sheet, put a storage shelf in front, and completely forgot about it. Out of sight, out of mind, you know?"

Bryan nods.

I crack open a beer and take a swig before continuing.

"I was juggling a lot of girls at the time. Once in a while, I'd sneak a hottie from the waitstaff upstairs for a quickie. That evening it was Sharon."

Bryan leans forward, newly intrigued.

"Sharon practically dragged me upstairs that evening. It wasn't sexual harassment, I swear, no matter what she claimed later. She lifted her skirt, dropped her panties and bent over—I mean *all* the way—her elbows on a shelf full of jars, begging for it.

"Getting inside of her was the only thing on my mind. I thrust as hard as I could... then she and the shelf vanished, leaving me staring down into a black hole, pants around my ankles. Breaking glass and crashing metal and Sharon's screams echoed up from below. I almost threw up."

Bryan's eyes bulge, unblinking.

"Holy fuck! I can't imagine what must've been going on in your head."

"*I'm fucked.* That was my only thought. The restaurant was packed and there I was kicking a hole in the dining room wall trying to find her, beside a party of six, screaming for somebody to call an ambulance. It was a fucking nightmare, man. You can't even imagine."

"How far was it from the first floor to the second? Ten feet? Twelve tops? How'd she get hurt so badly?"

"That shaft went all the way down to the basement, close to twenty-five feet."

"Holy shit. Talk about a versatile lover—she went straight from doggy-style to pretzel-style." Bryan laughs.

The look I give says I am not amused.

"Too soon?"

I finish my beer in one long gulp and blow a belch at him.

He scoots over and put an arm around me.

"Well, what's done is done and there's nothing you can do now but move forward. I won't lie, you've been shitty to me for a while, but I forgive you. We've been friends our entire lives and I won't let you going nuts and forgetting about me ruin that."

"I love you, man," I say, and I mean it.

"I'm not going anywhere. We'll get you through this together."

"Promise?"

"Promise."

It's late, and we've hit the perfect note on which to end the evening. The table beside us is littered with crushed cans, so I invite Bryan to stay the night rather than risk a DUI.

I'd rather sleep on the couch than spend another night alone, so I tell him he's welcome to my room, the only one in the house with a bed set up in it. Bryan agrees to stay over, thanks me for my hospitality and heads down the hall as I settle in for the night.

As I drift off to sleep, it feels good to know I'm not the only living soul beneath the roof of Forester House, thankful to have Bryan back in my life.

I awake in the morning to find an empty house. The bed in my room doesn't even look touched. Bryan must've gotten up early and let himself out.

I wish he would've woken me to say goodbye.

I call to thank him for coming over and to see when he might want to get together again, but he doesn't pick up.

I send a text message, but he doesn't reply.

I head into the kitchen to clean up from the previous night.

I'm surprised to find our empty beer cans laid out in a circle, rather than the jumbled mess I remember. In the middle of the circle of cans sit two paper plates, side by side. Smeared onto each plate is a word, in what looks like black finger paint: *Yes* on the left, *No* on the right.

I recall Bryan's fingertip, blackened from the dust on the table.

A knife is positioned between plates like the pointer on a Ouija board.

*What a joker, trying to creep me out.*

As I scoop up the cans, a sudden clatter in the next room makes me jump.

"Bryan?"

I stop cleaning and listen. The house is deadly silent.

The floor creaks in the living room and I smile.

*Bryan is still here. Of course he is.*

He always was a prankster. He's trying hard to give me a scare, even silenced his phone so it wouldn't ring when I called.

Had I told him about the weird happenings in Forester House, about the little things freaking me out? I don't remember talking about it but, then again, I had downed a twelve-pack. Perhaps it'd slipped out.

*That's okay. Two can play this game.*

I slide one sock-clad foot behind the other along the hardwood towards the living room, careful to stay out of sight, hoping floorboards don't squeak underfoot.

I arrive at the edge of the doorway, heart pounding with anticipation as I listen for him fooling around in the next room.

*Here we go. Pants-shitting time.*

*Three... two... one...*

"Gotcha motherfucker!" I scream and jump into the open doorway, flinging my arms and legs out like a starfish.

Bryan's not there. The room is empty.

Then I see that every book on the shelves beside the fireplace has been turned so the spine faces inward. A deep chill spreads through me as my gaze passes over the rows of backward books and arrives at the mantel.

The clock above it is no longer round or square.

It's gone, replaced by a scrawled sentence five feet across:

*Where is your father?*

I stand, staring and confounded. If this is a prank, it isn't funny.

There's something on the floor by the fireplace.

The polished silver lid to mother's urn.

Black dust lies thick atop the mantel, like spores freshly spewed from a fern. Mother's urn sits in a pile of the stuff.

I've never touched her urn, not with my bare hands. It feels as if it has eyes that follow me, judging, so usually I pretend it isn't there.

I take a deep breath, pick it up and look inside the tiny silver silo.

It's half empty. It should be full.

The ashes that do remain inside aren't the light gray color I expected. They're as black as the sand in my dreams, black like the dust that settles throughout this house every day.

Black like the writing smeared on the wall.

*Written in Mom's ashes? Bryan didn't do that. Bryan wouldn't do that.*

I replace the silver lid and return the urn to its spot. My heart throbs inside my ribcage; breaths come fast. The room sways and begins to spin slowly, round and round.

Feeling a sudden need to sit, I collapse into a stiff-backed leather chair facing the fireplace, but having a cushion beneath me isn't as reassuring as I'd hoped.

I grab the armrests as though I'm on a rollercoaster about to crest the first hill. I close my eyes and try to regain control of my breathing.

I'm *not* crazy, this *is* happening. The only question is *why*.

My pulse finally begins to slow. I hope when I open my eyes again the writing on the wall will be gone, that the books will be facing the correct way.

A familiar clatter causes me to open my eyes before I'm fully prepared to look.

My hopes vanish.

The lid to Mother's urn is on the floor again. The writing is still on the wall, but now a second sentence has joined the first:

*I hope you die.*

The urge to leave this house becomes impossible to resist.

As I try to stand, the upholstery melts beneath me. My hands plunge into a strange leather pudding, sinking halfway up to my elbows.

The sudden lack of leverage forces me back down, and I'm being absorbed into the melting morass the bottom cushion has unexpectedly become.

Despair takes hold as my lower body disappears into the cushions, leather rejoining seamlessly above vanishing thighs.

The chair sucks me in all the way up to my chest, covering me with unbroken upholstery.

As quickly as it melted the chair re-hardens, creating a mold around me. I almost get one hand free as the armrest returns to a solid state, leaving a thumb and four fingers protruding from little circles with neat stitching sewn around them. I imagine there's a matching stitched circle around my neck now as well.

I'm cemented into the chair. I scream for help, hoping someone will hear me. From somewhere inside the house, a muffled voice screams back.

*Is the house mocking me?*

The phone in my pocket chirps its *tra-la-la* ringtone and I instinctively retrieve it, flipping it open before the meaning of the act hits me.

I'm free of the chair as if it never happened.

The writing on the wall has vanished.

The moon-circle lid sits innocently atop Mother's silver urn, the mantel beneath it spotlessly clean.

My phone rings again and I see the caller is Mr. Thomas, executor of the Forester House trust. He's one of my least favorite people on earth, but I desperately need to hear another human voice.

"Hi, Mr. Thomas. This is Adrian. How are things?"

"From the sound of your voice, perhaps I should be asking you that?" The man speaks curtly. "I'm not interrupting your work on the house, am I? You sound out of breath."

"Yes, sir, working on the house," I lie. "Getting a lot done. It's looking better every day."

"Good, I'm pleased to hear that. Then you won't mind if I stop by tomorrow for an inspection of your progress? Let's say 8 a.m., sharp."

I hesitate as my mind tries to catch up. Too much has happened in too little time, even though the room around me now appears as if nothing has happened at all.

"Well?" His voice is insistent. "Is that a problem?"

"No, not at all. 8 a.m. is fine."

"Good. Also, the funeral home inquired yet again regarding the disposition of your father's ashes. Since you're without personal transportation, I took the liberty of having them delivered to my office. I'll bring them with me tomorrow so you can arrange for proper interment. Until then," he says, and hangs up.

I jump to my feet the instant the conversation ends, in case the chair attempts to consume me again. Once clear, I can't resist poking the leather to make sure it's normal. I turn to find the books once again positioned correctly.

I go to the mantel and take Mother's urn into my hands, lifting the lid to peek inside. It's filled up to the rim with ebony powder.

The round clock above the fireplace, so recently AWOL, casually indicates a few hours remain until sundown. I have to take a break from Forester House, even if only for a short while. Otherwise, I'm sure I'll lose my mind.

A few days ago I found a gift card for a coffee shop down the street; it had been a birthday present from me to Dad, tucked inside a card I hadn't bothered to sign. I'm not sure a more impersonal gift has been given for a father's final birthday, but I hope he hasn't already used it. A cup of coffee will buy me some time in the company of others, even though anyone I might know will likely scurry away without so much as a nod.

*Lawyers, you know how it is...* I imagine a former acquaintance saying while scanning for the nearest exit.

It's a marvelous feeling, locking the door to Forester House and walking away. If only it could last forever.

Fortunately, the gift card has the full balance remaining, buying me a few glorious hours of pretending to be normal. I don't have a computer or smart phone to keep me occupied like everyone else, so I find an out-of-the-way seat and stare out the window, watching the sun set as I guzzle coffees.

I return to Forester House fearing the worst, half expecting to find some unimaginable horror waiting in the shadows, but everything appears normal. Perhaps it's extreme isolation that's been affecting me all along.

I go through the house, turning on the lights in every room. Chasing darkness away is about all I can do to make the house feel more cozy. I long to hear the chatter of television or radio, but every request to the trust for *leisure items* has been denied.

I settle down in the parlor to read, on the same couch where Bryan and I had been pleasantly chatting the night before. The room feels so incredibly empty without him; it's hard to focus on my book. I find myself reading the same paragraph over and over.

I check my phone to see if I've missed his call but I haven't. I want to ring him again, but settle for a short text instead: *when u want 2 hang out?*

I stare at the phone, hoping for an immediate reply. Getting none, I give my book another go. It's supposed to be funny but everything reads like a tragedy.

Over the top of the page, movement catches my eye. I set the book down to find a dog in the corner, wagging its tail.

A name comes to me from nowhere: *Gretchen,* the beagle my parents had given me on my eleventh birthday.

When had I last seen her? It was hard to say, but certainly well before Mom and Dad bought Forester House. My memories are fuzzy and hard to access, as though belonging to someone else entirely.

*How old is she?*

I multiply dog years in my head.

*115? 120? That doesn't seem possible.*

Yet here she is, giving me that goofy grin. Her tail wags faster; she's happy to see me.

"Gretchen... come here, girl. That's a good girl."

I hold out my hand and she struggles to take a couple of steps forward. The poor thing can barely walk.

"Good girl!" I encourage her.

She stops, panting. Her eyes are different than I remember, deeper somehow. I sense disappointment and pain.

She takes another step. As her paw touches the floor, the walls of the room slam together like giant doors on a hinge, crushing her between them. It happens so fast the pitiful beast doesn't even manage a yelp.

Forester House rattles from the collision—it feels like an earthquake. I jump back on the sofa, shaken by the impossible scene playing out before me, staring in disbelief as the walls silently slide back into place.

I can't contain the mounting scream inside me any longer, so I release it.

A mocking shriek emanates in reply from somewhere within the walls, a disembodied cry for help that fades into sobs.

The shock of it silences me, and stillness gradually reclaims the house.

I sit, trembling, staring at brown and red splotches on the walls, the only evidence a dog was ever here. But there's no carcass, no bone, no gory mess on the floor.

Upon closer inspection I realize it's not splattered blood and shit on the wall either, simply the garish pattern of the parlor wallpaper, the same as it's always been.

I attempt to recall the poor dog's name, but it eludes me.

Then a realization hits: *I've never had a dog, not once in my entire life.*

My mind lurches as if on the edge of a precipice, and beads of sweat congregate on my forehead.

*I'm going to throw up.*

I run down the hallway. I need cold water. The house swirls around me, I'm going to pass out. I reach the hallway bathroom but the door is stuck. It's the final straw. I'm fed up with this fucking house.

I kick the door, and it screams.

I kick again, and it screams louder.

I kick again, using every last remaining bit of strength.

This time, the latch releases. The door slams into the bathroom wall and the screams I've been hearing grow clearer than ever before.

A man cowers atop the toilet seat, white-knuckled fingers clutching his knees. His eyes are deep dark holes in a screaming face, lips caked in black sand. A full five seconds pass before I recognize him.

It's Bryan. He won't stop screaming.

I call his name but he doesn't respond.

He recoils in fear as I step forward, but thankfully his piercing scream dwindles down to a whimper.

"Bryan, it's me, Adrian," I say. "What are you doing in here?"

His gaze passes through me like I'm an apparition. I place a hand gently on his shoulder and he shrieks as if struck by a serpent.

I help him to his feet and nearly carry him to the sofa. His eyes dart hither and fro like a wounded animal caught in a trap.

"I thought you left. I tried calling your phone," I gasp.

His brow furrows. He doesn't seem to understand me, as if we no longer speak the same language.

"The walls," he sputters. "The walls closed up, all around me."

"You got stuck in the bathroom?"

"No bathroom. Only black sand, everywhere... in my eyes, my ears, my mouth. I still taste it." Every word was a struggle. "Then it got into my mind." His restless eyes become still, fixing on a point behind me.

A chill touches me as I follow his gaze to Mother's urn. My only small comfort comes from seeing the lid in its place.

"How long?" he asks, voice as hollow as a spent shell casing. "How long have I been here? Weeks? Months?"

"Only since last night. Can I get something for you? A glass of water, maybe?"

He jumps to his feet, bulging eyes still locked on the mantel.

"Gotta get out," he whispers.

He shuffles towards the door but falls on his knees. He regains his feet and pushes towards the exit, flinging open the front door, charging onto the porch with nary a backward glance.

By the time I reach the doorway, he's running down the walk towards the front gate. He hangs a sharp left and disappears down the sidewalk.

Seeing no point in chasing after, I close the door and go back inside. The box of keepsakes on the floor by the sofa reminds me of everything I've lost, my family, my friends, my life... and for what?

I grab my favorite childhood stuffed animal, Theodore, from the box. He's so tattered by years of love it's nearly impossible to tell he once resembled a dog. I hug him close but discover he no longer brings comfort.

*Even Theodore doesn't love me anymore.*

The thought is angering, and I hurl the stuffed animal to the floor. The toy writhes and swells as if suddenly alive, seams stretching until the cloth body bursts open.

He's been stuffed with black dust.

I turn towards Mother's urn. The lid is off.

A new sentence is scrawled in black across the wall: *I hope you die.*

Every bit of energy in my body evaporates the moment I read it, replaced by an overwhelming feeling of lethargy. I manage to stagger to down the hall to the bedroom and sleep takes me the instant my head touches the pillow.

I'm dreaming. Soft lips are on mine, so warm, so exquisitely sweet. I'm pinned to the bed by knees planted alongside my hips. I'm naked but don't remember taking off my clothes.

The very real weight of a body pressing down upon mine brings with it awareness.

*This isn't a dream.*

*There's a stranger in my house, in my bedroom, kissing me while I sleep.*

The realization hits home, and suddenly I'm wide awake.

I push the person away to get a better look.

It's Sharon, the waitress from my restaurant. She's smiling, beautiful. She arches her back and unbuttons her shirt. There are no bandages, no injuries anywhere I can see, and I can see a lot.

"What are you doing?" I ask. My voice is high pitched and raspy. "I thought you were..."

She presses a finger against my lips, shushing me as she allows her blouse to fall away. Her breath is hot in my ear. "I'm fine, don't you worry. Come on, see how good I feel."

Silken hands slide across my skin to combat the images forming inside my mind, visions of this woman's twisted, bloodied body at the bottom of an elevator shaft. Intrusive thoughts are blessedly vaporized as her electric touch releases a shroud of bliss.

Our naked bodies roll from the bed onto the floor but I barely notice. We go at it for hours; our stamina seems to have no end.

I take her against the wall in the hallway, but she's insatiable. In the living room, she mounts me yet again on the sofa.

Afterward, I escape to kitchen to catch my breath and suck down a bottle of cold water. I turn from the brightly-lit fridge to find her silhouette behind me, elbows on the counter, every curve on her bent-over body shamelessly begging for more.

I can't resist. I slam the fridge closed, plunging the room back into darkness. I grab her hips from behind and push her into position. Her skin is taut and surprisingly cool to the touch.

The lights in the kitchen burst on. It's blinding.

A deep voice startles even more than the sudden illumination.

"Adrian, what on earth are you doing?" The man's voice is sharp, urgent and familiar. "Put that down!"

Still grasping Sharon's hips I turn to find Mr. Thomas, the executor for Forester House trust, standing in the doorway, hand on the light switch, a shocked look on his face.

"What the fuck, Mr. Thomas?" I shout. "Just letting yourself in now like you own the place?"

I turn to shield Sharon's naked body from him, but she's gone. Clutched in my hands I find only my toaster, plugged in with the lever depressed. Hot coils inside the machine cast a red glow onto the tip of my erection, perfectly aligned with the slot.

"What in the actual hell is going on, Adrian? Are you on drugs?"

The room swirls around me, like water down a drain. The toaster falls from my hands and the floor smacks me upside the head. Mr. Thomas's chattering voice fractures into pieces that skitter like spiders along the wall.

I throw up all over the hardwood.

People I don't know are coming and going. There are bright lights and odd faces asking questions I can't answer. I become aware of a blanket wrapped around me. *Mold* is a word that periodically cuts through the haze. *Toxins* is another. Hours later, the spinning stops and I find myself in an emergency room bed.

By the time the sun sets that same day, I'm back on my sofa at Forester House trying to free my wrist from a medical bracelet with *Adrian Greenburg* printed in dot matrix letters. It's impossible to remove, so I give up and instead read through my discharge paperwork:

*Diagnosis: brief psychotic disorder (trichothecene mycotoxin poisoning suspected but not confirmed). Prognosis: good, with reduced exposure. Urinalysis: trichothecene mycotoxins: negative; narcotics: negative. Remediation: environmental testing, professional decontamination of living quarters (if mycotoxins detected).*

Suspected black mold poisoning, to state it plainly. A damp old place like Forester House is apparently the perfect breeding ground. My urine test had been negative, true, but I've been told they're not accurate one hundred percent of the time.

Reading the hospital paperwork brings overwhelming relief; I haven't been haunted by my mother's malevolent spirit after all. I feel crazy for having even entertained the idea, for having let guilt get the better of me. Everything I've been experiencing matches up with the list of symptoms on the discharge papers.

I slide my hand along the coffee table and lift a blackened palm.

Happiness is an emotion I haven't felt for a long while, but it's threatening to blossom. Even Mr. Thomas had been unusually kind when he dropped me off, promising money for a clean place to stay while Forester House was decontaminated.

I'm starving and remember the leftover pizza Bryan put in the fridge. As I go into the kitchen and turn on the lights, a glimmer in the periphery of my vision draws my attention. What I see stops me dead in my tracks.

A dozen sharp knives are laid out on the table. They form the shape of an arrow pointing towards the counter. There's a box there, one I haven't seen before. The label on the side reads *Property of: Greenburg, Adrian (son). Human remains, cremated: Greenburg, Jeffrey.*

My father. Mr. Thomas had said he'd be bringing Dad's ashes. He must've dropped them here to call an ambulance when he found me about to screw a toaster.

A too-familiar sound draws my attention: the clatter of metal on the living room floor. As I look towards the doorway, black tendrils snake into the kitchen along the walls, giant fingers pulling malevolence incarnate into the room. An electric hum fills the air, like angry bees in a bag. I step towards the back door that lets out into the garage, ready to run screaming into the night.

*Mold poisoning,* I remind myself—but don't believe it.

The knives on the table begin to spin, stopping with each blade's tip pointed directly at me. I take a step to the left and the knives move along with me, tracking my location as if they're needles on a compass and I'm the North Pole.

*Black mold,* my subconscious whispers—but I know it's a lie.

The tendrils slither swiftly along the walls, forming giant concentric spirals, enclosing me in swirling vortexes, portals to an endless void. The illusion shifts abruptly, making the spirals appear to jut out like rapier-sharp terminus points, threatening to pincushion me between them.

I brace for impalement, but each spike billows into a thick black cloud the instant it touches my skin. Fine particles clog my lungs and clot over my eyes. I gag and spit against the grit as my vision grows dim.

I remember Bryan cowering in the bathroom and his haunting words: "*...black sand, everywhere, in my eyes, my ears, my mouth... it got into my mind.*"

*I* feel it, too, the fine black ash eating into my brain. I feel its rage, frustration, hatred of everything I've become. The words *late-term abortion* are spoken by a female voice inside my head, the voice of my mother.

Panic takes hold. I don't know what to do. In desperation, I grab the box from the counter and rip it open, flinging Dad's ashes into the air.

"Take him! I'm sorry. Leave me alone!" I scream to the black cloud as it condenses around me.

The air clears briefly as Dad's white ashes scatter, spattering across the kitchen floor. Every black granule hovers suspended in place, motionless, as if stunned. The hum grows silent.

Sensing my opportunity, I bolt for the door.

The buzzing resumes the instant my foot hits the floor, louder, angrier than before, but I don't stop.

Something whistles past my ear.

A butcher knife impales the wall ahead.

*Please be unlocked, please be unlocked.*

I grab the knob, grateful to feel it turn in my hand. I slam the door closed as I burst into the garage. Sharp thwacks rattle the wood behind me. I turn to find a half-dozen knives jutting through.

*I have to hurry.*

I shove cluttered yard tools and a lawn mower aside, searching for the gas can, hoping it's full.

*This ends tonight, consequences be damned. I'd rather live out my days in jail than be driven insane or murdered inside Forester House.*

Long black tendrils snake out from beneath the door, rising into the air, forming spirals as the buzz swells into a deafening roar.

I find the red five-gallon can. It's nearly full. Hope surges.

I haul gasoline into the kitchen as curling tendrils chase after.

There's a lighter in the drawer by the sink. One hand finds it while the other frantically twists off the gas can lid. I splash fuel across the kitchen and move into the living room to dump out the rest.

The rug beneath the sofa darkens with moisture. I snatch the hospital paperwork from the coffee table and crumple it up, flicking the lighter to set it aflame. I toss the ball of fire towards the kitchen and bolt for the door.

Brilliant light radiates from behind me as I exit Forester House. A long flickering shadow splays out across the lawn as I step onto the porch: a shadow shaped like a woman, arm outstretched, pointing at me.

At the end of the sidewalk, I watch, delighted, as the inferno spreads. Thirsty tongues of fire are already lapping out from beneath the eaves to taste the cool night air. Crackling flames chew through the roof and corkscrew up into the sky.

A wail of sirens rises in the distance, letting me know the charred carcass of Forester House will soon be bathed in flashing lights of blue and red. I reek of gasoline. Things will not go in my favor.

But I don't care. For the first time since my father died, I'm completely free. I have no redemption but have escaped retribution. For now, that must suffice.

Ash drifts down like giant snowflakes around me. I catch a piece and smear it across the palm of my hand. The long black mark reminds me of those words on the wall: *I hope you die.*

A loud electric hum joins the approaching choir of sirens in song.

Something lunges towards me from the burning house, pushing through the soft falling ash, plunging into my mouth. It's clogging my lungs, blinding my eyes. I gag and spit at the grit, blinking furiously as my vision grows dim.

The black sand nestles somewhere deep inside my mind, and I see everything clearly for the very first time.

I'm walking towards the fire, unable to stop. My legs force me back up the stairs, a puppet on a string. As I step into the burning hell of Forester House to die, unforgiven, I finally realize there are some things of which I can never be free.

# TEA HOUSE VIGNETTES

## by Sara Tantlinger

Layla should have left the rental house when the sugar morphed into ants. Her teaspoon rattled in the ceramic bowl as she jumped away from the scattering insects. She'd dipped the spoon into white grains of sugar, and it came back up full of black ants. The sticky creatures marched around the countertop, and a few had managed to sneak their way onto her left hand and up her arm. Panic directed hot alarm to settle in her chest as she tore off her sweater and threw it across the kitchen. Her palms slapped with frantic energy against skin as she beat away the small beasts.

They disappeared in an impossibly sudden way that could make the sanest person question their wits. Her mind was not slipping; she knew better. She knew this place. The feeling of tiny ant legs tickling her skin remained even though she couldn't spot another one on her body or the counter, not until she glanced back inside the sugar bowl. A few nearly dead ones twitched atop a mountain of snowy granules.

She pitched the whole dish into the garbage, not caring that the bowl wasn't her property. The owners had to know the place they fixed up and rented out as the charming *Tea House* was a cursed lot. Just like they had to know why Layla came back.

Her earlier discussion with the rental owner when she'd checked in had been brief. Layla greeted the woman whose name she could not remember. The memory almost surfaced, like the faint dying wisp of a thing the subconscious tucked away, saved for the right time to reveal itself, which apparently had not been today.

The woman stared at Layla with a scrunched face of vague

recollection, but such was the power of the house—a place that could bend minds if it so wished—and it seemed the house willed the women to forget one another.

"You've been here before?" the rental owner had asked, her brow creased in a question of what was perhaps curiosity or annoyance.

She'd nodded, taken the key, and glanced around at the impressive garden connecting the owner's property with the Tea House, an acre away. Roses and lavender, white blooms on trees, the scent of honeysuckle in the air. Flat stones curved a path around the flowers and shrubs, and wind chimes sang a gentle song in the breeze. An idyllic scene that left Layla's skin with chilled goosebumps despite the June heat. Incredible how so much darkness could lurk and live beside so much beauty.

"I was here two years ago," Layla replied. "It was different."

"Things change," the woman had said in a soft voice with a forced gentle smile—the kind of smile which held nothing but lies.

"I wasn't alone, last time."

She ignored the remark. "Enjoy your stay." The woman walked away, eyes focused on her phone where likely someone else had emailed to inquire about the availability of Tea House this summer.

*What the hell was her name?* Layla wondered and paced across the creaking wooden floor between the kitchen and living room. Hadn't there been a husband, too? She swore she'd met two people when she'd been here a year ago with Mia.

Layla assumed the rental owners knew things went wrong inside Tea House. Assumed they knew something hungry lived there, and last year, it had swallowed Mia. They acted like they didn't know a thing though, and Layla didn't bother in an attempt to retrieve more information from them because telling the owners, "Oh hello, your house ate my sister, know anything about that?" wasn't set up to be a great conversation.

Her sighs echoed as she stopped pacing and stood with bare feet on a purple Persian rug. Tea House possessed an acute strangeness, some phantasmagoric energy that made the whole place shimmer. When Layla stared straight ahead, the walls visible within her peripheral vision wavered like a mirage, yet they remained solid when she touched them or looked at them straight on.

The last time she'd been here with her sister, the terror had arrived so quick; an unannounced blight set upon them, equipped with unsettling movements hidden in darkness until the house revealed all of its teeth waiting behind the mouth of pastel walls.

And then Mia, gone. Taken by whatever inhabited Tea House, something still alive in its depths. She refused to be scared away this time. If she left now, she'd never have a chance to find any clue about Mia's disappearance, or to save her. The thought of Mia possibly being alive crawled into her mind the way the ants scattered, but hope was dangerous.

Layla would fight, and the house would fight back.

A mere three hours passed from her arrival time before the ant occurrence happened. Brewing a cup of tea from the large selection in the cupboard seemed an innocent enough task until the tiny things exploded like a volcano from the sugar dish and crawled everywhere.

The teacup stood long forgotten, and Layla shook out her sweater in case dead insects still clung to threads. While the sun faded outside and a muggy evening settled in, the air conditioning blasted inside. She hadn't been able to find a thermostat to adjust the temperature, so she settled for putting the sweater back on. She exhaled a deep breath, took a good moment to stop and look around the place. Where did she even begin in her search?

Pastel walls sent her stomach into a roil. The whole place looked more medicinal than cozy. Floral wallpaper decorated the hall outside the living room, and it all clashed with teal armchairs and a couch designed in spirals of more flowers—furniture that could have shipped directly out of her grandmother's house. Lace hung everywhere, from the heavy drapery around the windows, doilies on each stand and table, and from strange shawls hung up on hooks near the front door where a rather large statue of a peacock greeted guests. An unsettling number of portraits decorated every other wall—drawings, paintings, vignettes—all of young women posed with rather serious expressions on their faces.

Mia had loved it, said she felt like a Victorian lady waiting in her private rooms for her secret lover to come visit. Layla had laughed, let the warmness of Mia's excitement comfort her heart, and then left her alone there to meet the girlfriend their parents disapproved of. It was supposed to be a sweet date for the two girls to connect, have some privacy, and Layla had been the cool older sister renting the place for them, driving Mia all the way out here... How had it gone so wrong? The reviews for Tea House had been glowing. No one warned about restless spirits or standoffish owners who may or may not play a part in sacrificing lives to the damned place.

And if the reviews had said such things, would she have believed them?

She walked around in silence, alone with her despair until the unmistakable crash of shattering glass echoed in the house. Layla spun around; the crash had sounded so close, yet she saw nothing broken. Her heart pounded, a threat to beat right from her chest and land on the floor with a wet thump.

Something moved at the opposite end of the wall. It flickered and invited Layla to traipse across the wooden floor and reveal another secret slithering through Tea House. Wasn't this what she'd come here for, to understand the property, to find out what it'd done to her sister?

There was no other choice but to follow the flickering movement. She turned on her phone's flashlight and used it to inspect the walls. No light switch greeted her, just a single dead bulb on the ceiling. She kept her gaze straight ahead to alleviate the unsettling shimmer of quivering darkness. The hall ended in a mint green wall decorated solely with mirrors.

Square and oval shapes all trimmed in gold, each mirror showed Layla her distorted reflection half hidden in shadow and half overly bright from the light's glare. Dozens of Laylas walked closer to the wall of mirrors, and all bore the same perplexed expression. She didn't remember seeing this wall the last time she'd been here, but then again, the events of that night had unfolded so quick.

A small table stood below the mirrors, pushed against the wall. Unsurprisingly, a lacy fabric decorated the tabletop. Fake plants gathered in a small circle atop the lace and shielded the Wi-Fi box from direct view, hiding the current commodity from sight amid all the Victorian-style décor. Layla hadn't yet bothered to see if the internet worked here. A Google search wasn't going to help her find Mia.

She glanced at the time on her phone.

Impossible. How had two more hours disappeared? It had only been minutes. She retreated from the eerie hallway and checked the grandfather clock in the living room. It said the same thing: she'd managed to lose two hours, yet only minutes ago she'd checked outside the windowed curtains as the sun started to set. Now, velvet darkness ruled the sky.

The loss of time, it had happened before. How she'd burst into the house after Dani, Mia's girlfriend, had left a frantic voice message. She'd left half her items behind at the coffee shop where she'd settled in to work while the girls had some alone time. They searched together as evening turned to night turned into day all within a frighteningly quick span. Sunrise only brought pain, a glowing realization that Mia would never be found because the house had taken her deep into its shimmering world. Dani left, returned home, and forgot how much she loved Mia. She sank into a quietness that no one could pry open—and Layla knew it had to be the house's fault. It'd sucked some life from Dani.

But Layla remembered it all. She'd searched every inch of shadowy corner, tried to make sense of Dani's story. The girl said something came from the walls and absorbed Mia, took her.

Rage still lived within Layla when she thought of how people dismissed Mia's disappearance as a troubled teen who'd run away that night. Mia was a bright, brilliant star who dared to shine among the gray-scaled town they'd been forced to live in. Memories of Mia faded from the minds of Layla's neighbors, even from the minds of their parents, and maybe it was partially Tea House's power forcing people to forget Mia's vibrant existence, but Layla made sure to remember every day. Every hour. And it took a year to come back here, but she did it, which was more than the others could say.

A scratching within the walls caught her attention. She securely closed the curtains and then held her breath, listening. Had there been scratching the night the house took Mia? She didn't think so, but how could she be sure of anything here.

It sounded again, like rats in the wall chewing on plaster before settling back into somber quiet. She gave up on the noises and gave in to the urge to empty her bladder in the downstairs bathroom. The walls contained another pink nightmare, gauchely decorated with oversized paintings of more peacocks and portraits. The whole house itself felt too still, as if it were relaxing into a perverse quietness as it watched her.

She quickly finished her business and went over to the curved white sink to wash her hands, focusing on the clear water and not the way the house rippled with hunger. This place had tasted Mia, how could it not long for more blood?

A noise behind her, like a coin spinning on a countertop. She froze, listened, and then turned around as her hands clenched into wet fists from rinsing away the jasmine-scented soap. A golden disc, slightly larger than a quarter, revolved around on the tiled bathroom floor. It spun between her and the door in the small bathroom.

The golden circle whirled so fast, Layla thought it might combust into flame. She backed herself up into the corner, as far away as she could get, and searched for something to throw at the object or over it. Her hand reached for a nearby towel, but the moment she moved her gaze away, it whistled through the air at full speed toward her. She covered her face, but the disc hit her collarbone with the force of a hard punch before it fell to the floor and clattered on the tile. Dead.

An old coin. So harmless without its rapid movement, yet when she pressed her hand on the wounded area of her collarbone, blood wetted her fingertips. The breath she didn't know she held burst out like a pinpricked balloon. Labored breathing made its way through her body as she slumped over the sink. An ache and bruise blossomed from the still-bleeding wound on her collarbone. The thin sweater had offered no protection over her T-shirt.

Layla bent down to retrieve the coin, too curious about the image on it not to get a closer look. The coin pictured an etched cameo of a woman whose eyes had been scratched out. Scarlet stained the coin from the blood still on Layla's fingers. Crimson touched the woman's scratched face, and then screaming filled Layla's mind.

Mia's screams.

"Stop it," Layla said to the house. "Give her back to me."

Tears formed at the corners of her eyes, further distorting the shimmer of the walls. She sprinted away from the bathroom, deeply wishing she'd left earlier, but something had held her back. A warning that'd promised if she crossed the path while the coin spun, something much worse would have happened.

Breaths came a little easier when she emerged from the bathroom and found her way down the hall again, down where something still stood against the flickering darkness by the wall of mirrors. Layla stayed perfectly still, reassured herself the movement was not her reflection. No, someone else stood there. She still had hold of the coin and dug its rough edges into her palm with a tight squeeze as she walked forward.

"Why aren't there any damned lights here?" she muttered aloud in hopes her own voice would break the thick fear building in her chest.

In response, the darkness whispered. A black curtain fell upon the whole house. The lights on behind Layla in the living room flickered, buzzed, and then the bulbs burst from every lamp.

"Shit." She retrieved her phone, ignored the low battery alert, and pushed the flashlight back on. Two steps closer to the wall, and when she angled the light up and looked into the mirrors, she saw herself gripping a knife. Mirror-Layla held the blade up, grinned, her eyes replaced with golden coins that leaked blood as she took the knife and slashed vertical cuts down her cheeks.

Layla suppressed a scream as her reflection laughed. She tripped backward, landed on a knee that skidded hard against the wooden floor. The coin slid from her grip and rolled beneath the wooden table. Frantic, she touched her face, eyelashes, found normal eyes. No coins. No smile on her mouth, but her cheeks stung. Fingertips pressed against wet blood from a vertical slash on each cheek.

Shaking, she avoided looking up at the mirrors and searched for the coin on the floor.

Phone still gripped tight, Layla directed the light beneath the table and scanned the dusty ground. She needed to know more about the coin, how it connected to Mia, and if all of this could help find her sister. Her cheeks throbbed in rhythm with the ache still present on her collarbone. Let the damned house taste her blood, just let her find Mia...

There. It hid in the back corner of the wall entwined in cobwebs. She reached for the object when something else caught her eye—a yellowed piece of paper stuck to the wall with a thumbtack that shone like a black beetle. Fingertips reached for the coin first, and then she unpinned the slippery tack. It fell from her fingers and rolled in a circle. Like the coin in the bathroom, it didn't stop spinning.

She clutched the paper and backed away, urged her body to turn around faster, but her limbs struggled to obey her will even after what had happened with the coin. Everything felt like wading through an invisible mudslide as she fought to move, to stand up. The thumbtack danced in a wild spin until it flew toward her. Layla managed to move her head enough to avoid the tack connecting with her eye. Instead, it pierced her face below the vertical cut on her left cheek. The movement was so quick she didn't feel it until the numbness ebbed and sent hot electric agony in its place. The long metal stabbed the whole way through her cheek, and her tongue caught the pointed end.

With trembling hands, she hauled herself up toward the mirror wall and set the phone down. The beam of artificial light shot upward, but it was enough to see in one of the mirrors. *Deep breaths,* she told herself as she set down the coin and paper, forced an unsteady hand to pinch two fingers around the thumbtack. If this is what she needed to do, survive these trials of bleeding pain set by the house, she'd do it. She'd do anything to find Mia, and maybe the house hadn't realized that yet.

An animal yowl pushed its way through her lips when she pulled the tack out. She expected more blood to smear her face, but something thicker leaked from both the thumbtack wound and the vertical slits on her cheeks. She tugged open the sweater, and the collarbone wound, too, oozed a gummy substance. Her fingers rubbed the dark glue.

"Shoe polish," a familiar voice behind Layla said. The rental owner.

She grabbed her phone and directed the harsh glare at the woman who held a flashlight of her own, a ring of keys in her other hand.

"I knocked, but you didn't answer."

"What the hell is happening?" Layla wished for a weapon, but all she had was the coin, a thumbtack, and the... the paper! She flipped open the folded piece of old paper to reveal a drawing that matched the one on the coin. A scrawled vignette portrait of a woman with her eyes scratched out.

The rental owner stepped closer down the wooden hallway. "Do you know what they did to her, my great-grandmother?" She gestured toward the paper. "They covered her in shoe polish, took out her eyes."

"Who?"

"Angry neighbors. Sad excuses for humans who took out her eyes, replaced them with coins. Said it represented her greed. They buried her alive. Let her suffocate with thick polish on her face, down her throat. They thought she killed her husband, and maybe she did, but it was only to protect her children. And now I protect her. All the women in my family must protect her."

"Did she take my sister?" Layla had nowhere to move, the wall of mirrors was a dead end.

The rental owner stopped, frowned. "I'm sorry about the girl, but my great-grandmother gets lonely. She was so young when she died, you know. Her kids were only babies. So tiny. And she was just a girl herself back then, really."

Layla held the paper with the drawing, watched the woman in the vignette with coins for eyes grin. The inky lips moved, but no words sounded from the paper to Layla's ears.

"Give me that," the rental owner demanded, but Layla did not miss the note of fear in the woman's voice.

"What if I rip it in half instead?"

The woman shook her frazzled head. "Will only make things worse."

Layla didn't believe her, and as she gazed around the house in the half glow, absorbed just how many portraits of girls and young women lined the walls, her heart nearly disintegrated. None of these girls had been safe. Had they all been guests of Tea House?

"I couldn't protect Mia, so why should you get to protect your great-grandmother?"

The rental owner leapt toward Layla, but not before Layla ripped the drawing clean down the middle. As the owner of Tea House dove toward her, something else lunged out of the darkness between the tattered pages.

Coins for eyes and the rancid scent of rotten body mixed with shoe polish. The vignette came to life with a maw of darkness at her edges. The creature didn't spare a glance at Layla, just kept her coin eyes focused on the rental owner.

Inky black seeped from the creature's skin, oozed toward the rental owner and held her as if in a pit of tar.

"I'm the one protecting you!" the woman protested.

Spectral head tilted, the vignette-woman shook her long fingers at the rental owner, and then gestured toward Layla. Toward the cuts on her face and collarbone. Her blood.

"We're connected," Layla whispered. "I freed you." She spoke the words aloud to better understand them, to confess to the world what she'd done, be it for better, or likely for worse. How could spawning something from blood and gloom, something that used the house to swallow people like her sister whole, be a good thing to release into the world? This had never been her intention.

With strange gentleness, the shadows cascaded from the creature's skin and crept into Layla's head. So much pain, the way the vignette-woman's soul was bound to the house, to the person who controlled the place. The way shoe polish had congealed her edges as she was buried alive all those years ago. Doomed to repeat a cycle because of the curse of foolish neighbors.

A never-ending circle of agony.

"Oh," Layla muttered in surprise as the creature showed her, made her understand. "You lied," she said to the rental owner.

"You don't protect her, you bind her here. Make her suffer. Make them all suffer."

The vignette-woman gestured toward something Layla had not seen on the wall before, an object the darkness brought forth from its shimmering and placed into focus.

"Stop, put it away," hissed the rental owner. "You don't understand. She'll trick you!"

Layla found strength to grab her phone from the wooden table, and she directed the beam onto the new portrait that had formed on the wall across from her.

"Mia," she cried, and then her phone's low battery died, took the last light with it. Submerged in total obscurity, Layla felt the cold wisp of the vignette-woman, the prisoner of Tea House, torrent past her and toward the rental owner. The woman screamed, and though Layla could not see what happened, she heard unforgettable noises of a horrid, wet slurping, of something plopping onto the floor, of pleas to stop until the screams turned to silence.

Moments later, a glow from outside the curtains attempted to shed light into the living room. Morning already? Layla hurried to the drapes and cast them aside. Sunrise greeted her. The way time moved here, so quick and unsettling, but that wasn't why Layla's heart beat so frantic. She needed to turn around, and every inch of her body begged her not to; she'd never be able to unsee the damage.

She turned. The rental owner stood perfectly upright in the tarry substance that cemented her feet down. Black ooze spread from the woman's shoes all the way up her body and clung to the frame of her skin—she'd been vignetted like the creature from the drawing. Instead of a border like those in the portraits, her flesh had been pulled, stretched so the darkness of her edges faded out into the house's shadows. The oval of her face remained devoid of light. Small vines of ink took the place of blood. Meaty crimson innards spilled forth from a peeled-open abdomen. The rental owner's eyes, that had been the *plop* Layla heard, for the eyes sat still on the wooden floor, and in their place on her face shone two golden coins. The air stunk with slick metallic odors.

Layla sidestepped around the sticky mess and kept her gaze on the portrait of her sister.

"Hi, Mia."

A lavender frame, Mia's favorite color, captured her sister in a serious pose, which was particularly unlike Mia, who so often had a smile on her face despite the world that tried so hard to tear her down. The oval portrait captured Mia's brown curls, the almond shape of her bright eyes and the curiosity behind them. Unlike the creature and the rental owner, Mia had not been vignetted.

Layla traced a finger on the portrait's paint, wondered when the sun had vanished again, wondered why she couldn't remember her address, or the name of her sister's former girlfriend. The taste of her own name, her identity, she held it there on her tongue, but the flavor faded.

Yet, Tea House invited her to stay, to remember her sister, and even if she forgot all of their names, she'd always know the girl in the portrait was her family. Wasn't that what mattered?

"There's nothing left out there," the darkness breathed. "And you're already starting to forget."

"I don't want to forget."

"I'm sorry. It's what happens here. But you helped free me from my torturer. I can help you, too."

The guest of Tea House held the portrait in her hands and did not turn as the dim surrounded her on all sides. "How can you help?"

How could anyone help? She couldn't remember her own name at all, just knew she too was a portrait of a woman who Tea House consumed. "It didn't matter, getting rid of the rental owner, did it?"

"It did," the darkness replied. "You can protect us now. You can protect your sister. Keep her company. She misses you so."

"What do I have to do?"

The vignette-woman showed her. The woman who forgot her name placed the portrait she knew to be her sister down on the table, and she walked over to the dead rental owner, retrieved the keys and the woman's cell phone. As instructed, she grabbed a jar from the kitchen and placed it beneath the former rental owner's coin eyes that leaked blood.

"For the tea," the darkness murmured. "We'll have a party."

"Did she have a husband?"

"Yes. He'll come soon. We'll practice on him, and you will learn how to control shadows before real guests arrive."

She hesitated, but then her sister's voice broke through the haze. "We're whole now. Together." Familiar fingers decorated in her sister's favorite golden rings stretched out from the cloud of black near the mirror wall. Vignettes popped up everywhere from the velvet blackness, half-eaten souls who invited her to protect their portraits.

Tea House belonged to them now, and maybe together, that would be enough. The lanyard of keys rattled in one hand, and the cell phone of the dead owner lit up in her other hand. The new owner smiled as she read the email query from a small party wondering if Tea House was available next weekend.

# 27 FALSHAM STREET

## by Tony Richards

*hat a hole!* was Ian Coster's first thought. *I'm supposed to live in here?*

But he didn't see he had much choice. He couldn't afford anything better than this.

His gaze went around the room, and that didn't take very long. It was a narrow, perfectly rectangular room, some twelve feet long by eight feet wide. And there were only three items of furniture in view—a wooden single bed, a tall thin wardrobe of a different-colored wood, and what looked like a chair from someone's dining set.

The window was a sash one with the glass speckled and smeared. The carpet made a crunching noise when you stepped onto it like you had just stepped on a Brillo pad. And the walls were a mottled brownish color as if somebody had been chain smoking here for several years.

"We don't take social security," Mavda pointed out, the burly janitor who'd let him in. "What work you do?"

And when he replied *catering*, she nodded knowingly.

"Yes, we get a lot of such in here."

The really odd thing was that this place—27 Falsham Street—was in a very decent, central part of town. South Kensington, with Hyde Park a few minutes' walk away, several big museums nearby, the Albert Hall accessible on foot. A lot of wealthy people lived here, their expensive cars parked up and down the curbs. But then Ian didn't come from London and so didn't know this basic truth... a respectable façade can hide some quite unpleasant secrets.

From the outside, this five story house looked not too different than the rest. But some time back, whoever owned it had had it divided into dozens of small rented rooms. The toilet and the bathroom were both down the hall. The flights of stairs had no carpet at all, and there were very few lights coming up. He'd noticed several flies as well. A pair of them were circling this room's one electric bulb.

*Try looking on the bright side,* Ian thought. *It's in the heart of town, and I need that for work. The rent is low, in London terms at least. And I'll finally be sleeping in a proper bed.*

Ever since he'd moved down here from York, he had been sleeping on the couches of his friends.

One of the two flies he'd noticed started buzzing in toward his face. He batted it away with the back of his hand.

"Okay, I'll take it," he told Mavda.

He never saw her again, except when the rent was due. For someone who was charged with taking care of this place, Mavda didn't seem too keen on venturing out of her room, which was next to the front door and seemed a little larger than the rest.

Not long after he'd moved in, he tried to figure out how many people exactly were living in this house. Ian went up and down his dimmed-out third floor corridor and counted seven doors, excluding the bathroom and the loo. And there were seven more on the next level down. If that pattern was repeated throughout then there were more than thirty tenants all residing here.

But their rooms were very quiet. He'd hear a doorway bang occasionally, but that was all. He bumped into no one on the stairs or in the ground floor hallway.

*Just a place to sleep,* was the philosophy that he adopted. And that really was the sum of it. There wasn't even so much as a small communal kitchen. But he got his evening meals at work and in the daytime there were fast food joints.

His job in catering kept him out late, waiting tables at expensive functions and then spending a good hour or so just cleaning up the big leftover mess. Except before he'd moved to Falsham Street, he'd had to wait for a night bus to take him back to some friend's couch. These days he could mostly walk. This was late in May, the weather mild and pleasant even at this hour. Central London's streets were mostly empty, blackened friezes limned with yellow streetlight. But he enjoyed the quietness after all the evening's bustle, and he always went home at a gentle pace.

The silence inside his room was of a different kind, however. As soon as he got there, he felt trapped. He'd been here almost two weeks now and hadn't got to know a single other tenant. That being another London truth... people can live stacked like cards and still exist remotely from each other.

He went out frequently for walks, but nobody can walk forever. So he decided to explore more of the building.

Right at the back end of the ground floor hallway was a flight of stairs he'd not noticed before. It led steeply downward into some kind of deep basement room. The door was painted glossy black. It had three keyholes and was firmly shut.

Something like a dozen flies were humming round in the small space down there. As Ian watched, one of them landed on a deadbolt lock and crawled away into the little gap. Which made him glad he hadn't gone the whole way down.

Heading up the other way, he found out something he had previously not known. These steps led the whole way to a small rickety door which let out onto a flat roof. He went through it and gazed around at the terrific, distant-looking view—Hyde Park's tall trees and the pale dome of the Albert Hall.

But then he realized he was not alone.

Sitting down cross-legged by the parapet above the street was a short man with straggly black hair. His clothes looked old. His back was hunched, and he was puffing on a cigarette. But at least this was a chance to meet another resident, so Ian cleared his throat.

The man's face swung around, narrow and sharp-edged and with the kind of thin moustache that looks like it's been scribbled on. His gaze went very hard at first, but then he grinned.

"Ha! Another captive of this place, I would presume."

"Hope I'm not disturbing you."

"Nothing of the sort, pal. Glad to see a pleasant human face. Come along—sit down with me a while. Honestly, chum, I don't bite."

"Smoke?" the man asked, offering his pack. "Alex Musgrove, by the way. But everybody calls me Lex."

Ian told the man his name and took a cigarette, something that he very rarely did, but by this stage he had the desperate need to get to know some people round here. This fellow was somewhere in his fifties and he had a rather seedy look. Beggars can't be choosers, though.

They chatted for a while, exchanging information, although Lex's was mostly of the non-committal type. What did he do? *This and that.* How long had he lived here? *A fair while.* This was somebody who seemed to have good reason to conceal the details of his life.

"Catering eh, pal? That's not so good. Lousy hours and lousy pay, except you're young and you'll move on to something else. So, what do you think of Chateau Falsham?"

"Not too great, right?"

"That's an understatement."

"What exactly are the other tenants like?"

"Mostly very quiet. Keep themselves to themselves."

"I find that hard to understand. You'd think they'd want some company."

Lex's face took on a curious expression, deeply thoughtful and absorbed. Then:

"There's a story around that. I'll tell it to you one of these fine days."

He straightened up and studied his small wristwatch, which looked like a rather good one.

"Not right now, though. Got to see a man about a job."

And he stood up without any further ceremony.

"See you later then, my handsome lad."

He *was* handsome. Ian had known that since he'd been fourteen, and he'd turned twenty-one this year. He had blond and slightly wavy hair. A symmetrical face with good strong cheekbones. A mouth just a touch too small and eyes a lively apple green.

What use is a handsome face, though, when you have no one to share it with?

Several of the women at the catering firm had started coming on to him once work was done. He opted for one called Colleen, but where could they go at past two-thirty in the morning? She still lived with her parents and he had no wish to take her back to his place. So they wound up in an alley round behind the function hall, something Ian had never tried. But it turned out he found the entire thing uncomfortable. And deeply unsatisfying too. He came away wishing he'd never even done it.

In the bathroom's shower the next morning, he noticed something that was decidedly odd. The jets of water were all going at full blast, but a black housefly was steering through the drops. He'd never seen a fly do that.

And then—to his surprise—it landed on his dampened ribs. Simply sat there, rubbing its front legs together.

Disgust took over from surprise. He slammed a palm down on the thing. His hand came away smeared with red and black. Ian washed it quickly off.

And he was out from the shower the next instant, drying himself down with a stiff gray towel. He was standing in front of the basin now, a mirror on the wall above it.

He peered at his wet face. It looked a good shade paler than it had before. But then he realized there was something on the move behind his head. Something dark, constantly shifting. A low humming drifted to his ears.

And when he swung around, another dozen flies or so were moving through the air in swift tight circles, going different routes but in the same general pattern, so they almost were describing a loose ball. He swatted at the things with his free hand. They scattered for a moment but then came back in.

Ian swiped his towel at them, then wrapped it tightly round his waist and went back to his room, still dripping.

🌲

Colleen wouldn't look him in the eye that evening, and the other women had gone cooler too. Had he been too quick last night, perhaps even a touch too rough? Or perhaps she simply knew he hadn't liked it.

A dull unhappiness was settling over Ian. He'd come to London—or at least in part—to broaden his horizons, get some new experiences in. Instead of which his world seemed to be shrinking ever smaller.

To make matters even worse, this particular evening was the busiest so far. A fundraiser for a right-wing pressure group. Three hundred very well-heeled guests. An eight-course meal. An open bar. He and all the others were rushed off their feet, caroming back and forth as crazily as pinballs.

Things only started slowing down around ten thirty, when the band struck up. Ian was sweating by that stage.

"Okay if I go cool down a bit?" he asked his supervisor.

"Five minutes," was the response.

He'd worked at this venue before and knew precisely where the washrooms were. He pulled off his bow tie as he headed for them, breathing with relief as the door swung shut behind him.

Going to a washbasin, he cleaned his face. At least there were no flies in here. But then the door behind him started opening again. *One of the damned diners,* Ian thought.

And he was dead right about that, but not quite in the way that he'd expected.

He had noticed this particular woman several times during the past few hours. Even in so large a crowd she stood out like a neon sign. Somewhere in her mid-twenties and somewhere around five foot eight, she had short, fashionably-cut red hair, and she was remarkably slim and shapely. And she had the most amazing face, almost like a doll's face, almost painted on. Thin dark brows, huge cobalt eyes, and full lips that were nearly always pursed into a twinkling, rather impish grin.

She had on a glittering green evening gown. Her smile grew

even broader as she stepped inside. Ian turned toward her, feeling rather puzzled.

"S'cuse me, miss, this is the men's. You're not supposed to be in here."

"Oh? But then I never do what I'm supposed to."

And she moved in right up close. Her expensive perfume washed across him.

"What time do you finish work?"

"Miss?"

"It's a simple question."

"Erm... around two thirty in the morning, miss."

"That's fine by me. I'm always up till dawn. I'll spin around and pick you up and we can go and have some fun."

"It's Caroline, for what that's worth," she added.

And she leaned right in and kissed him on the lips, then pivoted away from him and headed out.

The rest of the evening went by in a blur. Ian was not certain how to take this. Only... wasn't this what he was really looking for? Experience? Adventure even? The chance to step inside some different people's worlds, to walk across a landscape that was not his own.

When he finally emerged from the banquet hall a horn sounded and headlamps flashed. A Mini Clubman—red with racing stripes—was parked right up against the curb. And there was Caroline behind the wheel, still with that green ball gown on.

Her face was even livelier than it had been during the meal, and her pupils were noticeably large.

"Okay, boyo. So, where do you live?"

"It's a dump... you don't want to go there. Can't we try your place instead?"

"No, you silly monkey! No we can't! Heaven's sake, my boyfriend's there!"

Which took him a good way aback but... experience? Adventure even? Getting just the briefest inside glimpse of different worlds? And so he told her his address.

"Oh!" was all she said when he opened up his building's front door.

A rather startled syllable. As if she had not fully understood the meaning of the words *a dump*. As if she did not understand the way some other people lived. Her blue eyes scanned the uncarpeted stairs, the lack of proper lighting as they headed up.

She looked confused a moment, unsure what to do. But then she forced another grin.

"Ah, what the hell?" And she almost laughed. "My God, but you're so pretty for a boy."

She slipped her high-heeled shoes off and then wrapped her free arm round his neck and kissed him again, harder than before.

And they were going up the stairs now. Side by side, holding hands like lovers in a park, the whole house quiet around them. And they had almost reached the second floor, when Caroline abruptly jerked and yelped.

"Something's got inside my dress!"

She was pawing at her midriff. And—as Ian watched—a fly came down from the shadows in the corridor, landed on her shoulder and then scuttled underneath her gown. Three more appeared and did the same.

Even more were circling her now. There were several crawling about in her hair.

Then about half a dozen landed on her face.

"Oh my God!" Her voice had risen to a high-pitched shriek and her slim hands were batting frantically. "This whole place must be absolutely filthy! I must have been crazy coming here!"

She glared at him with absolute disgust just before she turned and fled.

Ian normally fell asleep as soon as he got back into his room, but definitely not tonight. First, there was the utter disappointment... those deep kisses and the promise they were leading to, and it had all capsized and sunk without a trace.

But there was bewilderment as well. Why would flies even behave that way?

*That perfume she was wearing,* was the answer that he finally came up with. *Perhaps it drew them. Maybe it was that.*

That did not sound completely right, but he could think of nothing else that made the slightest bit of sense.

Just before he finally dozed off, he thought he noticed something moving on the ceiling almost directly above him. But the curtains in this room were very thin. The window overlooked the street. Uneven streaks of yellow light got in, and passing headlamps made the shadows shift.

So he gave it no more thought, letting his eyelids slip shut.

The next morning was Monday and there was no work. Ian slept late, got dressed slowly, didn't even bother shaving. Breakfast was a muffin and a coffee at McDonald's. Sunlight was caressing the whole center of the city when he stepped out on the street again.

Hyde Park was full of local residents and tourists. There were families and couples. There were whole big groups of people his age. Walking on the path beside the central lake, Ian wondered if he'd got it really badly wrong by moving here from York. He'd started to detest his job. He certainly did not like where he lived. And as for making some new friends...?

But hold it now, he already *had* friends. He had been trying to stay away from them and make it on his own so far, but that just wasn't working out. His cell phone was in his pocket, so he pulled it out and started dialing.

"Hello? Chas?"

"Ian, my man! How's life in fashionable South Kensington, no less?"

He had slept on Chas' couch for three whole weeks when he had first come south. The guy was an illustrator slightly older than him, mostly working from the little studio at the back of his place.

"I was thinking, Chas. My time's my own today. So if you're not too busy, why don't we hook up?"

"Of course—just get over here. A word of warning though, my buddy. Things round here have changed a bit."

And—his tone going all mysterious—Chas refused to explain what he meant by that.

It took two buses to reach Muswell Hill. Chas' flat was in a big Victorian house off Fortis Green.

And his door came open with a big "Tah-rah!" Chas had one arm tightly wrapped around a small woman who Ian had never seen before.

Her name turned out to be Beth. She and Chas had met less than a month ago, but she had already moved in.

"It was just like being struck by lightning, man. For both of us. Isn't that right?"

Beth nodded eagerly, then greeted Ian like an old close friend. The three of them took lunch at a nearby pub and then sat drinking in the garden at the back for simply hours.

It was a fine afternoon and Beth proved to be extremely nice. But just one thought was weighing heavily on Ian as he rode the bus back to his place: Chas had moved on with his life, but he was going nowhere fast.

Walking the last stretch to Falsham Street, he stopped in at a newsagent and bought himself a lighter and a packet of ten smokes. And once inside number twenty-seven, Ian headed for the roof again.

Lex was sitting there in the exact same hunched position as the last time, with a half-smoked Marlboro hanging from his mouth.

"Hey there, my new good-looking young friend."

Ian settled down beside him. "Did you get the job?"

"The...?"

"Last time that we met, you told me you were seeing a man about one."

"Not that kind of job, my old son. Don't go worrying your pretty head about it."

They went quiet for a while. Then:

"Lex?" Ian asked him cautiously. "You're not exactly on the straight and narrow, are you?"

"Did you ever hear me claiming to be any kind of saint?"

"Which means you have to have some cash. So why're you staying in a place like this?"

"I have what you might call *a past* which requires that I remain somewhat beneath the radar. And living in this anonymous rat hole goes a good way to achieving that."

Ian turned that over slowly, not sure that he fully got it.

"You said there was a story round this place. About the way we're all so isolated?"

Lex lit up another cigarette.

"You've seen the stairs what lead down to that basement flat? Well it's a proper little flat, not like the coffins further up, even with a kitchen and its own small bathroom round the back. A woman called Miss Franklin used to live down there. Lived down there for many years. A proofreader who worked from home. I got those kinds of details from the local paper, because no one ever saw the gal. She never went out and no one visited. Forty-nine years old she was. And just last year she lay down in her empty bath and slashed her wrists."

"I've heard this kind of story before," Ian cut across him briskly. "It was a couple of months later before people started noticing the smell and realized that she was dead."

"No, worse than that," Lex replied. "She closed her bathroom door before she topped herself, which means that there were two doors holding the smell in. And she did that around the tail end of October, just when the cold weather started setting in. No one even went in there until almost the end of the next March. Which means the bugs had five whole months to work on her. All that they found when they finally went in were poor Miss Franklin's bones and skin."

Lex pulled out a small newspaper cutting from a pocket of his jacket. It was from the *South Kensington Post*. The headline was *Local Woman Found Dead*. Ian scanned it right down to the final line, which told its readers the police were looking for no suspects.

"I keep this with me all the time, chum, simply to remind me of a vital truth. Living in a place like this can leave you cut off from the normal world. So bear that in mind and don't you ever let it happen, Ian lad."

Back inside his room and feeling pretty low, Ian threw himself out full length on the bed, not even bothering to remove his shoes. He lay there for a long while, staring at the ceiling, wondering how his life had come to this. The light had started fading out beyond the window. Finally, he fell into a restless doze.

In which state, a dream came calling. He was still living here but had grown older. He was lying in an empty bath. Beetles the size of his fist were crawling round in there as well, and they had massive curving mandibles. He wanted to get up but could not move. The beetles started chewing into him.

He woke up sharply, drenched in sweat. But he did not open his eyes straight away. Some of Lex's words were ringing through his head. *The bugs had five whole months to work on her.*

But there weren't too many beetles here in England that devoured meat. There weren't even that many cockroaches. So *bugs* could only mean one thing.

Maggots. Hatching from their tiny eggs, thousands of the squirming things. Very small at first, but gorging themselves on Miss Franklin, getting fatter by the day, filling themselves with her flesh.

Then turning into chrysalides. And changing.

A scratching noise reached Ian's ears and his eyelids sprang fully open.

It was now night, with streaks of lighting seeping in. And where it washed across the ceiling, Ian could see thousands of flies. Except they were not moving randomly the way they normally did. No, they were forming up into a big long shape. Almost like a living silhouette.

A human shape. A woman's one, a tapered waist and curls of hair. It was directly above him and Ian felt frozen to the spot.

In the section of the shape that had to be the face, the flies began to part at two small points. A pair of oval patches appeared. Sideways oval, and they looked like eyes.

And then another gap showed up, farther down the face and larger than the other two. A mouth, curved upward in a smile? Even... a hopeful smile, perhaps?

This silhouette had no right arm, merely a stump where the shoulder ought to be. But still more flies were crawling to that spot. And they were clambering on top of each other, hundreds of the buzzing things. Forming a dark column that grew longer as he watched. It was reaching toward his bed.

Four fingers and a thumb appeared, made of houseflies just as much. A hand that was coming open wide, almost like to grab at him.

A scream welled up in Ian's throat, but he held it in and turned it into action. He rolled sideways off the bed, hit the carpet, scrambled to the door. Only when he had got through it did he dare to stand up and run.

His only thought was getting out. And once out, he put as much distance as he could between himself and Falsham Street.

"You look like hell," his supervisor snapped at him when he turned up for work next evening. "Did you even bother showering before coming in?"

He'd not done that. He hadn't even slept. Ian had spent the rest of that night in the cheapest hotel he could find. And every time he'd tried to close his eyes, the sound of flies had filled his head. He couldn't seem to lose the buzzing even now, in spite of the fact that he was wide awake.

Heaven only knew how he got through that evening without being sacked. He couldn't concentrate and jolted at the slightest sound. And kept on seeing black dots moving through the air above the dining tables, even though they were not there.

The following day he found another room, not much different to the last but in a far less central part of town. Which meant he had to take the Tube simply to get into work. Its subterranean passageways were often pretty empty in the hours he kept.

There was just himself on the deserted platforms. Just himself in the bare, rattling carriages.

Just himself... and a few flies. When they approached him, panic always seized him but he tried to steel himself and drove them off with the backs of his hands. The problem was that they always came back.

*Flies can travel anywhere,* he realized, *and can get in almost any place they like.*

Those words turned into a constant mantra in his head. He even found himself mouthing them quietly sometimes.

Before much longer it was fully summer, and the heat in London soared right up.

And there were flies just everywhere. Whenever he went out onto the street, or opened up the window of his stuffy little room. They just came buzzing in and crawled around on everything. Except they didn't form up into shapes. He never saw them try it once. And that was something to be grateful for.

*Perhaps I only dreamed all that*, he kept on trying to tell himself. *A nightmare, a truly awful one, but really nothing more than that.*

He clung onto that thought the way a drowning man might cling onto a floating log and very slowly started to recover, the wounds healing in his mind.

Work, though, was a nightmare of a different kind. The wedding season was now in full swing, and while some venues had good air-conditioning, the same thing wasn't nearly true of all of them. He felt smothered by his formal clothes and there were plenty of bad-tempered guests. And there were loads of times when Lex's words came back to him.

*"Lousy hours and lousy pay, except you're young and you'll move on to something else."*

The question was... precisely when?

This evening's event was another busy one—in Knightsbridge this time, not too far from where he used to live. It was for something called The Fleet Street Club and turned out to be journalists, men and women and of every age. And it was a pretty noisy gathering. More alcohol than food was being consumed. There were some very flagrant egos on display. Heated arguments were in full swing. Bringing food to tables in an atmosphere like this was quite like trying to balance several plates while moving through a shooting range.

The heat soon started getting to him too. But after several months of working at this job, Ian had learnt to drop into a routine where his mind went almost blank. He moved between the tables like an automaton, doling out the next course on the list.

And kept on doing that for almost half an hour before somebody reached out and caught hold of his sleeve.

"Ian?"

It was a woman's voice, with a faint northern accent that he almost thought he recognized.

"Ian Coster... is it really you?"

He broke out of his trance and looked across. And stopped dead with astonishment when he did that.

A slim, delicate face was staring into his. An untanned but still healthy face, with pale green eyes and framed by long dark hair. This was Sophie Reynolds, and she came from York. They'd dated for a few months when they both had been eighteen.

She smiled hugely, pushed her chair back and stood up. She was wearing a white silk gown, a silver pendant at her throat, and she had always been nearly as tall as him.

"It's great to see you! Can you stop and talk?"

Ian turned that over quickly in his head.

"My supervisor's watching, so I'd better not. Maybe when things quiet down?"

"But... you're living in London too? I moved here just after Christmas."

"New job, then?"

"A good one too."

"That's terrific, Sophie. But I have to go."

And without another single word he turned away from her, pushing off toward the kitchens faster than he ought to have. There was now turmoil rushing through his head, and he had to face the fact he was embarrassed too. When they had been going out, Sophie had just started working at the *York Recorder*, a very small local paper with its offices above a hardware store. But she had obviously progressed to better things by far.

Once again, it was a case of her life moving on while his had not. He was getting angry now, though mostly with himself.

"Jeff?" he asked one of his colleagues at the kitchen door. "Can you take over at table sixteen for a while?"

And after that, time slowed down to a crawl, this whole evening dragging on interminably. Every so often he would find the strength to look across. Sophie was now chatting with a trio of distinguished-looking men, except she seemed to sense that he was watching her. Her head came up, she tried to meet his gaze.

Ian immediately turned away. Which felt pretty childish, but he couldn't help it.

No band struck up and there was no respite. Sophie was now talking to a grey-haired woman who appeared to be giving her some slow, careful advice. She was not glancing at him anymore. She had given up on that.

Was that a relief or a disappointment? Ian was not really sure. His mind was filled the whole way to the brim with desperate, conflicting thoughts. But it was nearly midnight by this stage. The room had become noticeably quieter and some of the older diners were beginning to depart. And so he turned the other way, going through the kitchens to the back door of the banquet hall.

He paused before pushing on the fire door's handle. It was another back alley out there, and on a hot night such as this he knew what might be moving through its claustrophobic confines.

But he badly needed a cigarette. He had been smoking on a regular basis ever since that awful night. This was Lex's legacy to him—a niggling addiction and a throaty cough.

Ian put a smoke between his lips, fumbled for his lighter, but then paused. He'd be in real trouble if he lit up here. He had no choice but go outdoors.

A soft humming reached his ears the moment that he pushed the door open a crack, and Ian almost slammed it shut. But then he realized it was the wrong type of noise... just a small car cruising past.

His heart was pounding fiercely though and his palms had turned slick with sweat. He paused awhile until his breathing had slowed down, and then he tipped his ear toward the gap and listened very carefully.

He was not certain straight away. But... there was not a *sound* out there. Not a murmur or the tiniest buzz. He opened up a little wider and peered out.

It was a very closed-in space that he was staring at, no larger than four foot wide with tall brick walls to either side, a floor of rutted concrete in between them. But it was not wholly dark. Where it opened out onto the road there was a streetlamp shining a bright vivid yellow. He could see nothing on the move against its glow, not even isolated dots.

He was still careful all the same. Reached out with his free hand, ran his palm across the nearest wall. All that it came back with was a trace of brick dust.

Maybe this whole thing was over. Maybe he was free at last. He stepped out into the small alley, taking a deep breath of air. And it was pretty warm, but nothing like as stuffy as the air inside. He felt himself relax and almost smiled. Lit the cigarette already in his mouth.

Then the fire door clicked shut behind him and he realized his mistake. There was no handle on this side—he'd have to walk around to get back in. But that was no problem in the slightest. Nothing was a problem anymore. The nightmares of the past had faded back. He needed to focus on the future now.

And he finally *did* smile. Loosened up his stance and propped one shoulder on the wall. He took a deep drag on the cigarette and flicked it casually, watching as its embers drifted down.

And when his head came up again, a silhouette was standing at the top end of the alley.

He stiffened up for the briefest moment, but then realized it was Sophie. There was no mistaking her, that very tall and narrow frame. Was she here by coincidence? Or perhaps she'd come looking for him? If the latter was the case then maybe this was an important part of where his future lay.

Except he'd behaved like a jerk all evening. Ian felt quite guilty now. But his mind was in an optimistic place and he felt certain he could put things right.

"Hey." He grinned.

Sophie nodded back but otherwise did not respond. And so was she mad at him?

"I'm really glad we've got a proper chance to talk," he tried.

She began walking slowly toward him.

"I was far too busy earlier on. I honestly did want to stop and chat but..."

These were lies though. He knew that. And so he let that final word die on his lips. If they were going to be friends again he needed to be honest with her.

Embarrassment took hold of him again. He stared down at his shiny formal shoes.

"The real fact of the matter is that I felt pretty awkward, Soph. You've obviously done so well for yourself, and in only three years too. And me... I'm still stuck in this lousy job. Only it shouldn't really matter, should it? We can get past that. I genuinely think that if we try to..."

And he faltered, unsure how to finish that. His jaw went tight and he looked up.

Sophie was now only a few yards from him and she was still closing in. But she was *still* in silhouette.

And she'd been wearing high-heeled shoes below her long white dress. But she was making not the slightest sound as she moved across the concrete.

Ian went rigid, his breath freezing in his throat. His cigarette dropped to the floor.

Time hung suspended for a single moment and then...

Sophie entire silhouette broke up into thousands of black moving dots. They churned briefly in the air and then began to swarm across him.

He was so caught up in horror he could barely move at first, but Ian squeezed his eyes shut, clamped his mouth shut too. He could feel the creatures all across his body. He was smothered with them, *caked* with them. He tried swiping at them furiously, but all they did was hum out of his reach then come back in.

They were gathering around his head now—it felt heavy with the weight of them. They were on his lashes. They were in his ears. He could even feel the things inside his nose. Ian wanted desperately to scream but dared not open up his mouth.

Even worse, he was suffocating too. Dozens of the flies were pushing up into his airways and there was no way to get them out.

He lost his balance, slammed against a wall, except he couldn't even feel the bricks. He was coated from head to toe, right the way up to his fingertips.

But he still fought to keep his mouth shut. Tried to draw some air in through his nose, but by this time it was fully blocked.

And he was starting to get very dizzy, starting to black out. When every single fly stopped moving.

Their humming and their scuttling ceased and were replaced by a soft voice inside his head.

*I'll let you live, my very handsome boy. But only if you stay with me.*

Was this a middle-aged voice he was hearing now, a genteel-sounding woman's voice? It was ringing clearly in his brain.

*I won't ask you to promise that... no, I'm not nearly that naïve. But I think you know now what will happen to you if you ever try to go away.*

And he already understood that flies could travel anywhere and get in almost any place they liked. And so there was no way he could evade this thing.

He didn't see what choice he had. He needed to breathe desperately. So Ian managed a stiff nod.

The moment he had done that, every fly was off of him. And they were forming up into a silhouette again, but not Sophie's shape this time. A shorter one. The one he'd seen that terrifying night. The oval gaps for eyes were there. The larger gap that was a mouth. Panting for breath and drenched in sweat, Ian watched as it grew broader, widening out into a smile.

Miss Franklin—what was left of her at least—turned away from him and moved a short distance toward the entrance of the alley. Then she stopped, looking back across her shoulder. And she raised one hand and curled a finger in a beckoning gesture. And then she continued on.

And when she reached the street and turned directly west, Ian knew exactly where the pair of them were headed to.

# GLIMMER

## by Jason Parent

I am heading there to die.

*We* are heading there to die. A laugh escapes me, an almost hysterical cackle, for I recognize the madness in the notions of wanting and seeking death. I know I should be careful what I wish for, but wishes have a way of dissolving on the tongue.

My daughter needs this, and I need her. I'm pressing the pedal to the floor, urging my SUV faster and faster, risking the danger for fear of the alternative. Of being too late.

The dotted lines separating the lanes tick by so fast they become a solid streak. The engine revs higher and higher. Should a deer... No, nothing else matters. Only Kylie. To hell with anyone or anything foolish enough to get in our way.

The remains of the hotel are close now, a charred husk, black against a black night—a megalith to opulence reduced to condemnation and obscurity. I hear my daughter's breathing, shallow as she lies on the back seat, her lungs forcing breaths through dry, colorless cracked lips, each accompanied by a whistling wheeze or a short moan. I want to scream, to tear out my hair, but I can't give into despair. Not now. Not when we are so close. So I force a smile despite her pain even though no one will see it.

"Hang on, baby," I say, unsure if I'm talking to my daughter or myself. "Just one more minute."

My knuckles whiten as I squeeze the steering wheel tighter. In slowing to look for the entrance, I notice the fence around the property. *Stupid!* How could I have forgotten about the gate? And what will I do if it's locked?

I'll ram the fucking thing, that's what I'll do.

My breaths stop hitching, then stop altogether as I turn the wheel and fishtail onto the path leading up to the hotel. Half of a massive, wrought iron gate is open, while the other half is missing, and I lose a wing mirror as I squeeze through the opening. Tall grass and weeds smother out pavement and clear passage. Once, the beautiful lane had circled an ornate fountain, cherubs splashing at play. Now, grass and brambles as high as wheat obscure my way. But I will not be swayed.

I plow through the brush, my SUV more than a match for the growth, letting my memory guide my way. Metal squeals as thorny fingernails scratch lines into my doors as if trying to peel their way inside the vehicle. I am not for them, however; I offer myself only to what awaits inside.

As I pass the fountain, tires treading too quickly over unseen ground, I see that the cherubs are gone. Instead, an empty pedestal guards over black stagnant water, while a mosslike fungus eats its way into the stone.

Behind it, cracked steps rise out of untouched earth to the mausoleum that once catered to the freshest stars and brightest up-and-comers: a hotel, speakeasy, and hedonistic playground that out-roared the roaring twenties itself. It was even rumored that Calvin Coolidge had often frequented the hotel. I chuckle despite the fluttering in my stomach and the clutter in my mind. *Too bad he didn't die here. It might have been nice to meet him.*

No levity can erase the terror that seizes me as I look upon those front doors. I freeze, heart thumping and car slowing, my cowardice immobilizing me when I'm mere feet from my goal. My throat goes dry. I cannot stop the memories from swirling.

I had been there once before, when the lawn was only thigh high. A childhood dare, boys challenging boys. We'd all heard the stories. What dies there stays there. It was true enough that the hotel had gone up in flames, more than a hundred souls trapped inside, the exits barred from within as if its occupants had formed some kind of suicide pact. Even though none of us had believed in ghosts, none of us were brave enough to spend the night.

Until I answered the dare. I walked in to a carnival of lights, something alive that should have been dead. People talking, laughing, having drinks at the bar, smoking cigarettes, all dolled up in the fashion of the time—their time, an age decades before my birth, before the Great Depression and a second world war, Johnny Carson and Vanna White. Before the world became a place only explored through a screen.

An invisible guest walking among echoes that time forgot, I watched in awe as a tuxedoed maestro's fingers danced over eighty-eight keys, the song like an echo carried on the wind. The spirits seemed so happy, locked forever in timeless bliss, that something inside me longed to commune with them.

To be like them.

All at once, the conversation stopped. The pianist halted his melody, his last note hanging like a bell toll in the still of night. And everything was still: spirits frozen in impossible poses, drinks being perpetually poured into never filling glasses, cigarette smoke like cotton candy puffs billowing in the air.

I looked closer, marvel relinquishing to unease, to knees buckling. Smiles had become strained, too big, lecherous. Mouths that had been laughing contorted into silent screams. The air weighed heavier upon me, icy cold and raising goosebumps on my crawling skin as I backed slowly toward the door. My elbows pressed against it and I tried to push it open, but it wouldn't budge.

My heart leapt into my throat. I pushed harder, put my back into it, but the door still wouldn't open. My breaths came short, my thoughts frenzied. I had to get out of there. I turned around to find the door barred and chained, a padlock holding the barricade in place.

Eyes tearing, I searched for something to break the lock or for another way out. My chin quivered; I could feel the scream building before it bellowed from my mouth. All eyes were upon me then, alien and unnerving, black liquid orbs filled with incalculable darkness, voids that, had I dared to gaze into them too long or too deeply, would have sucked me into their abysmal oblivion.

They *saw* me. The lights went out. Screaming, crying, warmth running down my legs, I turned to run. The door, no longer barred, gave way easily as I crashed through it. I kept on running, past my friends, out the gate, down the road, and into the night.

My parents picked me up some time later. I had no idea where I was, how far I had run, or how they'd been able to find me. I was still screaming when they tried to coax me into the car, screamed until my vocal chords bled.

But that was then. I was a terrified kid, moods too easily subject to fancy. I step on the gas. I am not that scared little kid any longer.

*Still, my daughter...* I have to consider her fear. I shake my head. *No. This is the only way.*

A loud crack as my front wheel mounts the steps and my bumper collides with stone. I yank up the emergency brake and climb out. Long reeds bend under the door then whip up to hit me like the rap of a belligerent father's belt. Its door ajar, keys still in the ignition, the vehicle chimes as I circle it. The night is eerily dark, starless, my high beams and the dome light providing the only illumination, creating a brilliant igloo connected to a tunnel showing me the way forward, a path up to the hotel's massive oaken doors.

My headlights flicker, and the hairs on my neck stand on end. The SUV is near mint, the bulbs fresh. I frown. *Could I have damaged it that badly...* No, the ghosts are already at play.

I will not be swayed.

I pull open the back door and offer a smile to my daughter, her chest still rising and falling albeit faintly. By now, my wife is probably aware of our absence, but I never told her of this place or my plans. She wouldn't understand or believe. But she's smart and curious, and I truly believe that once the SUV is found, she'll want to peek inside for herself, and maybe then we can all be together. Yes, I'm sure that's how it will play out.

It has to be.

Gently, I lift my daughter from the seat. She stirs as I cradle her in my arms, careful not to let my tears drop onto her favorite Dora the Explorer pajamas, the kind with the feet. Allowed to come home to die, as the so-compassionate doctors had put it, she at least gets to wear these PJs again, not those awful hospital gowns that made her look so...

*Sick.*

I chuckle and stifle a sob, remembering how much she loves... loved sliding over the kitchen floor on those feet. Her mom... she would get so worried about Kylie falling, but the two of us would share a laugh, a mischievous thing that was all our own.

She shifts but does not awaken. She barely weighs more than her pajamas, the leukemia having eaten away everything but her soul. Something lodges in my throat, and I choke on it before I can force it back down. As I plod up the steps, I shake off my reverie, wondering how I might open up the doors with my daughter in my arms.

They creak open as if caught in a breeze I cannot feel, though the temperature seems to drop twenty degrees all at once. In the slowly widening opening, a column of impenetrable darkness invites me in.

The hotel is welcoming us. I step inside.

I jump as the doors slam shut behind us, shrouding us in pitch black. No turning back now. I must be strong, for Kylie and for myself. I will not be scared away this time.

I take a hesitant step forward, and my shoe crunches something that sounds like cereal but is probably wood or—I swallow something bitter—exoskeleton. But without light, I cannot see. And for the first time, I begin to doubt my plan. *What if the spirits have left this—*

In a flash, the hotel comes to life. I flinch but quickly take in the scene. Round wooden tables are set about a tavern to my right. Men wearing sharp suits with tight vests, black shoes, and ties line bar stools or sit with women wearing everything from double-knitted cardigans or cocooning furs to thin, loose silk dresses, sometimes tiered or with fringe. Most of the women and many men sport headwear, felt hats and bonnets for the ladies and fedoras and newsboy caps for the gents.

At a piano to the left of the bar, a man with slicked-back black hair hammers away a jovial tune. Though his back is to me, his aggressive, almost manic, style of play recalls within me my first visit to the hotel, and I recognize him as the same tuxedo-clad piano player I had seen in my youth.

Everyone wears smiles. The biggest belongs to a man in the corner, sitting alone and flicking the lid of a lighter.

To my left is the hotel lobby. Filled with red-velvet and mahogany Bergère chairs and matching sofas on polished hardwood, the sitting area reeks of posh elegance. Besides a young bellhop in a red uniform and a man in a suit standing behind the reservation desk, presumably the night manager, the lobby is empty.

Ahead is a grand stairwell adorned with red carpet and banisters that appear to be solid gold. At its first landing, about twelve steps up, additional stairs continue to the left and right up to the hotel's rooms.

The giant candelabra over my head flickers. I look to the stairs then the sitting area, opting for the latter for fear I will not be able to get into the rooms above. Or that the stairs, in their true form, or the floor above, may not be able to support our weight.

I laugh at the ridiculousness of my fear. After all, I am here to die.

I head for a sofa and sit, laying my daughter atop it with her head resting on my lap. Stroking her hair, I wait, unsure what exactly I am waiting for. Kylie's breathing to stop, I suppose. I pray I have timed our flight well.

What an odd thing, to pray for my own daughter's death. But it is an end to her suffering and, selfishly I admit, my own as well. Taking deep breaths, I compose myself, gripping the armrest for steadiness and steadfastness. *We are where we need to be.*

The music stops and the lights go out.

A woman, beautiful and ethereal, appears as if out of nowhere, seated with legs crossed in the chair in front of me. She illuminates the space around her, her form somehow radiating bluish light like that at the center of a flame. Like the others, she is dressed in 1920s fashion: a dark, sequined dress hugging her curves, her lipstick and eyeshadow a matching shade. In that light, *her* light, there were only blacks, whites, and blues, her pale skin like cream under the light of a full moon, matching the pearls around her neck. Unlike the others, she does not play at being alive.

My breathing quickens as she slowly rises and approaches me, pausing only to puff from a cigarette holder that resembles a magic wand. In her dark, deep-set eyes, I see only sadness, grief as deep as my own. She walks closer and crouches before me. Her hand covers mine in a gesture of solace, as if across the planes of life and death, a bond of mutual empathy is forming.

I snarl with anger and pain as her nails dig into my hand. I look down to see a chunk of skin and tendon missing from the space between my thumb and forefinger, then back up in time to see the woman grinning maniacally, her clothes now tattered, face skeletal, empty black pits where her eyes had been. Ripcord flesh stretches thinly over bone as she raises her cigarette like a knife over my daughter's forehead. I leap up to tackle her as her arm swings down but instead pass through her, never making contact. She disappears at my touch, but her light remains like pixie dust in the air.

I scramble to my feet to check on my daughter. Her head is now on the sofa, an eight-inch rat—twenty with tail—is nibbling on her earlobe. Kylie cries out as the bastard bites down and comes away with meat.

Seething, spit hissing through my teeth, I snatch the rodent up by its tail and slam it onto the ground. Before it can roll onto its feet, I crush its head under my heel.

Something moves under my daughter's pajama bottoms, the fabric tenting near her knee. I reach into them and feel another leathery hairless tail. "How dare you violate my daughter!" I seethe with rage and raw hate for the vermin. As I pull it out, it squeals and shrieks, its claws and teeth seeking purchase in my daughter's flesh. I raise it in front of my eyes, snapping and twisting and pulling as I tear the animal in half. After dropping its remains to the floor and even though I know it's dead, I stomp on it again and again until my rage can subside.

Only then do I do what I should have done first: I check my daughter for other vermin. I see none, and my daughter still sleeps, or if she'd ever been awake, she must have fainted. I cradle her closer and wait for the next attack.

I set my jaw and settle in for a long night. I will not be swayed.

The lights snap on, and with them, a cacophony of voices. I throw my hands over my ears. The murmur of conversation has crescendoed into the roar of a freight train. The brightness, too, is amplified, so much so that I am momentarily blinded. The atmosphere is that of a carnival, or maybe a funhouse, or maybe the funhouse, with spinning floors, swirling walls, and strobing lights. That wretched piano man slams away at the keys, producing only noise. The rest of the guests seem not to notice.

*He sees us.*

The words are not spoken, yet I hear them through my ears as clearly as if they are. I look around for the speaker, but none of the spirits, caught up in their revelry, seem to know I exist.

The music stops and time halts, just as it had when I was a kid. One by one, each head turns my way, a smile impossibly wide on each face, glistening, sharpened teeth in each mouth. The man in the corner flicks his lighter, the only sound and motion remaining in that ghostly party. *Chink-chink, chink-chink.* He stops.

*And we sees him!*

I clench my fists and stand, letting my daughter's head fall upon the couch. "I'm not running! Not this time. I will not be swayed!"

The faces, undaunted, continue to leer at me, silent and unmoving. I scan their drawn, pale expressions for any motion, the slightest twitch, but receive nothing but steady salacious grins. I step forward. "You hear me? I will not be swayed."

A clink comes from behind the bar. A bow-tied bartender polishes glasses behind a sea of mannequin stillness. He turns to face me, his bushy handlebar moustache and crows' feet crinkling as he raises a bottle of what appears to be brandy. He points at Kylie, then waves me over.

I creep closer, weaving in between patrons frozen in place, doing everything I can to avoid touching them. They reek of cigarettes and booze, but those odors mask something fouler, ashy and acrid like bales of burning hair. Their beady, black-pit eyes follow me as I pass, never blinking, making me feel as if I'm stuck in a giant, still-life painting with only the dead to keep me company.

And my daughter. *I'm doing this for her.* The lie tastes bitter on my tongue, and I hadn't even spoken it aloud. I've soured everything. It doesn't matter. All that matters is that we can be together now. Our time will never end.

The bartender places a glass on the bar and pours from the bottle. The liquid is dark and syrupy and is certainly not brandy.

"What will it do?"

The bartender again points his long narrow finger at my daughter then slides it across his neck.

The gesture speaks as well as any words. It hits me in the chest like a boulder, and my resolve nearly crumples beneath its weight. It's one thing to let my daughter die naturally—if there's anything natural about a five-year-old being stolen from the world before she even has a chance to experience it—but to be the means to her end...

"It's better this way," I say as much to myself as to the bartender and Kylie.

The bartender nods and offers an earnest smile that lights up even his albino-white complexion. I take the drink and return to my daughter. Lifting her head, I place the glass to her lips. "Drink, baby," I say through sniffles and tears. As I slowly tip the glass, she responds as if by reflex, taking the liquid into her mouth.

With half the glass emptied, I lay my daughter's head back down. I stare at the liquid, sloshing it before my eyes. The lights go out as I toss it back.

I cough and choke, spit the contents from my mouth, not liquid but solid. And moving. A centipede drops from my lips and lands on my shirt. In the bartender's glow—he's standing much closer now, body shaking with silent laughter—I can see the critter squirming toward my neck as if it wants to return to where it had just been. I yank it off and throw it to the ground, then remember my hand and the glass it still holds.

Gasping, I drop it as many legged things crawl over the lip. The bartender continues to mock me in silence, his head tilting farther and farther back as he cackles like a madman until, with a finger across his neck, nail carving a slit through the skin, his head falls back permanently. Crawling, skittering things spew forth from the gaping hole.

I pick up the glass and hurl it at him, but it passes through the wall behind him and vanishes without a sound. "I will not be swayed!"

The lights snap on, and I shrink beneath the stares of the patrons. They circle my daughter and me, looming taller, closer, stretched thin like taffy and bent at the waist to glower down at me with lewd sneers and salivating mouths. Their eyes are like looking down train tunnels, those far-away specks of light at their ends twinkling with malice, sparkling eyes of cats toying with their prey. They are all around me, claustrophobically near, enclosing me in a ring of slender men and slenderer women, with no safe passage out.

*He sees us,* voices say in unison from tongues that don't move. *And we sees him.*

And though I cower, I still find strength. I have not forgotten why I came. "Do your worst." Eyes follow my movement as I sit beside my daughter. She coughs, the liquid I poured down her mouth sputtering over her lips. It looks like blood.

Her eyelids flutter. "Daddy?"

I press my hand over her mouth and squeeze her nostrils shut. "It's better this way," I whisper, my eyes filling with tears, my body wracking with sobs. I can't expose her to more harm from those malevolent spirits. It's clear the place wants us, but it's enjoying in our torment first. My daughter is no one's plaything. Her passing should be as swift and as painless as possible.

So my mind justifies as I clamp down harder. She is squirming now, her eyes wide open, staring at me accusingly, not understanding that what I do is for her own good. My strength is tested in that moment, and I hold firm. She will understand. Soon enough, she will understand.

Her body falls limp. The lights go out. Again, I am swallowed by the dark.

*Chink-chink. Chink-chink.*

That twisted man and his infernal lighter. It echoes through the hotel lobby so that I cannot determine where it comes from, so loud that it is more like the rattle of chains along pavement than the flip and closure of a lighter top.

A blue light appears close by, and I drop to my knees, crying fiercely and yet smiling. My daughter, my Kylie, has found her way. Enveloped in a bluish aura, she steps toward me in her Dora the Explorer pajamas, sweet smile on her face, arms out to comfort and be comforted, as perfect in death as she was in life.

The other spirits, still in their circle, appear around me, so many of them now that they bathe the entire lobby in their bluish glow. In their radiance, I can see the true state of the hotel: the charred husk I had seen on my way in filled with burnt and toppled furniture, exposed walls, and a patchwork roof that somehow fails to let in any light despite its many holes. Rats and other things scurry about, looking for their next meals. Cobwebs bridge gaps between railings and awnings and hang from fixtures. Anything cloth, carpet, tapestry, curtain, or wallpaper has long-since burned or rotted away, leaving only ant mounds of ash and dust.

Kylie's new home, and soon to be mine. I will not be swayed. With a shaking hand, I draw the pistol from my jacket pocket as my ghostly daughter steps closer. Her brow furrowed, she stares at me with doleful eyes, a world of compassion blessed with the innocence of one so young. But in those eyes, there is also understanding. She smiles softly then nods her approval as I raise the gun to my temple and pull the trigger.

Nothing happens.

I moan as I pull it again and again. Still, nothing happens.

My daughter reaches her tiny hand out, closes it over mine, and gently, tenderly pulls my hand toward her. She examines the gun with curious, fascinated eyes, then my hand, as if the feel of mortal flesh has become foreign and remarkable to her, the memory of her human form beginning to fade. She draws my fingers to her sweet, tender lips and kisses my hand.

Then bites off my thumb.

I scream and back away, covering my wound with my other hand. The pain shoots up my arm and into my brain, causing it to reboot. I fumble to understand what's happening, make sense of my mistake.

The spirit spits out my finger and grins that same leering, sharp-toothed grin the others wear as blood trickles down her chin. She is not my daughter. However much like my daughter that thing pretends to be, it cannot be her. Only a malicious reflection, a cruel manifestation of this wicked place.

Which means my daughter is gone. And I...
*I killed her.*
The circle of wraiths closes.
*And we seize him.*

I run for the door, a spirit in a flapper dress dissipating as I barrel through her. The door is barred and chained, the house apparently having decided to keep me this time. But the walls are dilapidated, the structure infirm. There has to be a way out.

I race through the lobby, around the stairwell, searching for a back door, only to find one barred in the same manner as the entrance. I check the windows, try to pry back the boards that cover them, while the spirits jeer and holler as if I am sport. They move in close, brush against my arm while licking their lips or smiling their awful grins. But they do not block my path, and I sense I am a mouse in a maze full of cats.

I head up the stairs, thinking to find a breach in the wall or an unbarred window from which to jump. Though I know the structure is unsound, the forces at play create an illusion of solidity that supports me as well as if it were real. The hotel is as whole as it was before the fire, at least when whatever controlling force is at play wants it to be.

Except not quite. As I climb the stairs to the left, I find myself impossibly back in the lobby, the spirits forming a corral between me and the stairwell. My gaze darts about, looking for answer as my mind tries to comprehend how I could be standing where I am. I turn to see the entrance, still barred, then again bolt up the stairs, this time turning right.

Only to find myself back at the entrance. My cheeks are wet, and it takes a moment for me to realize that the sobbing I hear is my own. The hotel has me, and it won't let me go. Worse, it won't let me die. I drop to my knees and bury my face in my hands.

At last, I summon the courage to raise my head. Nothing stirs. Lines of specters stand at my sides, silent and solemn. Before me, the Kylie-thing waits alone with outstretched arms. "Be with me, Daddy. Be with me forever."

The hotel is offering me an out, if I have the courage to take it. I stumble toward her and drop to my knees. "I'm sorry baby." Blubbering, I reach out to accept her embrace. "I'm so sorry."

I feel her teeth as they bury into my collar. Before my eyes roll back, I see the others coming. Hot, searing pain triggers from everywhere on my body at once. As I am ripped and shredded and torn asunder, I hear my scream, loud at first then as if from afar.

Then nothing. I arise whole and unblemished, radiating a bluish glow. My daughter is beside me, and she takes my hand. Looking up at me, she bares a bear-trap grin, and I recoil, an expression of an instinct that would soon fade.

I am no longer sad, no longer afraid. Instead, I am hungry. Ravenous, even, so much so that if I had to bear it long, I would surely go mad. But I rejoice as I retake my daughter's hand and stand with her facing the entrance, the others forming a half-circle behind us. She is smiling, and I am smiling, bigger than I ever have before, for I know my SUV will be found and others will enter.

The house will be fed. My daughter and I will live on, and I have no doubt her mother will join us soon.

# RUNNING THE NERVE GHOST

## by Simon Clark

From the house—that monster-faced bastion. Across the yard, creeping in silence, afraid of being caught. Excitement and terror mate, causing the heart to pound and hands perspire. Windows blaze, as violent as the crazed eyes of a murderer.

Inside the bedrooms, light falls as hard as a fist upon the faces of patients sleeping there—these are children sent by anxious parents, in the hope that sons and daughters regain their health behind the grim façade that seventeen-year-old Edward Dene saw as the brutal features of a monster.

Though Edward, himself, had been ill: long months in hospital, drawn this way and that across the no-man's land of coma: death prowling in front of him, waiting for him to approach within striking distance, while life tried to prevent the boy from crossing that grim terrain that forever lies between the living and the dead.

Eventually, Edward had recovered enough to be despatched to Breer Court, the house with the evil monster face and murderous eyes for windows, which haunted his dreams after Doctor Scripps had pushed those bitter-tasting pills through Edward's lips, pinching his nose shut until he swallowed them.

Out across the yard, to the forbidden East Wing, moonlight burning down from a black sky that glinted with tears from heaven—such cold stars, they were... those tears of God.

"Shouldn't have swallowed the pills," Edward muttered as jagged currents of cold air blasted from the north. "Should have pretended to swallow, then spit them out after Scripps had left. The pills give me nightmares, even when I'm awake."

Edward's friend, Hoggy, his face gleaming like a skull torn bare of its skin and meat, put his hand on Edward's shoulder—the sixteen-year-old was as kindly as a favourite uncle.

"Edward. We can go back if you wish. There is no shame in delaying our little adventure."

"No... Show me what you found."

Edward, despite the opiate driving strange and frightening images through his brain, was absolutely repulsed by the notion that he was capable of cowardice. After all, his brother was a soldier in France, fighting the awful legions of the Kaiser's army. Edward, therefore, refused to be show fear.

But he was afraid.

Terrified.

Hoggy spoke gently. "Edward, are you awake? Your eyes are all faded, like eyes in an old photograph. Do you want to go back to bed? Where you'll be warm?"

"No, show me what you found."

Soon they reached the East Wing... steps leading down...

"The crypt," Hoggy told him, lighting a candle and shielding its flickering flame from the breeze with a cupped hand.

Down the steps. Through a doorway. Underground now. A dungeon of sorts, with coffins resting on stone trestles that were deformed with bulbous fungal growths. Some coffins were broken, revealing glimpses of grave clothes and hair and bone.

"Show me." Edward felt dizzy. *I should not have swallowed the pills.* Cold air bit through his dressing gown and pyjamas, deep into his body. "You promised me treasure."

Hoggy, eyes bright in the flicker of the candle, pointed the way.

The smell here... musty, odours of damp mushroom... a perfume of death... leaking from these long boxes... rotting wood forming holes, exposing eternity sleepers.

Hoggy whispered, "We must go deeper into the crypt." Yet he

hesitated, his eyes now revealing tidal waves of anxiety. "Edward, should we be down here? This place with the coffins isn't good for my nerves."

"Dead people can't hurt us."

"We'll be found out and they'll punish us. The last time I wet the bed Scripps used his belt on me. I bled so much..."

Hoggy's voice became hollow now, far away sounding—maybe the voice coming, in a way that Edward failed to understand, from one of the coffins, the words slithering all whispery from the dead mouth of one of those cadavers that had been reduced to bone and rot and dust.

Edward thought: *Although I know I am awake, it's like I have a head full of dreams that scare me so. The pills do that to me... I will not swallow them ever again.*

He decided to concentrate on finding the treasure that Hoggy promised him was down here. *If I think very hard about one thing, then frightening thoughts will stop.* That's what he told himself as they moved deeper into the crypt, which lay beneath the East Wing of this forbidding sanatorium for sick boys and girls. Hoggy glided slowly forward—a ghostly figure in his own right. Hot wax dribbled down the candle over Hoggy's bare fingers—he did not notice! He felt no pain! Meanwhile, candlelight conjured their shadows into lurching ghoul shapes. The loathsome stroking sensation of cobwebs on Edward's bare face made him shiver. Even worse than that, dust had stuck itself to his lips—dust of the tomb: bone dust, heart dust, skin dust... all that dust which had flaked from the dead.

"What made me suggest we venture down here, I don't know." Hoggy's voice became wobbly, the way a child's does before they begin to weep. "My nerves... Mother sent me here on account of my nerves. An ever-present fear of anything and everything turned me into a recluse."

"Show me the treasure," Edward insisted, "then we will go back to our rooms."

Here, a table stood against a wall, this formidable item of furniture displaying a Bible, worm-eaten and decaying. An ancient tablecloth in purple velvet covered the table to such an extent the ends of the cloth hung down until they touched the stone floor. And there, at the far end of the vault, a pyramid—of sorts.

"The treasure." There was no satisfaction in Hoggy's voice. He could have been pointing out the grave of someone he loved.

Candlelight revealed the bizarre pyramid, which rose from the floor as high as Edward's shoulder. Moreover, the pyramid consisted of hundreds of flat objects.

"Photographs." Edward picked one out. "How can these be of any value?"

"Look closer."

Edward studied the image of a youth with a strangely mottled face and part open eyes. He lay on his back in a coffin, dressed in a smart suit of clothes and wing-necked collar. Edward picked more photographs out of the pile. All of them printed on oblong sheets of thin metal as was often the method in olden times. Quickly, he rummaged among the photos, causing some to slither down the pyramid slope to the floor with a light clattering sound.

"They are all pictures of dead people," he told Hoggy. "Dead people in coffins. This isn't treasure. It's horrible."

Hoggy then uttered these words in hushed tones: "If treasure be the truth, then this is treasure. You know, Edward, I think Doctor Scripps took these photographs... they are of his patients... the ones that did not..." Instead of finishing the sentence, he shuddered so much he closed his eyes, and his breath came out into the bitterly cold subterranean air in white clouds.

Those tin sheets, which were about the size of a book, still slithered down, triggering within Edward a bad feeling. Because he no longer rummaged through the photograph pile—no, photos tumbled for some other reason. Another force was at work here.

Edward gripped Hoggy's wrist. "I think there might be a rat."

Dislodged photographs became a cascade of mournful images of young men and women, elegantly dressed and all lying in coffins. Some with bunches of flowers laid on their breasts. A girl with a doll clutched in a dead hand. A youth with a hideously swollen lower jaw. A boy with fair curls around his head, coins lying on his eyes, mouth partly open, a woodlouse standing on his front teeth. And yet more pictures of young people with bandages tied around heads to stop their jaws falling open—or to prevent them from biting the living.

*No...* Edward Dene shook his head. *The dead do not bite the living... the opiate pill wormed that thought into my brain...*

The waterfall of photographs suddenly stopped. And the tomb was engulfed by a silence that felt so oppressive.

Then the pyramid became a volcano.

Because it exploded.

From the mound of photographs, a figure erupted. A strange, horrifying figure, ragged clothed, a mane of hair cascading halfway down its back: a disturbing individual, having two tiny eyes in an otherwise featureless grey disc of a face—the eyes looked as if they should have belonged to a rat, each tiny bead of an eye possessing a cruel glint of red fire.

The figure—the sprite, the goblin, the abhorrent incarnation, perhaps, of Edward's drugged mind—lunged at Hoggy.

Hoggy screamed.

Dropped the candle.

And that was the shocking moment the light died.

Darkness. Absolute darkness.

And yet, in choking darkness, which stank of mushroom and rot, there was such noise and movement. A rustling of something papery and dry. Hoggy gasping in shock and a sudden cry of: "Help! Edward! Get it off me!"

Then, from darkness, unseen, yet felt—oh, yes, felt!–the stinging, hurting grasp of strong fingers gripping Edward's arm.

"Get off!"

Edward had bellowed the command as he squirmed free of the creature's grasp. Though he saw nothing now, he judged where the table lay in the darkness, with its generous skirts of purple velvet. Edward ducked as talon fingers slashed through his hair: the creature had tried to catch hold of him again. Moving so fast he slammed painfully against the table leg, he managed to scurry beneath the tabletop. As he did so, he frantically, by touch alone, succeeded in pulling the swathe of velvet across the void beneath the table where he cowered. Now he was like the Arctic adventurer, sheltering within a tent, as a violent blizzard struck. And, oh yes indeed, down came a storm of such violence. Sounds of slashing, grabbing, pulling, searching—taloned fingers furiously trying to locate its prey.

Edward crawled back, where he pressed himself against the deadly cold of the tomb wall, screams of terror threatening to erupt from his mouth, but he forced his dusty fist against his lips to prevent the escape of any sound that would draw this frightful thing to him.

What of Hoggy?

From the darkness, the boy groaned in fear.

The creature appeared to abandon its search for Edward, because there came the *thud-thud* of footsteps, receding, fading, then the impression that the creature ran up the steps to the courtyard. Was it carrying Hoggy?

Ever since Christmas, 1915, Edward's brother, Richard, had been fighting in the bloody mire of no-man's-land in France. Richard would never abandon one of his own men, lying out there, wounded on the battlefield. He would risk his own life to save the man. Edward Dene would not abandon his own comrade, either. He scrambled out from under the table, then, holding his hands out in front of him, he hurried through utter darkness within the crypt, fingertips brushing against walls and the hard flat surfaces of coffins as he found his way out of that dreadful maw of the tomb by touch alone.

Cloud ghosting across the moon, obscuring its silver disc, thereby reducing the light it painted on the surface of the Earth. Even though Edward moved through a dangerous realm of shadow, he did glimpse the shaggy-maned figure that carried his friend away. Hoggy struggled in silence, perhaps too exhausted, or too frightened, to cry out. Indeed, his movements in that muscular grasp were slow, and absolutely ineffectual.

Edward followed the figure across the lawn to join a lane that led toward the forest. Gradually, he began to form an impression of the figure. Flaps of cloth hung from the torso and the arms: rags fluttering in the ice-cold breeze. The savage mane—that confusion of hair cascading down the back should, Edward concluded, belong to a beast not a human being. The figure moved powerfully.

What's more, there was a sense of intended destination for itself and sixteen-year-old Emmanuel Hogg.

The creature's legs never seemed to tire. Not like Edward's legs—wasted limbs that had barely moved for months when he lay, burning with fever in hospital. And now his legs trembled as he tried to run faster, and his breath spurted from his lips in clouds of white mist. Despite his exhaustion, he soon entered the forbidding dominion of the forest where, by this time, the figure carrying Hoggy was over a hundred yards away, the gap widening.

*I will catch up. I will rescue Hoggy.* The words matched the speeding beat of his heart, thrusting blood through his body. What he could do to defeat the abductor of his friend, he did not know. Just how could he, the weak invalid Edward Dene, become a slayer of monsters?

So gloomy now. He could barely see the loping figure. Yet he had the dreadful impression that his friend hung, limp as an old coat, in the creature's vicious grasp. *Dead? No, he can't be. Must have fainted. After all, Hoggy suffers from nerves. Fear has overwhelmed him, that's all.*

The figure carried Hoggy over the railway line that ran through a cutting beside the wood. Just then, a steam train rumbled across Edward's intended path, slowing as it did so, before stopping and blocking his pursuit. He climbed the mound that ran along the cutting, his elevated position granting him a clear view into brightly lit carriages. He immediately realized that this was one of the hospital trains employed to convey wounded troops from the battlefields of Europe back to hospitals here in England. Inside the carriages, narrow beds replaced passenger seats, where nurses in crisp white uniforms moved to-and-fro administering care to their patients: men blasted by bullet and shrapnel. All the men wore bandages, though the bandages were not pristine white— most were drenched in crimson. Men without arms. Without legs. Many had their faces entirely covered with bandages. A nurse bent over one of those shattered victims of war, took hold of the sheet that extended halfway up the soldier's chest, then gently pulled the sheet upward, until it entirely and tellingly covered his face.

Nobody in the carriages noticed Edward out there in the

darkness. He felt so helpless and sad, because much of the doctors' and nurses' work there on the hospital train would be futile, just as Edward's pursuit of the creature that carried his friend away would be futile, too.

After wiping his eyes, Edward turned around and began walking slowly back toward the forlorn structure that was Doctor Scripp's sanatorium for those unhappy boys and girls.

Vivid memories of Hoggy struggling in the creature's arms, then Edward finding his way blocked by the hospital train, filled Edward's skull to such an extent he moved as if in a trance across the courtyard toward Breer Court.

Edward crept past the East Wing, which contained the crypt, intending to sneak back indoors through the window they had left open earlier for precisely that purpose. He paused when he saw the crypt's entrance, and that dark throat of the stairwell going down to the vault full of coffins. How could anyone include such a grim tomb in a structure where people lived? Whoever had designed the house must have been touched by madness...

"Hello there, sir."

Edward's heart gave a painful heave at the sound of the voice. What had spoken to him? The creature that had abducted Hoggy? It had to be.

*I'm next. It will carry me away.*

"Stranger... yes, you... won't you stay and talk to me?"

In confusion he looked around. Nothing but the empty yard, moonlight glinting on granite slabs that formed the paved surface.

"Up here."

And there, above him, above the awful yawning doorway to the tomb, an open window, where a figure stood—a feminine figure with soft curls of hair. He could not see a face or any detail, other than a dark silhouette, for such a bright light shone behind the figure.

The soft female voice spoke in such a friendly way that those warm tones sent strangely pleasurable tingles through Edward's stomach.

"Hello," she said. "Won't you stay for a while? I'm so lonely."

Edward stared up at that intriguing feminine shape in silhouette. Hitherto, he had believed that the East Wing was not occupied by a single living soul. Yet, clearly, he was wrong. This dilapidated part of the house did, indeed, have a tenant. Edward sensed she was a beautiful tenant at that. And, excitingly, she was interested in him.

"You know," she said, "you let it out."

"Let what out?" He was surprised by the boldness of his voice.

"The ghost. You let the ghost out."

Edward stared up at the figure, a womanly shape cut from shadow and nothing more. Just then, a door opened across the yard. In a flash, Edward ducked into the shadows, terrified that one of the sanatorium staff would see him. His blood ran cold when he saw Doctor Scripps appear in the open doorway, a cat in his arms. The doctor put the cat down, making a bad-tempered shooing motion.

In such a soft voice that Doctor Scripps could not possibly hear, she whispered, "Come up here, before he sees you. No... the door is locked. You must climb up."

He saw that there were iron brackets embedded in the brickwork, possibly fixings for a long-vanished rainwater fall-pipe. Across the yard, Doctor Scripps stepped out through the doorway, no doubt to refresh himself with the night air. Fortunately, he strolled away from where Edward had concealed himself in the shadows. However, when he returned to the door, that is when, very likely, he would notice Edward. Punishment for rule-breaking would follow, together with a telephone call to Edward's parents, informing them of his bad behaviour. That would be shameful for Edward, and he was determined not to be caught, so when the doctor's back was turned, he quickly scaled the wall.

When he climbed into the room, the girl was gone.

"Hello?" he whispered. "Where are you?"

"Here."

Edward turned toward the sound of her voice, noticing for the first time two doors in the far wall, one leading into a sitting room, lit by an oil lamp standing upon a table.

He said: "Why don't you come out and speak to me?"

She replied in a soft voice: "I find it difficult... You see, I am one of the doctor's nerve cases. Strangers frighten me."

"I'm Edward. Don't be afraid."

"I'm Robyn. Pleased to meet you, sir."

"Sir? I'm a boy."

"Hardly that. I see a handsome man."

Edward once again sensed her interest in him—and that was exciting. His skin began to tingle, and he wanted to see her face.

Her soft voice came again. "I shall come into the room. Please be strong. The way that I look will shock you."

A tall, pale figure glided serenely into the room. The girl, for it must be her, had placed a muslin cloth over her head, a large cloth at that, which not only covered her head, but came all the way down her body, so it formed long skirts, down as far as her ankles. She resembled an actor dressed to play the part of a ghost. He could not see her face through the muslin cloth, yet she appeared to see perfectly through the fabric, because she walked toward him with such confidence. Bare hands emerged from folds of the muslin. The fingers were long, the skin soft looking—those bare hands, alone, were somehow endearing to Edward. They were such pretty hands.

Edward's heart raced. "Why have you hidden yourself beneath the sheet?"

"My nervous condition renders me painfully shy. Just one glance from a stranger... that would be enough to cause me to faint. I am eighteen years old, and fear that I will never have the opportunity of living a life as other women do."

Edward knew of several patients here with similar maladies. Some fainted at the merest glimpse of a spider. Others would, if they stepped outdoors, throw themselves down on the ground, their eyes tight shut, moaning terribly, such was their fear of open spaces.

Robyn spoke boldly. "I have been here for twenty months, never leaving these rooms. In all that time, I have not felt the human hand of friendship touch mine. Would you touch my hand, Edward?" She held out a pretty hand.

With excitement igniting fires inside of him, he reached out his hand, relishing the moment she grasped his fingers. He had heard people talk about *love*. Now the word detonated inside of him.

She murmured, "All the time I've been here, Edward, no one has kissed me."

Now he became the bold one. He stepped forward and kissed her shrouded form, feeling the warp and weft of fabric threads with his lips—and feeling the shape of wonderful lips beyond that milky veil.

He had never kissed anyone like this before. Such heat flowed through his body and he was sure his skin would burst into a great and glorious fire at any moment. He wanted to kiss her again; however, Robyn stepped back.

"It is true," she began in calm tones. "You allowed the ghost to go free."

"The ghost attacked my friend and me. It carried Hoggy away, and he hasn't come back."

"Nor will he. He is with the others now."

"Where?"

"I do not know. And I dare not even imagine where the ghost takes those it has chosen."

Edward stared at the tall figure in front of him, shrouded in muslin—so ghostly, so eerie. Is Robyn a phantom, too? *Pull aside the cloth. See her face. Confirm that she is flesh, not spirit.* Though he knew he would never unmask her, not without her permission.

She said: "With my prayers, I caged the ghost within the tomb. You released it."

"That wasn't our intention."

"Nevertheless..."

"How do you know so much about the ghost?"

"I have an abundance of time to sit here in my little suite of rooms and think. You see, I believe that the ghost is us. We, the patients, constructed an evil spirit from our sorrow and our anger... together with all those secret desires that torment us. Therefore, this dreary building is haunted by the ghost we conjured from the misery we feel, knowing that we will always fail to become well again, and that we can never return to a life of happiness in the outside world."

"But how can we make a ghost that carries people away?" Edward recalled that Robyn had told him she was a nerve patient. Might she be insane? Her explanation of what haunted this place was so strange.

"Edward. We make our own ghosts. Everyone does."

With that, covered from head to ankle with creamy muslin, she picked up an oil lamp and glided across the room.

"Follow me," she said. "We will go down into the crypt. Our prayers will anchor the ghost there, and everyone will be safe again." She led the way into a corridor that smelt of damp forest in winter. "I stole the key that unlocks the door to the crypt from inside the house."

Edward thought: *I don't want to go back down there again. Not into the tomb.*

But he instantly pictured his brother. Richard would never retreat from danger. He was brave, so Edward decided he would be brave, too.

Down the steps. Down into gloom. Down into that vault of morbid despair. The lamp Robyn held only offered the weakest of light down here, as if even the radiance felt afraid to venture far from the burning wick. He knew he should do the chivalrous thing and enter the evil confines of the tomb before the lady. But she quickly went first, gliding along the avenue formed from coffins lying there at waist height upon their stone plinths.

"Imagine," she murmured, "putting your dead relatives in a cellar beneath your home. How macabre... how unsanitary."

Move deeper into the crypt, gloom filling the void, in the same way the slimy snail utterly fills its shell. And this gloom was slimy, too... just how that could be he did not know. But that unctuous gloom ran its own deathly cold fingers over his bare face, touching his lips. Shadows kissed his eyes—an obscene sensation that was terrible and foretold of the time he would rot in his own grave.

And just then!

Did a wet hand touch his?

He froze in shock, his heart pounding a grim beat against the bones of his chest. His entire body shuddered. The wet hand tightened around his, making him gasp in horror. He looked down, expecting to see a decaying paw which had wormed itself from a nearby coffin.

No. The hand belonged to Robyn. And the hand was not wet. His imagination was playing cruel games. Maybe he was becoming a victim of nerves as well, just like those other sanatorium patients, who spent their days sitting in silence, faces expressionless, as a never-ending diet of pills drowned their brains in opiate. Though he could not see Robyn's face through the muslin, he fondly believed she smiled at him. Then, just for a moment, she moved closer, leaning sideways so her head lightly touched his head. He felt the hardness of her skull through soft fabric, and his belly flooded with warmth.

"Come," she whispered. "We will pray, and the ghost will be trapped once more. Our piety is stronger than its occult power."

They walked, hand-in-hand, she holding the lamp, its fragile glow revealing old brickwork with dusty hangings of cobwebs. They walked, flanked by coffins on their stone trestles. Most of those long boxes had decayed to the extent that there were holes in the wooden panels, revealing pale hardness of bone within—the orbit of an eye socket, the grin of jaws without lips, the flickering movement of a rat within ribs that glistened with damp.

Robyn led him to the end of the vault, with its pyramid of photographs of young people lying in coffins, robbed of their lives, and awaiting the final journey to the grave. She set the lamp down on the velvet-shrouded table, the one that Edward had scrambled beneath little more than an hour ago.

"We will pray," she told him. "In order to anchor the spirit here. However, if I fail, I will shout *run*, then you must run away as fast as you can, because you will be in danger. Understood?"

"Understood."

Robyn tightened her grip on Edward's hand as she began The Lord's Prayer.

"Our Father, who art in heaven."

Edward joined her in prayer, so that they spoke the verse together: "Hallowed be thy Name. Thy kingdom come."

Photographs on the mound began to slip down the sides, those tin sheets faintly rattling.

"Thy will be done."

More photographs tumbled down; images of people died young. Heads framed by coffin wood, lips shrunk back, revealing teeth. The flesh of faces mottled, where blood had congealed in the web of veins beneath the skin.

"On earth as it is in heaven."

Then the spectre was back. Rising from the mound of photographs where it had made its lair. The figure in ragged clothes—two tiny eyes peering from a grey face, the head possessing a grim tangle of black hair.

"Give us this day..."

Eyes gleaming, the horror stepped free of that pyramid of morbid portraits.

"Run," she whispered to Edward. "Run. Don't look back."

Edward thought of his brave soldier brother. "No. I will not desert you."

"Then watch what I do. And remember me forever."

Letting go of Edward's hand, she ran toward the monstrosity, which had fixed its tiny, yet oh-so-hungry eyes upon her form. Clad like a ghost herself—shrouded, eerie, silent—she flew directly at the creature, driving her body against whatever substance shaped the monstrous thing in front of her.

As with what happened to Hoggy, the creature grabbed hold of her, then raced through the tomb, heading for the steps that led to the courtyard. This time, Edward did not scramble beneath the table. Instead, he leapt onto the creature, where he hung on tight to its greasy rat tails of hair—and there he rode, on the back of this abomination.

With amazing speed, the creature raced up the steps, into the outside world, where a cruel moon illuminated the pathway to his and Robyn's destruction.

Breer Court became a blur, such was their speed. Then buildings gave way to lawn; the doctor's cat, in the process of chasing a mouse, darted away under a bush the instant it caught sight of what approached. And the creature's pounding feet crashed against the ground, a sound greater than thunder to Edward's ears, while the smell of the monstrosity was a visceral thing—hard spikes of odour pierced the delicate tissues of his nose, driving the vile smell of something like burnt hair into the centre of his brain.

Moments later, the forest. Edward clung onto the hard, gnarly back, riding this nightmare brute. And he, a fragile rider, clad in dressing gown and pyjamas, icy talons of air clawing at his scalp as the north wind blew.

Just as Hoggy had done, Robyn squirmed in the creature's grasp. Maybe the fierceness of its grip crushed the breath from her lungs because she made no sound, even though her mouth clearly yawned wide beneath the creamy shroud: the overstretched mouth the embodiment of Munch's depiction of the tragic and silent screamer.

The creature thrust its way forward with such immense speed through the forest that on one occasion its foot struck a fallen tree trunk with enough force to make it explode, turning the darkness white with pulverised fragments of wood. Edward's breath came in terrified spurts. And the violence of movement jolted his own bones, sometimes causing his head to whip forward to smack into the back of the creature's neck so Edward's own face was immersed in the tangle-wood of hair—an experience as revolting as plunging one's face into the foul liquid of the sewer.

As well as having to duck to avoid low branches that threatened to slash his head from his shoulders, Edward repeatedly had to renew his grip on the slimy hair, lest it slip through his fingers, which would result in him falling off the brute. He could not allow that to happen. *Save Robyn.* Those words pounded through his skull. *Break her free of the ghost.*

Captive, rider, and steed burst out into the open, essentially three individuals fused into one, the harsh glare of the moon blazing down upon the meadow. That is when Edward glanced down at where his hands grasped bunches of hair, parting tangled fibres, so revealing a bare patch of the thing's neck.

The face of a human skull pressed hard against the underside of the brute's skin, moulding grey flesh into something that resembled a skull mask. Hoggy's face. Edward was sure he saw a distinct resemblance there, despite this being a face deprived of flesh. But how can that be? How can Hoggy's skull be inside the brute's body and somehow pushing outward against the barrier of skin?

And then the dreadful understanding: the ghost consumed its victims. Eating them? Absorbing them? He did not know how the process worked, but he was certain that was the fate of anyone the ghost carried away.

Edward tried to grasp hold of Robyn. If he could pull her free? Then, when they fell to the ground, they could run for their lives. He grabbed hold of Robyn's left arm. The arm felt so thin beneath the fabric—a hard stick. As the creature ran, he tried to put his arm around the young woman in the hope of wrenching her free. Yet when his hand found her waist he froze in horror: to his reaching fingers it felt as if he had grabbed a bag of bones, just a collection of loose ribs, vertebrae, limb bones and the like, contained by the muslin sheet with which she had shyly enclosed herself.

"Robyn."

Taking a gulp of air, he tried grabbing hold of her again. But, to his horror, the muslin cloth was empty now, just a banner of creamy white that flapped and snapped in the breeze as the ghost ran.

Finally, Edward accepted he could do no more. He released his grip on the mane that seemed more like wet slime than hair. For a moment, he flew through the cold moonlight. Then gravity claimed his body. The ground rose to meet him—unforgiving... brutal... a violent adversary.

The next day Doctor Scripps called Edward to his office. The doctor, a thin man of forty, black bearded, wearing black-rimmed spectacles that contained a cold grey eye behind each glittering lens, stood beside the desk, his stance magisterial, his demeanour cold.

Edward sat on a straight-backed chair, clad in pyjamas and dressing gown.

Doctor Scripps counted brown pills from a packet into a small dish on the desk.

The doctor said: "You have been wandering, boy. Yes, wandering about parts of the house which patients are forbidden to enter. You must know that Mr. Emanuel Hogg and Miss Robyn Lamont have run away together. What you might not know is that Miss Lamont is in the advanced stages of leprosy, hence her confinement to the East Wing. If you do not know what a leper looks like, then see for yourself." He rested his finger on an open medical book, containing photographs that made Edward's blood run cold. "Your parents would be acutely distressed if they knew you wandered about the grounds at night, Mr. Dene. Look at the bruises on your face. They are evidence that you have become a danger to yourself. Therefore, your medication is forthwith doubled. Then you can rest safely in your room, like your fellow patients. Yes, my boy, you will be just like them."

Edward Dene swallowed the bitter pills, now placing his trust in the science of medicine, truly hoping that the opiates would make him well again, so allowing him to go home to his family. Should the pills fail to remedy his condition, however, he would return to the crypt beneath the East Wing. There he would find the ghost, and he would allow it to run away with him. Away, into darkness everlasting.

And then he would be happy once more, back with his friends, Robyn and Hoggy. And they would become one with the ghost that could run so fast that neither Doctor Scripps, nor the sorrows of life, would ever lay their cruel hands upon them again.

# DEATH RATTLE

## by Tim Curran

I t was a milk run, so Jantz took it. And why not? The pay was good, the job fairly easy. All he had to do was man the Maiden Rock lighthouse for twenty-four hours. He'd been an assistant keeper ever since he got back from the war in Europe, so he knew his stuff. The regular light keeper, Breen, had a family emergency and his assistant was out on a medical leave, so they needed a guy in a pinch and they were willing to pay Jantz a week's pay for just one day of work. It was a good gig. Besides, it would keep him out of the bars and, truth be told, he'd been hitting the sauce a little hard these past few months.

Breen took him out there in a launch before he left town. "It'll be pretty easy duty. The light's automated, so just keep the gennie in the basement full of gas, wipe down the lens, keep the windows clean, man the radio. That's about it."

"Sounds like my kind of job."

Breen opened the throttle. "What were the old salts yarning you about on the dock?"

Jantz laughed. "The usual. Telling me about the ghost of Maiden Rock."

"Stories, that's all."

Jantz figured as much. Every light seemed to have a ghost story connected with it. "Anything to that Mary McBane business?"

Breen shrugged. "Maybe. Way before my time."

Either way, it was hardly unique. An old woman named Mary McBane had been out fishing the shoals with her husband just before World War I and got caught in a storm. He died from exposure. She made it to the light, but the keeper was drunk and he never heard her knocking to get in. In the morning, they found her frozen to the door, an ice sculpture.

"Those old timers like to go on," Breen said. "Like little boys around a campfire. Only spirits at Maiden Rock come in a bottle."

They had a good laugh over that.

Ghosts of all things.

Jantz took his supper in the watch room, which was just below the lens room, where the beacon was. He had beans and franks, washed down with strong black coffee. It was going to be a long night, and being that he didn't have an assistant, he was going to have to keep an eye on the light all night long. Well, there were worse ways to make buck.

He'd already been through the entire lighthouse three times, just to get a feel for it. There were six levels. The galley was at base level, the sleeping quarters above it, then the reading and living rooms, service room, watch room, and lens room at the very top. Most lights were laid out pretty much the same.

The radio was in the watch room, along with the log book, so it was a good place to station himself. When he finished eating, he paged through a few magazines to pass the time. He wished like hell he'd brought a portable radio with him. Some music might have been nice.

*Or a bottle of good whiskey,* he thought then. *Even a bottle of rotgut.*

He put that out of his mind. Drinking and light-keeping did not mix. He held out his hand. It trembled. The booze was the only thing that calmed his erratic nerves. It had been like that ever since the war.

God, how he hated the silence.

It reminded him unpleasantly of his Aunt Gretta's house in Marblehead when he was a kid. It had always been quiet as a tomb. If you dared break that silence, you were in big trouble. She would sit there in that dusty old room with the peeling wallpaper that she called the *parlor,* just listening. Waiting for him to make a noise.

God, the old witch. Like some bloated, pale spider sitting astride her web, the threads of which ran through the entire house. In the back of his mind, he could still hear the tapping of her cane.

Well, he wasn't going to think of that evil bitch and the terrible things she'd done to him as a boy.

Still... it brought his mother to mind. He'd never known his father. He'd died of a lung infection when Jantz was a boy. But his mom... a sweet, kind, frail woman. A real darling. There wasn't anything she wouldn't have done for him. She just worshipped him. The two of them had been very happy together. Then she had a heart attack, followed by a second one four months later. By then, she was pretty much an invalid. The third and final one came when he was at school. She'd collapsed on the front porch, chatting with the mailman. They'd called him into the principal's office to tell him the bad news.

So long ago. Christ, the years had a way of getting away from you.

The sun was going down now and he could hear the sea angrily thrashing against the rocks far below. He kept thinking about his mother, and that invariably led to Aunt Gretta because he'd had to go live with her after Mom's fatal attack.

Feeling suddenly uncomfortable, possibly even vulnerable, dark thoughts crowding his mind, he turned on the lights in the watch room. The shadows dissipated and so did that awful constriction in his chest. He could feel a terrible anxiety rising in him. A drink would have been nice. He stepped out onto the gallery deck and looked out over the angry sea. The wind was picking up and it felt good in his face. Above him was the light slowly rotating and the widow's walk, below just the jagged rocks and the endless sea.

*Down there,* he thought. *That's where Mary McBane must have frozen to death.*

Odd, but when he pictured Mary McBane in his mind, he saw Aunt Gretta. But they wouldn't have been anything alike— Mary was a fisherwoman, tough, sinewy, seasoned by the elements, he imagined, and Aunt Gretta had been a sedentary creature, a swollen pale slug stitched into the black, flowing tent of a dress, her cane always attached to her right hand. He could see her in his mind—a roiling, blubbery sea of flab, her face puffy like that of a corpse, watery blue-veined eyes like diseased ova set in raw pink sockets.

*Fucking bitch.*

He gripped the gallery railing, the wind cold in his face. He wasn't going to think about her because it made his guts crawl like cold worms. Even her memory terrified him, made him feel small and helpless.

*Get in here, bad boy.*

*When I call you, you do not run away, Mister David Jantz. If I have to come looking for you, I'm going to punish you. Do you understand that? Do you understand what I'm saying, you noisy, dirty little boy?*

He stepped back inside, poured himself some coffee with a shaking hand, sipping it slowly. That woman, that awful, awful woman.

*Your mother might have coddled you, but I won't. She was always weak. But I'm strong. This is my house. If you eat my food and live under my roof, you will follow my rules. Now put out your hand. Put it out, I said!*

Jantz stared down at his knuckles. It was crazy, but they were hurting, throbbing as if she'd just whacked them with her damn cane.

He went back to his magazines, pretending that he wasn't haunted by his memories, poisoned by his own ugly childhood.

He had just finished updating the log when he heard the booming sound from far below. For one confused moment, he thought it was the wind outside or perhaps steam in the pipes. But when he heard it again, he knew it was neither: somebody down there was knocking at the door.

*Way out here? At this time of night?*

It was inconceivable, yet the knocking went on. And not just a casual rapping that he would not have heard at all, but a powerful, insistent pounding. *Boom, boom, boom.* Whoever it was, they were not about to be denied. He stood up and went to the stairs. They spiraled down and down into the shadows.

The knocking was even louder out here, echoing with volume and... something like manic desperation. As he gripped the stair railing, he told himself it was probably some old fisherman. Maybe a friend of Breen's. He thought that in the front of his mind, but in the back where things were not so well lit, a voice whispered, *It must have sounded like this that night Mary McBane froze to death.*

But, no, he wasn't going to tangle up his brain with that kind of bullshit. Whatever this was, it would prove to be perfectly reasonable and perfectly prosaic. That's all there was to it.

He moved down the steps slowly, very slowly, stepping lightly. Doing his damnedest not to make any noise. He wasn't entirely sure why that was, but he felt it was important somehow. Regardless, his footfalls reverberated off the metal stairs, bouncing all around him in the shaft of the stairwell.

*Boom, boom, boom.*

"I'm coming, I'm coming," he said under his breath.

By the time he got down four levels to the base, the knocking had weakened considerably. The way, he figured, it must have slowly weakened that night as the life ran out of Mary McBane's body. In fact, when he got to the door, the knocking had ceased altogether.

*Just like that night, I bet.*

He stood before the door, feeling a creeping dampness coming from beneath it. The sea could not be denied. Its dankness lay over his skin, a chill running up his spine. For some reason, again, it reminded him of Aunt Gretta's house. It had always been cold there, clammy from the pervasive sea air. In the haunted depths of his mind, the voice of a frightened boy said, *please, Aunt Gretta, not the closet! I'll be good! I won't make any noise!* Then the memory faded, leaving his throat feeling tight, his mouth dry. He balled his sweaty hands into fists and hated.

*The evil witch is dead. Let her lie still.*

He shook his head. It was crazy how the dead silence of Maiden Rock was bringing it all back to him. And what was even crazier, was how it seized him up there by the door. He needed to open it, but he felt frozen, his skin marbled with gooseflesh.

He wouldn't allow it.

He threw the door open and a chill wind entered the lighthouse, circling around him, blowing his hair back. For one uncomfortable moment, he smelled a perfectly vile stink of putrescence. It reminded him of rotting things stranded by the tide on the gray beach near Aunt Gretta's house. Then it was gone, replaced by a pungent, sweet smell of sandalwood.

*That was the perfume she used to wear. Do you remember?*

There was no one out there. He grabbed a lantern and stepped out onto the rock. In the wind, he circled the light, even looking in the little shed where the fuel for the generator was stored. There was nobody on the rock, no boats moored to the little dock.

Shivering, monstrous serpentine shadows stalking him, he went back in, banging the door shut. It echoed through the tower. God, just like when Aunt Gretta used to shut him in the closet and slam the door.

He turned toward the stairs and swooned with terror. There were wet footprints on the floor leading toward the steps. It wasn't possible. It just wasn't possible. They were his own. They had to be his own. He had stepped in something wet and—

*They're not from you going out, but someone coming in.*

Then, as he stared mindlessly at them, they seemed to evaporate and disappear. Breathing hard, he wiped cool sweat from his face. He was hallucinating. One day without a drink and he was already hallucinating.

Back in the watch room, the stark terror gone but apprehension clinging to him tenaciously, Jantz brewed another urn of black coffee and made it strong. His nerves were jumping like hot wires, but he needed to blow his head clean, purge the dreadful memories from his mind. He swallowed down one cup, poured another, smoked one cigarette after the other, leafing through magazines with shaking fingers. His eyes locked on the transmitter on the desk across the room. He wondered if he called the coasties if they'd come and get him.

*How can they? You agreed to this.*

But it had never been this bad before. He'd pulled plenty of long, lonely shifts in lighthouses and it had never bothered him like this. God, the solitude was eating his guts out. It was like... it was like—

*It was like when that fucking witch locked you in the closet.*

*Do you remember that? Do you remember what it felt like?*

*The draping cobwebs. Everywhere you turned, your fingers broke through webs. They tickled your face, broke against your mouth. Tiny, leggy things crept up your arms and that one time one of them tried to crawl into your ear.*

*You could cry, you could scream, but she'd never, ever let you out.*

*Because you were loud. You slammed a door. You dropped a glass. You dumped your school books on the floor.*

The memories were like the webs in the closet: they tangled him up, stuck to him, trapped him. He knew he had to stop this, but he didn't know how. Usually when they stole in on him like this, he'd take a drink. Then maybe another followed by another. Yes, and keep going until he was numb and piss drunk.

He sipped more coffee.

He'd never felt this alone in years. What was it about this place? Why was it all getting to him here? And a tiny, frightened voice in his head that sounded very much like his own when he was eight or nine said, *It's the ghost. It's the ghost of Mary McBane. She's crawled out of her frozen grave to torment you. She hates you the way she hates all light keepers.* Part of him wanted to laugh at the very idea—Christ, it was like something from one of those horror shows on the radio—but he found nothing funny about it.

*Aunt Gretta. You fucking witch.*

*You fucking sadist.*

*Guess what, cunt?*

*I'm glad. I'm glad you died the way you did.*

He heard a low buzzing noise and it brought him out of it. A bug? This time of year? It buzzed like Aunt Gretta's screeching voice. Sometimes the heat woke them. He looked around and began to panic. The walls. Jesus, it had looked like the walls were breathing for a minute there. He grabbed his coffee cup. There was a dead fly floating in it.

"Shit," he said, dumping it into the sink and washing the cup out.

He filled it with more coffee, made his log entries. Everything was fine. Out the window, he could see the light cutting through the night. He heard the buzzing again. A white knife of fear stabbed his guts. There were two flies in the coffee cup this time. How was that possible?

He lit another cigarette, telling himself it was just this old rotting light. It was probably full of vermin.

*It reminds you of the soup, doesn't it?*

God, yes, but it did. He did not want to remember, but it came to him regardless—the fly in the soup. Aunt Gretta had given him canned chicken noodle soup for supper (as she did most nights) and there had been a dead bluebottle fly in it. He had gone to dump it out and she became irrational, lips pulled back from nicotine-stained teeth, eyes bulging from her seamed yellow face.

*Pour it out? Pour it out? I give you food and you want to dump it out? You will not! You will eat! You will eat what I serve!*

*But there's a fly...*

*Eat that soup, bad little boy! Eat every goddamned drop of it, you shit! You dirty little shit!*

And he had. Hell yes, he had.

He heard the buzzing again, only it was louder, insectile and shrill, rising in volume, seeming to fill not only the room but his skull with a black, terrible droning. It was coming from the coffee urn. It wasn't possible, but he heard it. Trembling, beads of sweat rolling down his face, he lifted the lid of the urn. It was filled with flies. Hundreds of them rose in a black seeking cloud, boiling around him. They were in his face, in his hair, crawling under his clothes and trying to get into his mouth. He thrashed and slapped at them.

Then they were gone.

*Dry out,* he thought then, breathing so hard he was nearly hyperventilating. *You've got it bad. You have to get into dry out.*

He realized that he was on his knees on the floor, the lid still in his hand. He threw it and it bounced off the wall, clanging in the corner. He tensed instantly, instinctively. You weren't supposed to make noise—*she* didn't like it, *she* would punish you for it.

Suddenly, that maggoty reek of death filled the room, the stench of tidal flats: slimy black mud and dead fish crawling with sea lice. And... *sandalwood.*

Jantz felt tears roll down his face because he knew he was no longer alone. Someone stood behind him reeking of watery graves and salt spray, dripping with briny water.

*"The noise, bad little boy, what did I tell you about the noise?"* Aunt Gretta's voice said, reedy and strident, like a saw-toothed file scraped over the strings of a fiddle. *"What did I tell you? What did I tell you?"*

His head rotated slowly on his neck, making him look, making him see the ultimate horror his narrow, crowded mind could show him: Aunt Gretta... but Aunt Gretta risen from a murky grave on the seabed, a bloated waterlogged carcass in a rotting shroud crawling with tumescent sea slugs and draped with green kelp. Her distended, puckered face was barnacled, mouth shriveled to pulsating black blowhole. Her eyes were pink like open sores, the flesh rotted away from her mouth in scabrous ulcers, revealing speckled gums and black, gnarled teeth.

Jantz saw this, his mind ripping open with what seemed an audible tearing noise, garbled and nonsensical sounds pouring from his mouth in the voice of a terrified child. Her cane went *tap-tap-tap.*

*"I... I... I'm sorry... I didn't..."*

Her image blurred, shimmered like heat waves, then the cane came at him, whooshing through the air as it had so many, many times when he was a boy. It struck him in the arm and then in the belly, cracking him in the spine when he doubled over, then in the face knocking out two teeth in a gout of bloody drool. Then it collided with his head, putting his lights out.

Before his eyes irised shut, he saw her standing over him, squatting, a stream of acrid urine clogged with sediment and curds of flesh spraying down in his face. It was cold as grave slime.

When he woke, his mouth was full of blood. He lay there, his mind whirling, spinning, wobbling on its axis. His body ached. He tried to stand and he fell over, striking the floor and wrenching his arm. He cried out with the pain, his voice loud and piercing, bouncing off the walls and coming right back at him.

*Good God, what are you doing? You have to be quiet! If you're not, if you're not—*

He crawled across the floor, telling himself that this wasn't happening, that it *couldn't* be happening, but he was hurting, his teeth on the floor, blood and saliva hanging in gouts from his mouth. The radio. He had to get on the radio.

*Get me out of here, they have to get me out of here before she comes back.*

He used the wall to pull himself up until he was standing uneasily. He moved slowly and very *quietly* toward the transmitter. Turning it on, the static seemed unpleasantly loud, jarring. He picked up the mic as his heart pounded with a fluttery, feathery rhythm like butterflies were taking wing in his chest. A squealing sound erupted from radio, making him cry out.

Then:

*"That's it, bad boy! Get on the radio and broadcast to the world all your dirty, filthy secrets! Tell them what you did! Kick over the ugly rock of your life and show them what crawls underneath it!"*

Aunt Gretta's voice wailed and buzzed, filling his head, shearing through his thoughts, punching into his brain like a knife and dropping him to his knees. His head pounded and his teeth— what there remained of them—chattered incessantly. He could feel her slithering into his mind, trying to take control of him. All the dark, repressed memories in the cellar of his soul had come to life now, uncoiling like snakes.

*Don't let her!*

*Do you hear me? Don't let her!*

*The evil cunt will work you like a puppet!*

*She'll fill you head with words!*

*She'll make your mouth speak them!*

He jerked as if he had been kicked. He jumped to his feet. There were things in his past, fearsome ghosts haunting the dead bones of his childhood, dread and disturbing secrets that could never, ever see the light of day.

*Listen!*

He could hear it plainly: she was out there. She was coming up the spiraling staircase. He could hear the horrible tapping of her cane on the metal steps. What she had started, she would finish. What he was, he would be no more.

He knew what he had to do.

But it would take guts.

Just like last time... real guts.

*But you're too afraid of her. Your belly is filled with jelly and chicken guts and cool, shivering pudding. You don't dare.*

*You don't dare raise a hand to your Auntie!*

But if he didn't, then that old hag, that carrion-smelling human buzzard, would peck away the good, healthy red meat of his life, leaving nothing but a well-picked carcass behind. She'd open him up until all the dirty, repressed secrets gushed from him like poisoned blood and he couldn't have that.

*Tap-tap-tap,* went her knobby cane in the hollows of the lighthouse. *Tappity-tap-tap*

Closer, closer, oh dear Christ, she was so much closer. He could already feel her cold, scaly lizard hands on him, squeezing, nails digging in.

It was at that moment that something in his mind gave way, something built long ago crumbled, broke apart, shattered into loose bricks, mortar, and rotting joists. And when that happened, why, there was nowhere left to hide and the much-abused, battered, and so very desperate ten-year-old David Jantz came scrambling out. He revealed himself after all those sheltered years of hiding, the unclean light of day shining in his face. He screamed his guts out because *she* was coming and *she* would do unspeakable things to him, make him do the foul, obscene things that had fragmented his mind in the first place—she would scratch him, beat him, bite him, burn him with cigarettes and when all the fight was stomped out of him, when he stared up at her with blank shell-shocked eyes, she would demand that he do *things* for her, touch her in all those hot, moist, vile places that sickened him and turned his soul black with cancer.

*Tap-tap, tap-tap.*

Oh, so much closer now. The sound of it burned into his brain, making him hurt in ways far beyond mere physical discomfort. This was bigger, badder. His thoughts knotted together, tangling, snarling—some of them were from little David Jantz and some from big David Jantz—ropes knotting into ladders and braids, what was unreal was real, what was sane was insane, want couldn't be *was,* and who he thought he was was not who he was at all.

His breath coming in short, sharp, and painful gasps, he crawled to the door on his hands and knees, blood and spit mixing in a cool jelly in his mouth. He found the shadows and grabbed at them, covering himself with them like blankets, wearing them, disappearing into their ebon recesses.

*"Where's my bad, bad little boy?"* said the metallic screeching of Aunt Gretta's voice. *"Where will I find him and what will I do to him?"*

That terrible voice cut into his mind, bisecting his brain, deli-slicing his gray matter into shuddering sections. He could see her dark, crooked shape coming up the steps as he had so many years ago. A bulging, undulant croaker sack filled with hopping, sliding amphibious motion. Her face a smear of white grease.

He screamed as he had when he was ten—silently. It came out with great violence, yet it made no sound save in his mind where it was the wild, bestial shrieking of animals being put to death.

*Do it!*

*Do it now!*

*You know how!*

*Don't be a little cowering sissy!*

*Do what has to be done!*

She stood mere feet away now, stinking as she had when he was a boy, like rotten eggs stewed in vinegar. Her flesh was the glistening, bumpy yellow of raw chicken. He remembered then how he had to do it, how he must time his movements expertly. His heart drummed, his body convulsed, his eyes no longer blinked. Then with a hot rush of wind from his lungs, he jumped out at her, hitting her with outstretched hands, pushing her down the stairs.

She screamed with rage because he had bested her yet again. Her anguish and cries echoed up the stairwell as she thumped down and down, end over end, each meaty, wet thump making him squeal with joy.

Then... silence.

He uttered a tiny elfin giggle because he had her, he *really* had her. He'd killed the wicked old cunt just like last time, only this time it would be for good. He ran down the stairs, his feet pounding, the steps clanging and ringing out. He was loud, oh so goddamned beautifully *loud*. And look at her there at the bottom of the steps, all twisted up, torn and broken like a Raggedy Ann doll with its stuffing pulled out and its limbs pulled from the sockets.

*See how easy it was? Now toss her into the sea like you did last time and be done with her. Let the rotting weeds and crawly things have her.*

He stood over her.

He *squatted* over her.

And yes, yes, oh most certainly, *yes,* now he would do something disgusting and certifiably offensive to her. But as he unzipped his pants for the anointing of the dead witch, the ultimate baptismal via his bladder, her yellow waxen face seemed to ooze and melt, a smoldering sulfide grin splitting it open like a jagged crack in a window pane. Dead, yes, but not dead enough. Smiling up at him from an ulcerous oyster-gray face honeycombed by tunneling sea worms, a sweet and sickening stench issued from her in plumes of charnel steam that burned his ocular membranes like mustard gas.

She seized his sweaty wrist with the scaled, flaking claw of a vulture, pulling him down onto her. She stared hungrily at him with eyes that were writhing yarn balls of grave worms. He screamed. He fought. But then she was beneath him, a wriggling well-fattened slug that was soft as a baked apple. A sucking black whirlpool of corruption. He sank into her, the rotting shroud of her dress splitting open to reveal the white flaccid dough bags of her breasts and the necrotic black depths between her legs that crawled with brine shrimp. And there, she forced his trembling hands.

*"My sweet, sweet boy,"* she hissed. *"Oh, my sweet sweet little boy... oh... yesssss..."*

They took him away the next morning in a straitjacket, juiced on Thorazine because it was the only way to stop his perpetual screaming. Several hours later, Breen, the light keeper, returned with his assistant to resume their regular duties.

As the monolithic tower of the Maiden Rock light came into view, the assistant swallowed and said, "It's safe then? Really safe?"

Breen nodded, steering the launch through the choppy seas. "Safe enough, safe enough. Old Mary McBane only kicks up her heels once every ten years, venting her hatred of our profession. She's spent now and resting comfortably in Hell."

"Poor Jantz," said the assistant. "What you suppose she did to him?"

"Who can say, son? Probably showed him what he's most afraid of because that's what she does, so they say. His night was a long, long one, I'm guessing."

"Poor guy. But better him than us."

Breen didn't comment on that. "Seemed a likeable sort. I imagine, given time, he'll remember his name. Then maybe the rest will come back. Maybe."

# HONEYMOON IN BURNING BEDLAM

## by Richard Gavin

The amber glass of the cell's window has once again begun to haemorrhage. All the panes in this house bleed, but each one bleeds uniquely. The mullioned window of this cell seeps a viscous fluid that is gold and scarlet in colour and that smells of orchid and cloves. My view of the front courtyard grows obscure from this fragrant honey, so I use the rag in my hand to smear enough of it away to see that the lawn has, as I'd suspected, sprung back into form.

The great lawn is composed not of grass but of thousands of unique nails, each one bent and rusted in some fabulous way. This tangled carpet of spikes is frustratingly resilient. Whether clipping them with wire-cutters or mashing them down with an iron spade, the nails always rejuvenate, growing firm and full whenever I try to clear a path to the main gate.

I have only recently resigned myself to the fact that escape from this bedlam through the front courtyard is impossible, as impossible as bounding from the turreted roof, or sneaking out through the labyrinth of tunnels beneath the cellar. I have tried both and failed abysmally. Maybe I am meant to stay. Maybe I'm the Minotaur at the heart of this maze.

"Darling," my spouse calls, in a voice as cold and glassy as her skin. "I've found another spot. Could I trouble you?"

"Of course." I fold the rag in my hand to hide the stain of the window's honey-blood, then I kneel before my spouse and study the portion of her thigh to which she points with a gleaming finger. "Yes, the fire has discoloured it a bit," I confess.

She has silver looking-glass skin, my bride. Her body is a cold and supple mirror. She has a voice like spring birdsong. Her hair is a great wave pattern that I have brushed onto the back of her domed head with oil paint (lavender and lampblack). She has no face at all.

Of late my spouse has taken to stretching out on the front lawn so she can watch the afternoon clouds float by. I admit that I quite like the way the courtyard trees are distortedly reflected upon the spongy glass of her breasts.

She has come to discover that the iron lawn functions like a bed of nails; its crooked spikes apply soothing pressure to her body. Unfortunately, the tips tend to scratch her reflecting skin.

These rusty grasses are engulfed by streams of fire whose flames leap and send up shimmers of stifling heat and woolly black smoke into the atmosphere. It makes it seem as if the air is weeping, as if the sky is overcrowded with processions of mourners hidden in flowing veils.

I put the rag to its original use, dampening it with more fluid from the little tin of mirror polish. I begin to wipe my wife shiny. "Good as new," I tell her, studying my own face as it stares back at me from the funhouse maze of her parted sex.

"Darling," she purrs, "will you show me more of the madhouse today?"

"Yes, of course."

We will indeed explore more of this bedlam today, she and I, but I cannot truly guide her, for I am as lost as she; we are prisoners in this burning bedlam. This fact seems to exhilarate her. How I wish I could share in her delight.

But my biography, insofar as I know it, really begins with an experience of profound disappointment. As a boy I was routinely shipped off to summer at the waning farm owned by three of my uncles. My feelings toward that place, with its stinking barnyard and its lilting wooden house, varied depending on my mood on any given day. I was then, as now, helplessly compelled by whims.

A Wednesday afternoon could be idyllic, but I could easily go to bed that night wanting to poison the coffee of each of my keepers.

One of my uncles (the oldest and therefore the most out of touch with my generation) was, bless his heart, forever seeking ways to keep me entertained. Typically, he would fail, but one of his efforts was to rescue a stack of old comic books that he had enjoyed when he was about my age. Their pages were brittle and smudged and smelled of mould. I despised comic books, and always resented the presumption that all boys my age liked them. I hated all those heroes and found their even, white teeth deeply distressing.

The only thing I enjoyed in any of those issues was the advertisements. I thrilled to the idea of owning a genuine monkey's paw or X-ray spectacles that would allow me to see the skeleton that hid within every bag of human skin. But the one ad that never failed to make my pulse quicken read something like:

*Build Your Own Haunted House!*
*Ghostly Apparitions! Screaming Skulls! Ghouls in Chains!*

The kit was relatively inexpensive and could, according to the faded type on the quarter-page ad, be shipped worldwide. I was oblivious to the fact that the mail-order company that had offered this product during my old uncle's childhood had almost certainly shuttered their doors by that time. But the dream of owning a genuine haunted house consumed me utterly. I fantasized about being sent a yellowing land deed and a ring of antique keys, possibly a hand-drawn map, or a bloody history of the home I had purchased.

I begged my uncles for any chores that were worthy of compensation and worked myself ragged chopping firewood and shovelling shit until, two weeks before summer's end, I was able to mail off my payment.

"You won't see that little toy of yours for weeks, maybe months," my eldest uncle blurted out over our supper of potatoes and smelt. I looked at him, my face no doubt screwed up with confusion. Had this whole ordeal been some cruel and elaborate joke? Did my uncle know something I did not?

He stared at me icily. My other uncles kept their attention on their plates. It was as if they were afraid to make eye contact with their eldest sibling.

My old uncle then calmly set down his fork and pulled from his vest pocket the sterling silver locket of snuff that he was never without. The container was designed to look exactly like a pocket watch, complete with a crown and a chain, and my uncle wore it as such, never tiring of playing the prank of producing the locket and inhaling a pinch of the pungent leaves from inside when some unwitting stranger would ask for the time.

"Those mail-order houses are a racket," he added.

Crestfallen by this lesson, the next day I was returned empty-handed to the city by my mother.

Months lapsed, and I had all but forgotten about my hard-earned haunted house, until one evening in late May, when we received a telegram informing us that my eldest uncle was dead. My mother dutifully piled me into the car, and we drove all night to the farm for my uncle's pending burial.

"I almost forgot," my now-eldest uncle said the night after the wake, "there's a package for you."

I was rather stunned when the massive carton was produced from a closet and set upon my lap. Its size did not translate into weight, for the box sat light upon my thighs. I then recognized the company name on the label, and whatever grief I'd been carrying in my soul was instantly purged. I raced to the room I lodged in every summer and carefully unsealed the box.

Inside the cardboard I discovered still more cardboard: slabs that were decorated with decals depicting rotten grey wood, and pairs of yellow eyes peering out from the blackness between the slats. I spied what looked to be stair banisters strung with cobweb, like tinsel on a Christmas tree.

My palms were damp. I could hear my pulse thumping in my ears. But the overnight drive and the death ceremony had begun to weigh on my eyelids and limbs. Excited as I was, I maturely resolved that the task of unleashing a mansion of horrors on the world was one best left to the alert. I undressed and crawled into the bed that seemed to have shrunken in my absence. Before I drifted, I carefully leafed through the kit's instruction manual, leering with delight over the illustration of a boy and girl who were visibly revelling in the awfulness they had assembled. Their expressions were ones of depraved joy.

I looked more closely and spied a woman (perhaps the mother of those two monsters) trapped inside the house that the two children loomed over like giants. Down inside the haunted house, this woman's body was being gripped by a set of ghostly hands, which tore at her housedress and clenched her throat. Her eyes popped from their sockets. Her facial expression was a frozen, silent shriek.

*She'll never escape*, I thought, and this idea sent me into a peaceful sleep that was replete with beautiful, bruising dreams.

The next day took me from the dizzying heights of promise to the dank pit of disappointment. My late uncle had spoken the truth: it was all a racket. I'd spent hours in the living room of the farmhouse, carefully sliding lengths of decorated cardboard into one another.

I am ashamed to admit that even when the so-called haunted house began to reveal itself to be little more than a two-foot-tall box hiding underneath macabre labels, I was still hoping for some startling miracle to occur when the project was finished. Maybe the box would begin to swell like a rapidly growing toadstool until the farmhouse containing it burst into splinters, or sheeted ghosts would suddenly gush out of the sloping roof, filling our living room, ready to scare my relatives to death.

Heartbroken by this lack of magic, I found the sight of this childish craft unbearable. Carting it to the vacant kitchen (my mother and uncles were still in town at the lawyer's office discussing the will) I carefully opened the latch of the wood-burning stove and shoved the haunted house into the fire. I did not even care enough about it to sit and watch it burn. Instead I stomped through the house and yelled at the top of my voice, for by now my late uncle's mocking laughter was deafening me.

Defiance was required. I flung back the respectfully shut door to the bedroom where my uncle's corpse had been discovered. I spent several minutes singing at the top of my voice and bouncing on the bed where he had died.

It was then that I spotted the mock pocket-watch sitting on the nightstand, glinting in the sunlight. Realizing that this would be a much better means of crossing his mocking ghost, I stole the silver locket and carried it arrogantly by its chain through every room in the farmhouse. Eventually, I took it out to the knoll that connected this ugly farm to a wooded grove that I rather liked to look at.

Settling onto the knoll, I spent some time fumbling with the oversize locket until I found the release that opened its cover.

There was still a fair amount of snuff inside the hollow case. I studied the curious blend of tiny plant matter. Some of the dried flora resembled the bulbs of roses no larger than the nail of my little finger, others were gluey greenish nubs that smelled like skunk spray. The only thing I recognized were lilies of the valley.

I was either honouring or mocking my dead uncle when I took a pinch of the reeking plant matter between my fingers and snorted it the way I'd watched him do countless times.

My regret was immediate and fierce. The snuff seemed to ignite inside my nostrils, searing my flesh. Half blind with tears, I tried to purge it with a sneeze, but it was no use.

The pain gradually ebbed and what replaced it was a pleasant swimmy feeling. I reclined on the grass and snapped the silver cameo shut, noticing for the first time that the image of a fool in a jester's cap had been skilfully embossed on its lid. Close study made the pair of horns that jutted up from the fool's brow very apparent. This detail made the fake pocket watch incredibly special to me, far more than its connection to my family.

As I became more and more giddy, it was obvious to me why my late uncle was never without his snuff. I resolved that I would follow his example and then helped myself to another pinch.

I was preparing to rise and go ransack the farmhouse so that I could find and claim the entire cache of my uncle's snuff, when the sight of massive plumes of black smoke caught my attention. They were rising from somewhere beyond the grove, pushing above the treetops like great squirming grubs. Even my tainted nose could smell the distinct burning scent.

Content with this gift of disaster entertainment, I stretched out on the bed of grass and watched the black smoke for faces.

No faces appeared, but something better did: a woman in a ragged dress who slowly emerged from the trees and came trundling along the path toward my uncles' farm. She seemed to be moving straight at me, but then in a blink she would veer from the path, staggering to the right or to the left. You might think that these movements were comical, but on my life, I vow that they were petrifying.

The woman had me enthralled. My fascination with her increased when I saw that she was carrying a sparrow in a cage. She stood before me now, holding the bird before my face. Its cage was a human ribcage, smallish, perhaps the remains of a child. The sparrow itself was quite lovely.

The bones thrilled me because, paired with the fact this woman had emerged from a grove I had never ventured into, I believed I was in the presence of a genuine cannibal. I had always suspected that the forests surrounding this farm were swarming with cannibals. (Other boys at school bragged about how they would become womanizers or policemen when they came of age, but for me there was no finer aspiration than to be devoured alive by cannibals.)

The woman did not tear at my flesh, nor did she introduce herself. She did, however, let me run my fingers along the slats of the ribcage.

"I've come to show you the way to the burning bedlam," she explained, sliding her thin hand over my own.

I know I said something in response, but I cannot recall what. The next thing I remember was following slavishly behind this vagabond lady. She held the caged sparrow out before us as though it were a lamp lighting our way through the darkness, but our walk took place on a cloudless, arid afternoon. Even the trees refused to cast shadows.

Still dizzy from the snuff, it finally occurred to me that this woman might be luring me off to rob me, so I fumblingly hid the silver locket in the pocket of my shorts. I then asked my guide how much further we had to go.

"The bedlam is a long way from here, a day's journey at least," she said flatly. "We will spend tonight at my house. It's not far. You'll need to rest by the time the moon comes up."

"But won't the fire be out by then?"

"How old are you, little fool?" The woman stopped in her tracks to ask me this.

"Eleven," I replied. I did not want to look into her lavender eyes any longer.

She spat on the dirt between my sandaled feet. "Asylums can burn for years and years. Every child your age knows that!"

The mosquitoes were buzzing around my ears and drinking my blood by the time the tiny cream-washed house came into view. It sat on a high cobblestone street and looked as though it had been clipped out of another neighbourhood and pasted all by its lonesome, like a random picture in a scrapbook. In the little square window facing the street there hung a skinned rabbit, its raw body twirling lazily in the dying sun like a giant pendant of red marble.

"Are you a butcher?" I asked the woman as she pulled me into the house. Flies were haloing the rabbit corpse, crawling upon its lidless eyes.

"No," was my guide's only reply.

The house was a single long room that held a table with a blue china pitcher. There was a spinner's wheel, and an antique bathtub that had been turned upright in the far corner, as though it was trying to climb the walls with its claw-feet.

The woman took two plates from the fireplace mantle and poured onto them cold tomato soup from the blue pitcher. We ate in silence. When night fell (my guide was wrong; there was no moon tonight) I snuck a few pinches of snuff to help me sleep.

I awoke to the sound of morning rain. The skinned rabbit was no longer hanging in the window.

My hostess came through the front door just as I was rising.

"A very good morning to you," she chirped. "I need your strength before we move on. Help me move this tub outside. I want to collect the rain. There might be enough to fill it."

It took us both some time, for I was young, and the woman was frail, but eventually the claw-foot tub was making all kinds of clinking noises as the rain splashed into his metal hull.

"If you like," the woman said as she placed her arm across my shoulders, "we can stop off here once we're done at the bedlam. I can lay you down in this tub and send you to heaven."

Her offer sent a jolt of realization through me.

"I *knew* I'd seen your face!" I cried, pointing at her. "My uncles showed me your picture in the newspaper! You're the lady who drowned her children!"

"Shh..." she said, pulling me near, stroking my hair. "Shh... shh... shh... They visit me still, child. They visit and they tell me that breathing in rainwater makes you feel all bright inside. That's a pretty thing to know, isn't it? No matter what happens, child, just know that I'm willing to give that to you."

I pulled away, but slowly. I felt my head nodding. "Do you think the rain will put out the asylum fire?"

She chortled and cupped my cheeks. "No, silly child, but let's be off nonetheless."

We made a stop at a mountain ash where we hung the sparrow in its ribcage from a bough with a pleasing vantage. We then continued our mission in the rain.

The black smoke was growing thicker, and eventually I was able to smell something being scorched, and later still, was able to see flames and a great stone fortress.

We came to it, and I saw the glorious sights.

"Your bride is the asylum."

"What?" I replied.

"Your bride's at the asylum," the woman said, changing her wording and therefore her meaning.

"I'm too young. I don't want to get married."

"What you want doesn't matter. Your uncle even left a dowry. It's in your pocket right now."

I felt myself blanch. Disgusted, I wrenched the silver locket free. "This?" I cried. "I don't even want this anymore."

"How many times must I tell you? What you want doesn't matter."

Then, coolly, the woman plucked the dangling bauble from my hand and swallowed it whole.

I must have fainted at the sight of this, and when I awoke, I was a grown man, with a band on the ring finger of his sinister hand.

My bride's skin had taken on the mirror-silver shine of the snuff locket.

How exactly I was hurled from adolescence to manhood in an instant is a mystery I don't like to contemplate. Knowing that so many years, so many *prime* years, had tumbled through an oubliette in my soul makes me weak in the knees. This knowledge used to upset me very severely indeed. During those spells, my gleaming bride would confine me to a solitary cell in the highest tower of the bedlam, one whose padded walls stink of urine and blood.

It is only fitting that my bride devoured a symbol of time, for she has altered the course of life. Women always seem to somehow embody time. I have always felt that they were functioning on cycles that were somehow different than mine... realer, more patient.

My bride makes things better. Whenever I become agitated by my lost years, or frustrated over being condemned to this stone madhouse, she comforts me with long deep kisses. Her breath is infused with my late uncle's snuff. Kissing my bride makes me feel bright and weightless, the way she'd said her children had felt when the rainwater that had been filling their lungs had ceased to frighten them. Perhaps the giddy intoxication I feel when I breathe in my wife's smoky kisses is what people call love.

I am standing again at the seeping window which has turned amber from the heat. I am watching the burning lawns and I realize that I have again been tricked: it is not the bedlam that burns, but the lands that frame it, that conceal it from the world.

"Polish me again, my darling."

I live to please her. Our honeymoon is permanent. Yet every day I try to burn this bedlam so that we can get back to that world beyond. Though I know these stone walls are really nothing more than decals on cardboard, I cannot seem to make the fire catch. I tear off pieces of the walls and toss them onto the burning lawn, but the stones somehow regenerate, turning into walls firmer and more stubborn than their predecessors. The discarded pieces just smoulder on the lawn, sending up great slugs of black smoke. No doubt these smoke signals fascinate a few who live on the other side of the grove.

I am as trapped here as the helpless cartoon mother in the instruction booklet. Perhaps I really did build my own haunted house, for I stalk these halls as futilely as a ghost, and I can never seem to find my keepers to plead for my sanity.

# THE LAST HAUNTED HOUSE STORY

## by Philip Fracassi

L ook at you. Look how cute you are.

You and your friends.

Yes, please. Come in, come in.

Come on inside.

The front door is locked, of course, but there are lots of openings. Windows I've left loose. A cellar door unchained; the chilled dark beneath is perfect for youthful exploration.

Ignore the rumors. You're brave children.

And look!

You brought sleeping bags.

Delightful.

I've been so lonely. Too lonely. For too long.

Oh good! You found the broken window. Shame you didn't notice the cellar door first. I love the feeling of warm life in my cold bowels. All that pumping blood. All that fear. But the window will do nicely. Yes, come in. That's right.

If I may...

It's just a little cut! Yes, the broken glass is sharp here. You'll soon find that everything here is rather sharp. Your friend is crying, so sweet. Ah! Oh! The blood... I can taste it. On the floor, on the windowsill...

Don't argue, don't argue, children.

Come closer, come deeper inside.

There's so much I want to show you.

There, are we all better now? You and your friends?

You found the living room, how nice. A perfect place to settle in and play some games. Tell a few stories.

I see you brought flashlights. That's too bad. I always prefer candles. The flames create wonderful shadows on my walls, in my hollow corners. Good and scary, those shadows. Who knows what hides within them, right?

Come on now, let's all get cozy. Sleeping bags are rolled out, I see. Snacks! What a cozy night. A sleepover in my great belly.

And now my favorite part.

Story time.

Each one of you has a haunted house story to tell, and each one is suitably frightening.

Wonderful.

I have a haunted house story as well.

But I'll wait my turn. Let the dark grow darker, the shadows deeper. Wait until everyone is firmly settled for a long night of fun.

By the way, I've quietly sealed the windows, locked the doors. Trust me when I say, there's no way out.

Of course, the cellar doors are still unchained.

But I'm afraid you wouldn't make it through the cellar.

Now, if you don't mind, I need to poke and prod your friends a bit. I need one susceptible so I can join you.

Didn't I mention?

Oh yes, I'll be joining the fun. I always do. It's a devilish pleasure to slip inside the flesh. So warm and squishy and *alive*.

Two girls and two boys. How appropriate. Children, all of you. It makes me sad to think... well, regardless. I must admit how much I adore children. The adults who visit me are filled with so much suspicion, so much anger.

It's not very tasty.

No, it's the innocence I crave. The early, naked pangs of lust. The raw tang of fear. The idiotic pride. They are all spices in the stew.

Speaking of which, this girlfriend of yours is not to my taste. Did you know she's abused at home? Her mind is quite dark and self-destructive. Also, she senses something. She's smart, this one. If broken inside.

Let's see... oh, this young man is something altogether different. And yet, he also has secrets. A lust for you! My darling! So sharp and strong... Did you know? I wonder. He has quite the imagination, this one. A pornographic mind. Such savage desires. But also... doubts. Insecurities. He's lonely. A sad sack of meat if there ever was one. He doesn't even know I'm here; touching his insides, rummaging through his thoughts, dissecting his mind, his emotions. So common in boys. They don't know how to look inward. Not like girls do.

Not like you, my cherub, my cream filling.

I'll try the other boy now. My heavens, you're all just like a box of chocolates! I'll never know what I'll get!

Oh my, oh my. I like this one. He's *nice.*

Yes, yes. He's *perfect.* I'm just going to sink in deeper...

Oh God yes.

Like a warm bath.

He's fighting me a bit, which is natural. Instinctive. Still, it makes taking over all that more fulfilling. Ha! He's like a tiny fish at the end of the line. Fight fight fight, little one! Ha ha, marvelous!

But enough... yes, there we go. I feel a bit like Goldilocks finding the perfect porridge, the perfect bed.

Yes, of course I know all of the stories. All of the *feelings* you humans have. I relish them, honestly. It's my favorite part when greeting visitors.

Taking their memories.

Glorious.

Good gracious, if you could hear him screaming in here! He knows, now that it's too late. Now that I've taken over. Now that I've moved in.

Of course, you don't hear the screams, but I do. I love them. They're the perfect orchestration to this new perspective. It's wonderful, seeing you with his eyes.

I look around at you all. I practice a smile. I wiggle my fingers, feel the scratch and pull of his clothing against the skin.

By the way, seeing myself through his eyes? It's intoxicating. My walls, my ceiling, my floors. Look, look! The intricate crown molding, the lovely stone fireplace, the caked filth, the sticky spores, the damp air. I breathe it all in through my new orifice.

It smells heavenly.

It smells just like me.

Like home.

"Brad? What do you think?"

*Brad.*

I turn toward you, still smiling. You're so pretty, darling.

I can't wait to get you alone.

"About what?" I say. The words come easily. They always do. A talent of mine, you know. I'm an extraordinary ventriloquist. I've had, after all, lots of practice. Decades, in fact.

"Jesus, what's wrong with you?"

Hmm. The other boy. Maybe he's not as dumb as I thought.

I decide to take care of him first.

Ignoring the little snot's question, I search deeper into Brad's thoughts, his mannerisms. His screaming has slowed, but he's still with me. Going mad, I assume.

"Nothing, I just don't like it here," I say, and drop the smile. Yes, Brad is quite the coward, isn't he? The one who always gets dragged along into your adventures. The nerdy one, the bullied one. Did you know Brad owns a gun? Did you know that if I hadn't stepped in, he might have used it one day? Maybe even on another child?

You should really be thanking me.

"Come on, Brad. It'll be fun. This place is harmless," you say, flashing your lovely green eyes my way. Your cheeks are so plump, your hair bursting with blonde curls. An angel fallen from heaven, truly.

I pretend to sulk, buying time. Honestly, I really don't know what the question is. I was busy, you know? Taking over.

"Well..." The other girl pipes up, trying to take ownership from you. I hate her. Her voice is shrill and vexing. I fight back the scowl reaching for my new lips. "I think we should play Truth or Dare," she says, wiggling her eyebrows like a whore.

How trite. But... yes. A game. Of course! Well, this will be much easier than it should be. Usually it takes time, you see. To separate them. You know, one uses a bathroom. One wants to explore a place the others don't dare. Two will sneak off for a fuck. One time? Three boys locked a fourth boy in the cellar. As a joke. When they let him out, I was already working him from the inside. The revenge was so sweet that the boy I'd taken over wasn't even upset. He was cheering me on, the rascal.

But this? This is a much more civil way to go about it. Yes, this will be a very pleasant way of doing things.

"I know what to play," I say, doing my best to look eager, to sway them. "Let's play Hide and Seek."

As soon as I say it, I'm prepared for the pervert boy's predictable argument. His need for male dominance.

"That's a kid's game," he says, probably hoping someone mentions Spin the Bottle. Not unheard of... but no, not tonight. Not while I'm playing.

"You scared?" I say, turning toward him. When he meets my eyes, I show him just a *glimpse* of the real me. Just enough to give him a goosebump or two. Enough to let him know who's in fucking charge here.

"No," he says, and I relish the weakness in his voice. The defeat. You'll never play with your hand again, little one. And isn't that just the saddest thing of all?

"One! Two! Three!"

The game is afoot now.

"Four! Five! Six!"

Even encased in this flesh I still feel little feet tramping inside me, tickling my innards of stairs and hallways, touching my walls with dirty fingers, making me tingle with shameful anticipation.

"Seven! Eight! Nine!"

I feel your feet especially well, my luscious gumdrop. My love. Oh, I'm sorry. You want so badly to go into those rooms, but they're all locked. Sealed tight. Trickery, on my part, leading you like this. Steering you.

The other boy, up the stairs you go. I'll be with you shortly.

And finally, my poor, abused young lady. I'm sorry, but it's down into the cellar with you. The only path I've left open.

But you, my angel, you just keep going down that hallway. Yes... keep going and you'll find the closet at the end.

My special closet.

Inside now, inside! Lovely.

"Ten!"

I open my eyes. The eyes of the boy they call Brad, who is weeping, weeping deep inside me; sobbing for his mother, wanting out, wanting to go home! Every now and then he'll begin to shriek deliriously.

Ah, it's *music*.

Worry not, boy. It will soon be over.

For all of you.

"Ready or not!" I yell, unable to contain my glee. "Here I come!"

As promised, I start with the lustful boy. Frankly, I don't appreciate the way he thinks about you. It's not respectful. Not decent.

You're worth so much more than your skin.

I reach the top of the stairs, enter the upper hallway. I feel his heart pumping, pumping above my head.

The attic.

I sense his breathing, feel it mixing with my own stale air. To give you a comparison, for you it might feel as if a small mouse were scurrying about inside your chest, tickling your ribs, nibbling at your heart. Sucking your oxygen.

I'd let the attic ladder drop, of course. I knew the enticement of that mysterious black square in the ceiling would hook him. That one craves isolation. He *enjoys* the dark. I knew he wouldn't fear spiders or their webs, worry about drooling ghouls hunched in shadowed corners.

And so... up, up, up he went.

Damn the distraction! The boy's mind—that of our new friend Brad—is growing distant. This isn't a good thing. It will be much harder to keep myself hidden within the flesh once he's gone, his working consciousness a necessary ingredient to keep up the charade. To help keep things... cohesive.

Still, there's time enough.

But we mustn't dilly-dally.

I take a step toward the ladder, look up toward the opening with Brad's eyes. With a thought, the ladder folds upward, the door to which it's bolted swings up into the ceiling, neatly. Silently. It won't move again, not unless I want it to.

"Hey!"

"Where are yooouuu?" I yell loudly in a playful sing-song, mostly to cover his protestations. Not that the others could hear him. Not that they could do anything about it if they did. But still. Decorum.

"Hey! Let me out!"

Banging on the attic floor. I close my eyes, relish the feel of his fear, the sweet taste of budding terror.

Slowly, I thicken the dark that surrounds him. On his flesh it will feel suddenly cold, sodden with an unknown moisture. It will coat him like diluted syrup.

"Hey! Enough, man! You got me! Open the fucking door!"

"But there's no way to reach it!" I yell. Then I can't help myself. I begin laughing.

"You think... ow!"

Slow nibbles at first. The dark is hungry—always *so* hungry—but it is mine to control. The shadows always wish to feast, never taste. They devour instead of dine. Soon, I'll release the dark completely, but not yet.

I want to savor him.

He begins screaming now, and I shudder with pleasure as he fills my mouth. That thick, penetrating darkness residing in my uppermost chamber snips away his skin in sharp, tiny bits and bites. It pokes at his eyes, yanks at his hair, tugs at his lips, clogs his nostrils, seeps beneath his clothes and infests every inch of him.

"Please no! You guys! Help me! Please God... Oh no. No! Help!"

Pounding and pounding, but growing steadily weaker. The voice more shrill, more desperate. Then, more quiet.

God, he's delicious.

I wait as the blood is slurped from his bones, the organs consumed in gnashing, savage swallows. There's no holding back the shadows anymore. With a rush of pleasure I release them.

They attack like dogs, snapping and chewing, *devouring*, until the body is gone. Now, only the spirit remains.

And that, my dear, is mine.

Forever.

I walk Brad's little body down the stairs and, moments later, I'm standing at the kitchen door which leads to the cellar. The abused little girl is down there with her flashlight, investigating my walls, the barren shelves, the packed earth. I feel her move toward the stairs leading to the storm doors, the ones which would lead her out into the night, lead her to freedom. To escape.

And we can't have that.

I open the door, look down the stairs with Brad's eyes into the black, cool depths of me. Hearing movement, she scurries away from the storm doors (excellent!) and hides behind the old shelves, painted in dust and vermin droppings, veiled in lacy webs, each heavy with blood-fat spiders.

"Here I cooommmee..." I whisper into the depths, not daring to speak too loudly, no longer trusting the sound of the boy's voice. It rattles and creaks unnaturally, worsening as control of the body slips away. The hands tremble constantly, and now I feel one of the teeth come loose, popping free with a squirt of blood. I swallow the slick tooth easily, eagerly.

Not much time now, my sweet. You and I will be together soon. Wait for me, it's almost time. Just a small chore and a few minutes more, as they say.

I go down the creaky stairs, step onto the earthen floor, close my eyes and relish the sensation of her beating heart, pulsing fresh life into my lower depths. I push away the urge to simply *take* her. I don't normally play with my food, not really. But tonight, I must admit, it's hard to resist a little tomfoolery. Something to sweeten that meat.

"I know you're down here," I say, not caring anymore that the fool boy's voice sounds like broken glass in a tin can. "I can smell you."

A sharp intake of breath from her hiding place. She's turned off her light, of course. Smart girl. Without the light, however, she doesn't realize the movement of the spiders. Already they're nesting in her hair, crawling across her sleeves, up her collar toward her neck, her ears, her face.

Staying silent, she pulls away from the shelves, leans against the moist stone of my walls. I'm embarrassed to say that Brad's tiny pecker stiffens at this, and I laugh out loud. It sounds wrong, I know, like splitting wood instead of a young boy's giggles, but the time for deception is dripping away, away. The game is almost over.

I crouch like a villain and spin toward her, wanting her to see the glint of my eyes. I switch on my flashlight with a trembling hand, dance the beam across her. Exposed, she winces.

"Okay, Christ, you got me," she says, feigning control. "Let's just get out of here."

I click off the light.

Above and behind me, the cellar door closes with an air-splitting *crack*. The room is smothered in darkness.

"Brad? Hey, turn your light on." Oh my, I think she sounds worried.

She should be.

"You have a light," I whisper, then drop to all fours.

"Damn it, Brad... God, you asshole..." she says, but her voice is cracked. Tears wet her face. Her breath is fast, hard.

One of the spiders bites the back of her neck.

"Ow!" she yells, then begins sobbing like the scared little girl she is. "Something fucking bit me... damn it, I can't turn my phone on!" She's hysterical now.

But then, like a miracle, her light does come on!

It shines down toward her feet, where I'm hunched, looking up from the rich soil, split lips stretched into a rictus grin.

"Boo!"

She screams and I reach for her, but she's fast, this one! Stronger than she appears. I watch, bemused, at her screaming, her panicked flailing through the dark, fleeing like a cat from a cage toward the storm doors.

Too late, little girl. It's much too late.

I bring a loose roof beam down onto her skull and she drops like a broken doll to the earth. Her light is thrown aside, rolls over once, illuminating nothing.

She tries to stand, and I fell another beam, slam it down across her back, pinning her.

I could bring the roof down on her head if I wanted, but there are other considerations. Others who need sustenance. I'm many things, but selfish? I think not.

I wait a moment, wait until the soil beneath her body begins to churn, shifting and bubbling like boiling water. The worms have come, as have the mites and the millipedes; the red ants flow in from the corners. Humming a broken melody, I walk to the stairs and sit for a few minutes, watch as she begins to sink into the chaos of the churning earth. To *them*. She tries to call out, to scream for help, for mercy, but they find the opening and fill it, seek her throat and what lies within.

I give them their feast, thinking of you.

When she's gone, I stand shakily, walk young Brad's legs up one final set of stairs to find you. Finally, my sweet cherub, your wait is over.

It's time.

Brad's body is failing quickly.

But I don't wish to abandon him yet. Not yet.

First I must find you, am I right? Hide and Seek is still in play.

We must finish the game.

Yes, of course, of course. I know precisely where you are. It doesn't take away from the fun.

You are in the closet that is not a closet.

You are in the closet that is a mouth.

"I'm coming!" I bellow, not knowing if the words are decipherable. The muscles of this body are stiffening, the organs shriveling; the skin flakes to fine powder, as if the boy had walked through a sandstorm to reach this hallway, this deep throat of mine.

Still, you wait. Huddled in the dark at the end of this tunnel crafted of rotting wood, stripped, sagging floorboards, cracked plaster walls. I'm old, you see. Old and tired. But visitors! They are always welcome, always helpful, yes. Fresh meat hardens my beams, fresh blood fills the swelling veins behind my facade. New souls energize my spirit.

Not to mention, all those delicious feelings.

Lust, fear, anger, regret, despair.

All of it goes into the stew, and I swallow it down, yes I do! I swallow it down in great big gulps!

And so, as I limp toward you, I am grateful for the sustenance your friends have brought.

But you, my dearest. You are *special*.

I have something unique in mind for you, turtledove. And I am coming... coming as well as I'm able.

But I am also changing. And that, I think, is just fine. Yes, I think you'll love me just as I am, won't you? Even now, I feel the thick roots sprouting from the gums where teeth once snugly sat. As the hard kernels come free, I spit them out like spent candies. The roots fill the gaps quickly, long and sharp, puncturing the fleshy lips and cheeks. I laugh, somewhat hysterically, as the face I wear is cut to ribbons.

The sounds I make must be awful for you. Yes, I sense your confusion. Your growing fear.

But I'm close now.

I'm just outside the door.

"Knock knock," I say, but there is so little of the mouth left I doubt you hear anything but snapping wood, the last, dying gurgles from the torn flesh of young Brad's throat.

You push open the door and look into my eyes.

Silently, you study the long splinters of my teeth, the cracked plaster of my skin, the empty windows of my eyes. To your everlasting credit, you don't scream. When I reach for you, your eyelids flutter like butterfly wings, and you simply droop, like a plucked flower, into my outstretched arms.

Gently, I push you back, back into the closet that is not a closet. The door closes behind me and I rock you in my stiffening arms; I *embrace* you, pull you in close.

Finally, the last of the flesh falls away, and now there is only me as I truly am. Empty rooms and a damp, stony heart. Hard knobs for elbows, coarse brick in the place of bones, brittle shingles smeared like wind-blown grass across my skull. Inside my mouth is a rotted, sun-bleached plank of a tongue surrounded by twisted wooden daggers instead of teeth. My eyes are nothing more than weathered panes of glass, sided with worn shutters.

Look upon me in my true form, my love. Look at my deranged body that is both a prison and a castle. A fortress, and a tomb.

I kiss you, in my own way, and pull the light from you slowly. When it comes, the windows of my eyes burn with it, pulse with it... *SHINE* with it! Look at you! So beautiful; basking in the warm yellow of my feverish consumption.

I push you back even farther, past the walls which slide away, past the frailties of my body, into the shadows. Together, as one, we fall through the dark, floating forever downward; two twisted leaves plucked by the wind from a dead autumn tree.

I pull you tight as we spin and dance. I pierce every inch of you, and each gasp of your pain thrills me.

And now, in this sacred space, as we continue to tumble and fall through the blessed dark, I bring my mouth to your ear and I tell you a story.

It's the story of a haunted house, and it's the last one you're ever going to hear.

# Publisher's Afterword:
## A Real Haunted House Story
### by Joe Morey

Many years ago my wife Bobbi and I experienced our own real haunted house story. One morning, her sleeping mother inside a small lake house in Clear Lake, California would not wake up. To this day, we are unsure what happened to her because no autopsy was ever done. She lasted three days this way, and according to the caregivers who came and went to check on her at times, she was talking in her sleep as if she was wrestling with the devil, but still would not wake up. She took her last breath on Saturday, and died exactly at 3: 00 PM. Susan, the caregiver came running up the stairs of the guest house, yelling, "She's gone. She's gone. She's dead!" It was shortly thereafter that events started to unfold.

I will have to consolidate all of the events of the haunting, and as far as I know no one ever saw an actual apparition, but there were plenty of other poltergeist activity over a two month period, and beyond that I imagine. The report was from the caregivers: lights turning on and off of their own accord. Doors gently swinging open when there was no one there, and no wind. A woman's voice was heard, but it was as if it were from a great distance, and as if she was looking for a way back from the beyond to the house she had lived in for so many years. Probably the most eerie experience was that Bobbi's father woke up one morning with the two single beds pushed together when they were not that way the night before he went to sleep. Not only that, he woke up to find he was sleeping on pins and needles, and I mean literally. None of us have any explanation for this event, but it is quite frightening to think that late in the night when the bedroom lights were out that the two single beds slid slowly together in the dark, and pins and needles mysteriously materialized beneath his sleeping form. It gives me a chill to think of it again. There were more incidents, but now it is time to relate our moments with Bobbi's mother's tormented spirit. Probably the most prevalent incident that happened multiple times is that we heard her mother's footsteps while she was wearing her slippers. The reason we believe they were hers is that she shuffled and dragged her feet, and she did this toward the end of her life. Bobbi and I both heard this in the kitchen on separate occasions after she was gone, but the most frightening moment was when we were sleeping in the bedroom with the lights out that we heard those ghostly shuffling feet walk between our beds. Of course, it startled, and scared us both, and I quickly turned on the light, but there was no one there. No apparition. Just silence inside the house.

My son, Chris Morey had an experience as well. We had to check on the lake house, and Chris was down visiting. He was sleeping on the couch with the back door open and the screen door closed and locked fortunately. Out of nowhere, a large black dog appeared snuffling and barking at the door as if the ghost was standing right there. Chris woke up, heard a woman's distant voice, and he turned his head when he heard, and then saw the master bedroom door swing slowly open by itself. He turned back and the black dog was gone. Of course, he was rattled, and the story rattled us as well.

Our last experience that I recall was when Bobbi and I stayed in the guest house, and the bedroom door opened slowly of its own accord. There was no wind. I had had enough, and I turned to her, and said "This is the last time we are staying in this house!" We only went back to the house a final time after renovations had been done to put it up for sale. The real estate agent mentioned that she had a strange experience in the house, and wondered if the house was haunted. We shook our heads, and handed her the keys. The haunted lake house sold two months later, but there were never anymore reports of hauntings to our knowledge after that. The ghost had seemingly fled the house, or did it?

Was it Bobbi's mother who haunted the lake house? Or was it, when she passed away something slipped through from the other side when her soul left this plane. Did something evil slip in? Could a demon have passed through the cracks into this reality? Bobbi and I will never know the truth of this because we will never go back there. We are both glad that we are not living through such haunted circumstances again. Trust me, it is far less frightening to watch a horror movie than to have a real life haunted house experience; I guarantee you that. So there you have it, the highlights of a real haunted house story. Do you believe it? I hope I have convinced you. More than likely, someone in your family has a haunted story to tell you as well. My advice to you is to seek them out, and hear their story, and make up your own minds, but Bobbi and I are convinced; we do believe in haunted houses, and we now believe there is something more after death. I can only hope that it is something better than this life.

13 Haunted Houses is Weird House's first anthology, and the very first anthology I have ever published in my years of specialty small press publishing. I tried a number of anthologies in the past, but they always stalled, and were never completed. I have to thank Curtis M. Lawson for stepping in and helping me with this project. He is an excellent writer, an excellent editor, and took the reins from me and invited the great writers you have read in this book. You might say that I filled in the gaps with other great writers to make this an entertaining, and frightening read. Special thanks must go to Cyrus Wraith Walker for his excellent book design and spooky wrap-around haunted house cover. Curtis and I hope you have enjoyed Weird House's: 13 Haunted Houses anthology, and you will be pleased to know that we are currently working on a number of other anthologies as well that are both unique and interesting. I do think it is important to remember one thing about haunted houses, though: If you walk past an unoccupied, dilapidated, and eerie looking Victorian house with a wan yellowish light emanating from one or more of the upper windows, here is my advice: "Do not go in, and leave as if your life depended upon it!"

Joe Morey
Editor and Publisher
Weird House Press

# About the Authors

## Ramsey Campbell

The *Oxford Companion to English Literature* describes Ramsey Campbell as "Britain's most respected living horror writer". He has been given more awards than any other writer in the field, including the Grand Master Award of the World Horror Convention, the Lifetime Achievement Award of the Horror Writers Association, the Living Legend Award of the International Horror Guild and the World Fantasy Lifetime Achievement Award. In 2015 he was made an Honorary Fellow of Liverpool John Moores University for outstanding services to literature. Among his novels are *The Face That Must Die, Incarnate, Midnight Sun, The Count of Eleven, The Darkest Part of the Woods, The Overnight, Secret Story, The Grin of the Dark, Thieving Fear, Creatures of the Pool, The Seven Days of Cain, Ghosts Know, The Kind Folk, Think Yourself Lucky, Thirteen Days by Sunset Beach, The Wise Friend, Somebody's Voice* and *Fellstones*. His Brichester Mythos trilogy consists of *The Searching Dead, Born to the Dark* and *The Way of the Worm*. His collections include *Waking Nightmares, Ghosts and Grisly Things, Told by the Dead, Just Behind You, Holes for Faces, By the Light of My Skull* and a two-volume retrospective roundup (*Phantasmagorical Stories*) as well as *The Village Killings and Other Novellas*. His non-fiction is collected as *Ramsey Campbell, Probably* and *Ramsey Campbell, Certainly*, while *Ramsey's Rambles* collects his video reviews, and he is working on a book-length study of the Three Stooges, *Six Stooges and Counting*. *Limericks of the Alarming and Phantasmal* is a history of horror fiction in the form of fifty limericks. His novels *The Nameless, Pact of the Fathers* and *The Influence* have been filmed in Spain, where a television series based on *The Nameless* is in development. He is the President of the Society of Fantastic Films.

## James Chambers

James Chambers received the Bram Stoker Award® for the graphic novel, Kolchak the Night Stalker: The Forgotten Lore of Edgar

Allan Poe and is a three-time Bram Stoker Award nominee. He is the author of the short story collections On the Night Border and On the Hierophant Road, which received a starred review from Booklist, which called it "…satisfyingly unsettling, with tones ranging from existential terror to an uneasy sense of awe"; and the novella collection, The Engines of Sacrifice, described as "…chillingly evocative…" in a starred review by Publisher's Weekly. He has written several novellas, such as the dark urban fantasy novella, Three Chords of Chaos and Kolchak and the Night Stalkers: The Faceless God. He edited the anthology, Under Twin Suns: Alternate Histories of the Yellow Sign and co-edited the Bram Stoker-nominated anthology, A New York State of Fright, and an anthology of ghost stories, Even in the Grave. His website is: www.jameschambersonline.

## Douglas Wynne

Douglas Wynne is the author of the novels The Devil of Echo Lake, His Own Devices, The Wind In My Heart, and the SPECTRA Files trilogy (Red Equinox, Black January, and Cthulhu Blues). His short fiction has appeared in numerous anthologies, and his writing workshops have been featured at genre conventions and schools throughout New England. He lives in Massachusetts with his wife and son and a houseful of animals.

## Sarah Read

Sarah Read's stories can be found in various places, including Ellen Datlow's Best Horror of the Year vols 10 and 12. Her collection OUT OF WATER is available from Trepidatio Publishing, as is her debut novel THE BONE WEAVER'S ORCHARD, both nominated for the Bram Stoker, This is Horror, and Ladies of Horror Fiction Awards. ORCHARD won the Stoker and the This Is Horror Award, and is available in Spanish as EL JARDIN DEL TALLADOR DE HUESOS, published by Dilatando Mentes, where it was nominated for the Guillermo de Baskerville Award. You can find her @inkwellmonster or at www.inkwellmonster. wordpress.com.

# Emma J. Gibbon

Emma J. Gibbon is an award-winning horror writer and Rhysling-nominated speculative poet. Her debut fiction collection, Dark Blood Comes from the Feet, from Trepidatio Publishing, was one of NPR's best books of 2020 and won the Maine Literary Book Award for Speculative Fiction. Her stories have appeared in The Dark Tome and Toasted Cake podcasts, and various anthologies. Her poetry has been published in the HWA Poetry Showcase Vol. VIII and various magazines including Strange Horizons and Kaleidotrope. Emma lives with her husband, Steve, and three exceptional animals: Odin, Mothra, and M. Bison (also known as Grim) in a spooky little house in the woods. You can find her online at emmajgibbon.com.

# Evans Light

Evans Light lives in Charlotte, North Carolina, surrounded by thousands of vintage horror paperbacks. He is author of Screamscapes: Tales of Terror, the upcoming I Am Halloween, and more. He is editor of Doorbells at Dusk and the In Darkness, Delight horror anthology series, and co-creator of Bad Apples: Halloween Horrors and Dead Roses: Five Dark Tales of Twisted Love.

# Sara Tantlinger

Sara Tantlinger is the author of the Bram Stoker Award-winning The Devil's Dreamland: Poetry Inspired by H.H. Holmes, and the Stoker-nominated works To Be Devoured, Cradleland of Parasites, and Not All Monsters. Along with being a mentor for the HWA Mentorship Program, she is also a co-organizer for the HWA Pittsburgh Chapter. She embraces all things macabre and can be found lurking in graveyards or on Twitter @SaraTantlinger, at saratantlinger.com and on Instagram @inkychaotics

# Tony Richards

Tony Richards lives in London, England, and is the author of numerous novels, including his ongoing Raine's Landing supernatural series, and over 100 short stories, the best of which can be found in his new collection After Dark from Weird House Press. Widely-traveled, he often sets his fiction in locations he has visited, and his work has been shortlisted for the Bram Stoker and British Fantasy Awards.

## Jason Parent

Jason Parent is an author of horror, thrillers, mysteries, science fiction and dark humor, though his many novels, novellas, and short stories tend to blur the boundaries between genres. From his EPIC and eFestival Independent Book Award finalist first novel, What Hides Within, to his widely applauded police procedural/supernatural thriller, Seeing Evil, to his fast and furious sci-fi horror, The Apocalypse Strain, Jason's work has won him praise from both critics and fans of diverse genres alike. He currently lives in Rhode Island, surrounded by chewed furniture thanks to his corgi and mini Aussie pups.

## Simon Clark

Born, 20th April, 1958, Simon Clark is the author of such highly regarded horror novels as Nailed By The Heart, Blood Crazy, Darker, Vampyrrhic and The Fall, while his short stories have been collected in Blood and Grit and Salt Snake & Other Bloody Cuts. He has also written prose material for the internationally famous rock band U2.

Raised in a family of storytellers – family legend told of a stolen human skull buried beneath the Clark garage – he sold his first ghost story to a radio station in his teens. Before becoming a full-time writer he held a variety of day jobs, that have involved strawberry picking, supermarket shelf stacking, office work, and scripting video promos.

He lives with his wife and two children in mystical territory that lies on the border of Robin Hood country in England.

## Tim Curran

Tim Curran is the author of Skin Medicine, Hive, Dead Sea, Resurrection, The Devil Next Door, Dead Sea Chronicles, Clownflesh, and Bad Girl in the Box. His short stories have been collected in Bone Marrow Stew and Zombie Pulp. His novellas include The Underdwelling, The Corpse King, Puppet Graveyard, Worm,and Blackout. His fiction has been translated into German, Japanese, Spanish, and Italian.

# Richard Gavin

Richard Gavin's work explores the relationship between dread and the numinous. His short fiction has been collected in six volumes, including grotesquerie (Undertow Publications, 2020), and has appeared in many volumes of Best New Horror and The Best Horror of the Year. Richard has also authored several works of esotericism for distinguished venues such as Theion Publishing, Three Hands Press, and Starfire Publishing Ltd. A resident of Ontario, Canada, his website is www.richardgavin.net

# Philip Fracassi

Philip Fracassi is the author of the award-winning story collection, Behold the Void, which won "Best Collection of the Year" from This Is Horror and Strange Aeons Magazine.

His newest collection, Beneath a Pale Sky, was published in 2021 by Lethe Press. It received a starred review from Library Journal and was named "Best Collection of the Year" by Rue Morgue Magazine. His debut novel, Boys in the Valley, was published on Halloween 2021 by Earthling Publications. His upcoming releases include the novels A Child Alone with Strangers (Aug 2022), and Gothic (Feb 2023).

Philip's books have been translated into multiple languages, and his stories have been published in numerous magazines and anthologies, including Best Horror of the Year, Nightmare Magazine, Black Static, Dark Discoveries, and Cemetery Dance.

The New York Times calls his work "terrifically scary."

As a screenwriter, his feature films have been distributed by Disney Entertainment and Lifetime Television. He currently has several stories under option for film/tv adaption.

For more information, visit his website at www.pfracassi.com. He also has active profiles on Facebook, Instagram (pfracassi) and Twitter (@philipfracassi).

Philip lives in Los Angeles, California, and is represented by Elizabeth Copps at Copps Literary Services (info@coppsliterary.com).

# About the Editors

## Joe Morey

**Joe Morey,** creator, former editor, and publisher of Dark Regions Press (1985 – 2013). In 2010 – *Dark Regions Press won the HWA Specialty Press Award.* Also, the books under his editorship won Bram Stoker Awards, and other awards from around the world. Joe Morey has been publishing for thirty-eight years, and in actuality published a small press 'zine, titled: REGIONS in 1984 before turning the press into Dark Regions Press all those years ago. He has decided to start a new specialty press: Weird House which will specialize in publishing horror, fantasy, dark fantasy, science fiction and poetry collections. The emphasis will be upon beautiful signed and numbered hardcover editions embellished with art, and carefully designed to add a level of sophistication and elegance. He has loved horror, fantasy, and science fiction since he was a child, and that will never change. Weird House will be his last specialty small press.

# Curtis M. Lawson

**Curtis M. Lawson** is an author of unapologetically weird and transgressive fiction, fantastical graphic novels, and dark poetry. His work ranges from technicolor pulp adventures to bleak cosmic horror.

Curtis is a member of the Horror Writer's Association, and the host of the *Wyrd Transmissions* podcast. He resides just outside of Providence, RI.